ANOTHER CHANCE AT LOVE

ALEXA ASTON

Love,
Alexa Aston

COPYRIGHT © 2021 by Alexa Aston

Published by Oliver Heber Books

OLIVER HEBER BOOKS

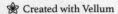 Created with Vellum

PROLOGUE

MAY—NIGHT OF THE SENIOR PROM

Willow Martin gazed at her reflection in the mirror. Her long auburn hair had been art-fully twisted into a chic chignon by her grandmother, Boo. Boo had also helped Willow sew the lavender dress she wore that enhanced her violet eyes.

"There. You look lovely," Boo declared. "Dylan Taylor won't know what hit him when he sees you."

She usually didn't bother with make-up but with it being Senior Prom, Willow had played up her eyes and mouth. She'd made sure the lipstick was the kind that didn't come off.

Because she planned to do a lot of kissing tonight.

Actually, more than kissing. She looked into the mirror again and wondered if this time tomorrow, she would be able to tell the difference in herself. Tonight, she was a virgin. Tomorrow, that would have changed.

Dylan had changed her in small ways. He wasn't the kind of boyfriend to tell her what to think or order her to lay off the ice cream and potato chips. She'd seen too many of her friends being controlled by the boys they dated, and because of it, she had avoided dating and only gone out in groups until this, her senior year. Somehow, at a Labor Day cookout, she and Dylan, who had been friends since kindergarten, paired off.

Suddenly, everything became right in her world.

They'd spent all senior year together. Willow couldn't imagine being closer to anyone than she was with Dylan. Not Jackson, her brother, who was three years older and attended USC. Not Boo, who had taken in Willow and Jackson when their parents had been killed while skiing fifteen years ago. Everything with Dylan was easy. They never argued. Although they enjoyed different interests—Dylan being on several of the school's athletic teams and Willow known for her artistic talent—they also liked to hike and fish together. She loved being around his parents and especially his little sister, Grace. At twelve, Grace was a budding artist herself, always showing her work to Willow and asking for advice. Willow had won a full scholarship to UCLA and planned to study art. Where Boo was a sculptor, Willow's favorite medium was paints, both oils and pastels. She longed to study in Europe someday.

If she did, it meant leaving Dylan behind.

That was why tonight would be the night she gave herself to him. She wanted her first time to be with this boy she loved. They would have the next two weeks of school and then the summer together before she went off to Los Angeles and he stayed home to attend community college in nearby Salty Point. They had talked about how different their lives would soon be and how far away they would be from one another. Dylan had told her he wanted her to be free of any entanglements when she went to college. He wanted her to meet people and experience new things.

Left unsaid was that her heart told her he would

be waiting for her when she returned—and that was the problem. A huge, elephant-in-the-room-nobody's-talking-about problem.

Willow didn't want to settle down in Maple Cove as Dylan did. She wanted to see the world. Explore new places. Taste different foods. Soak up the architecture and art in different countries. Already she knew she would apply for the Junior Year Abroad program UCLA offered, so she could study in Paris. To be in the city of so many great artists over the centuries and see their works in museums was at the top of her to-do list. In fact, she already knew she would love Europe and would most likely make it her home after college graduation.

That meant no Dylan.

Tonight would allow her to show him how much she really loved him. It would also be the most treasured memory she would hold in her heart, one of this perfect boy, on the cusp of manhood, and how he would forever own a piece of her, as she did him.

"You're looking awfully starry-eyed, Willow," Boo said, studying her carefully. "I hope you and Dylan have thought of protection."

Leave it to Boo to know what was on Willow's mind and heart. As always, her grandmother was frank and forthright, pulling no punches. She doubted many grandmothers discussed the use of condoms with their granddaughters.

She turned and enveloped the much shorter woman in her arms. "That's taken care of, Boo. I promise."

"Good," Boo said emphatically. "No sense in getting pregnant and tying yourself to this town."

"You've lived in Maple Cove for decades," she reminded her grandmother, who had just turned seventy-three the week before.

"That's because I got out and lived for a good long while before I met your grandfather. I saw things and did things and when I met him, I had no regrets when he wanted me to stay in Maple Cove and settle down. I could turn my back on that big, beautiful world because I had my Murray. My wonderful love for ten years."

Willow had never known her grandfather. He had died of sudden cardiac arrest at forty. Boo was only thirty-five and had raised their only child, an eight-year-old boy who became Willow's father.

Boo reached up and cupped Willow's cheek. "I want you to go to California, my precious. Study art. Drink a little too much. Make friends you'll have for the rest of your life. Dylan is a good boy. Steady as a rock. But he's tied to this place. You need to be free to explore your art. Find your style. Know yourself. It won't hurt, though, to make love to that boy because he'll be gentle with you. Treat you like a true lady. Dylan will be the one you can judge every man by in your future."

"But for now, you think I would be settling if I stayed with him. Or came back to Maple Cove for him."

Her grandmother sighed. "I do, honey. You have a grand future ahead of you. More talent than I ever possessed. You're going to be known in the art world. I guarantee it."

"Boo, you are an amazing sculptor," Willow protested.

"I'm damned good," she said proudly. "Made enough from my art to provide for you and Jackson and still have some left over. But you're better."

"Dylan and I have talked. Once I leave for UCLA, we agree there won't be anything to tie us to each other."

Boo nodded sagely. "That boy is smart enough to know to let you go. I like that. This way, you won't try to run home too often or sit in your dorm room and miss out on the parties and all the fun because you have a boyfriend back home. Same for him. Dylan needs to live his life, too. Find a nice girl and make a home with her here in Maple Cove."

"I know." She bent and wrapped her arms around her grandmother, who barely topped five feet. "I love you, Boo."

"And I love you more, my sweet girl. Now, go have some fun tonight."

They went downstairs and five minutes later, Dylan rang their doorbell. As he entered, Willow couldn't help but admire his coal-black hair, freshly cut, and warm, gray eyes that gazed at her admiringly.

"You look beautiful, Willow," he said, a slow smile spreading across his face. "Just. Wow."

"You look pretty handsome yourself," she replied, fully appreciating the way he filled out the dark suit that his mother had bought him to wear to prom and graduation.

"I got you this," he said, indicating the white cardboard box he held. Opening it, he said, "It's a wrist corsage. I know how particular you are, and I didn't want you to have to pin anything to your dress."

"Thank you."

She held out her wrist and allowed him to slide the corsage over her hand. "I love it."

He grinned. "Mom said you'd like it."

They stood staring at one another. She tried to drink in this moment. The tang of his cologne. The approval in his eyes. How her heart beat wildly in her chest at the thought of finally having sex with him.

Reaching for her hand, he said, "We'd better go. Carter and Emily are waiting in the car."

"Have a wonderful time, you two," Boo said.

"We will, Boo," Dylan said. "I promise to have Willow back by—"

"No curfew tonight," her grandmother proclaimed. "Stay out the entire night. Watch the sunrise together."

"Really?" Willow asked, knowing her grandmother's permission extended to what would happen after prom tonight.

"Really. Enjoy yourselves."

Her hand felt warm and protected in his as they went down the front sidewalk to the car. Dylan opened her door and then came around and joined her in the back seat as she greeted Carter and Emily. Carter Clark was Dylan's best friend, and Willow suspected Emily would one day become Mrs. Carter Clark.

"Next stop, Maple Cove High," Carter proclaimed.

They arrived at the school parking lot less than five minutes later, producing their prom tickets at the door and entering the gym Willow had spent all morning at, helming the decorations.

"Wow!" Dylan said, squeezing her hand. "This is fantastic."

"Thank you," she said, glowing with pride at how everything had turned out.

She looked around at the transformed gym, which she and her decorating committee had turned into a Paris boulevard. Willow had worked for months designing murals upon sheets which the committee hung along the gym's walls. There were scenes of sidewalk cafés and flower shops. Clothing boutiques and restaurants. She had even painted the Eiffel Tower on one and the Arc de Triomphe on another. Finally, one entire wall was her rendition of the Tuileries Gardens.

Tables had been placed in front of her scenes throughout the gym, along with fresh flowers in the center of them. The entire scene looked like Paris in the springtime.

"No wonder you won an art scholarship," Carter said. "It's like Paris has come to life right here in Maple Cove."

"Let's dance," Dylan said, pulling her onto the dance floor and slipping his arms around her.

They began swaying to the music, lost in each other's eyes. Love for him poured through her, and Willow had to refrain from kissing him in the midst of everyone. That would be for later. When they had their private celebration.

As they danced, she decided it was time to clue him in to her plans. "I'm ready for us to be together tonight, Dylan."

He frowned. "We are together, Willow. I want us to be all summer. Until you leave." A shadow crossed his face.

"No, I mean *together*."

Realization dawned in his eyes. "Do you mean..." His voice trailed off.

"I do. We're going to go to Gillian's after prom. She's gone to visit her cousin in Portland for the weekend. We'll have the house all to ourselves."

"She knows?"

"Yes. And I have protection," she assured him.

Dylan sighed. "You are the best girlfriend ever." He glanced around. "I suppose we need to stick around, though I'm itching to leave now."

"Why? No one's stopping us from leaving."

He laughed. "Because we're supposed to stay? Besides, we just got here. You worked so hard. You need to enjoy this night. Savor it."

"I think we can enjoy being together even more," she told him, pressing against him.

His smile lit up his face. "You're on, you wicked girl."

He released her and grabbed her hand, weaving through the crowd. People kept stopping them, telling her how great the gym looked. She tried her best not to be impatient and politely thanked everyone.

They finally made it off the dance floor when the principal stopped them. He, too, was full of compliments.

"Our star quarterback and resident artist. You make the perfect couple," he told them. "I suppose I shouldn't reveal this, but you've been named King and Queen of the prom. We'll announce it after dinner." He glanced up. "Oh, it looks like the food is ready to come out now. Excuse me."

After he left, Dylan shrugged. "I guess we better stick around. We can leave right after our royal dance."

Carter and Emily waved them over, and they joined them and two other couples for the meal. When it ended, the Senior Class sponsor announced them as King and Queen, and they danced the spotlight dance alone, their classmates watching in awe. When it ended, applause broke out, and they left the dance floor.

"Do you mind walking to Gillian's?" Dylan asked. "I hate to ask Carter for the keys." He grinned. "Because once I get you in bed, I plan to keep you there all night."

"Not at all," she said, eager and a little bit nervous

at what they would soon be doing. Thinking about making love and actually going through with it were two different things.

They left the gym, and in the empty foyer Dylan pulled her into his arms for a long, slow, delicious kiss. Willow leaned into him, feeling the blood race through her veins as her body caught fire.

He broke the kiss. "There's more of that to come," he joked, and then gave her a hard, swift kiss.

Threading his fingers through hers, they went to the glass doors and stepped into the cool evening. Immediately, one of her twinges tingled within her. The premonitions didn't come often and always were the harbinger of bad news. She froze, worried that something had happened to Boo.

"Willow? Do you have one of your feelings?" Dylan asked, concern in his voice.

"Yes," she whispered, dread filling her.

He hesitated a moment and then said, "We can go back inside, Willow. We don't have to do it."

Before she could reply, a squad car pulled up in front of the school. Sheriff Walt Willingham stepped from the car and began making his way toward them.

"Hello, Sheriff," Dylan called out.

Anxiety filled her. A sick feeling washed over her.

The lawman came to a stop in front of them. "Dylan. Willow." He paused, frowning. "Did you know I was coming?"

"No, sir," Dylan said. "We just came out to get some fresh air. Is it... Boo?"

Sheriff Willingham shook his head. "No, son. It's your family."

Dylan's fingers tightened around hers. "Something's wrong?" he asked, panic in his voice. "They were going to go over to Salty Point for dinner this evening."

"They did." The sheriff sighed. "They were coming back along Boxboro Highway when an eighteen-wheeler crossed the line and struck their car head-on." He shook his head again. "There's no easy way to say this, son. Your folks and Grace are gone."

A sound came from Dylan, like a wounded animal. He dropped to his knees. Willow followed him, wrapping her arms about him. Willingham said a few more things, but she doubted Dylan heard anything else.

The night which was supposed to be one to celebrate their love had turned into tragedy.

CHAPTER 1

PARIS—TWELVE YEARS LATER

Willow put down her brush, and with a critical eye, studied the painting she had worked on over the last two weeks. It had taken her a long time to capture the right shade of the woman's dress, with the dark folds of the skirt deepening the color. Once she had nailed it, everything else fell into place. The streaks of light as dawn broke. The massive oak tree reaching to the sky. The gazebo steps the woman stood upon.

Perfect.

She cleaned her brushes methodically, humming as she did, and then stripped off her paint-splattered clothes and showered in the tiny bathroom of her studio. During her twenties, she had lived in Berlin, London, and finally Paris, and had never gotten used to the miniscule shower stalls in Europe. Or the lack of storage. Or the high rent on her studio and flat. At least she was finally making good money from her art and could afford this separate space. Especially since Jean-Luc worked out of their flat in Montmartre, an artsy residential neighborhood. They were fortunate to have a two-bedroom flat, with one bedroom serving as Jean-Luc's art studio, where he created his sculptures.

Willow dried off and applied makeup, something she rarely did. Tonight, they would be celebrating her thirtieth birthday, which should be a time of joy. Her gut told her it might be the end of things, though, as she slipped into a deep purple wrap dress and then combed her fingers through her auburn tresses. If she let them dry naturally, they would fall in waves about her.

She dug through her purse and found her phone, which she turned off anytime she worked. She had missed three messages, one each from Tenley and Sloane, her closest friends, and the other from Remy.

"Business before pleasure," she muttered to herself as she listened to the voice mail from her agent. Remington Moore lived in New York and had represented Willow her entire career. She didn't bother with a business manager, mostly because she didn't trust anyone but herself with her money.

Especially Jean-Luc.

They had lived together two years. In recent days, Jean-Luc had made a few comments that led her to believe he might want to make their arrangement something more permanent. It wasn't what she wanted. Not anymore. Jean-Luc was the stereotypical artist—moody, wildly creative, and utterly charming. He flattered her endlessly and was a marvelous lover, but he could also be very self-centered. He also went through money faster than anyone she knew. Having grown up in a frugal household, she had made sure to keep their finances separate. Because she was much more successful in her career, Willow paid the rent on their flat, while her lover bought groceries and wine and often brought flowers home for her.

The problem was that Willow didn't really love Jean-Luc. She had been drawn to his good looks and talent, but she had committed to moving in with him too soon when he pressed her to do so. After a year-and-a-half of living together, she realized her lover was merely convenient. Someone to come home to and have sex with. She realized it was merely sex. They had never truly made love. That physical connection had never been followed by a deeper, emotional connection. Willow still didn't really know who Jean-Luc was. They didn't communicate as a couple should. When she tried to delve deeper, he would grow angry or tell her she wanted too much from him.

A wave of sadness washed over her. Her heart told her tonight wouldn't be a celebration.

Instead, it would be a bittersweet parting.

She sighed. None of her romances had turned out as she had expected. She had only taken a handful of lovers over the years, beginning in college. Not one of those relationships had developed into anything lasting. She had lost her virginity to her college boyfriend because it seemed everyone had already done so by nineteen. She had felt awkward being what seemed to be the only virgin on campus. He claimed she loved her art more than she did him, which was true. He tried to force a commitment from her before she left for her year of study abroad, which she refused to bend to. She had told him they should see other people while apart. When she returned to Los Angeles the following year, they had tried to start something back up and still drifted apart.

Twice she had struck out during her twenties,

once in London and again in Berlin, choosing to be with men who had more looks than substance. One had continued to pick fights with her as she became more successful and his star in the art world began to fade. That breakup had been a nasty one. The other, a playwright, had cheated on her with his new leading lady. Willow had been hurt at the betrayal more deeply than losing the actual relationship.

When she met Jean-Luc, they had instant physical chemistry and after only two months of dating, they had moved in together. Willow had been lonely at the time, having recently moved to Paris without knowing a soul. She liked having someone to come home to and wanted to have not only a lover but a companion to discuss art or politics. Unfortunately, Jean-Luc had never fulfilled that role. It was if she had put their relationship on a back burner and let it simmer, ignoring it for too long. Perhaps turning thirty today and starting a new decade in her life was the wake-up call she had needed. Her heart told her that they weren't meant to stay together.

Yet ending their relationship on her birthday was a downer. Maybe she could put on a happy face tonight and try to celebrate. Then she would speak with Jean-Luc tomorrow, and they could decide what to do. Part of Willow wanted him to fight for her—for them— and yet deep inside, she knew he would come up lacking.

And she would be alone yet again. Perhaps she was destined to never marry. She kept making mistakes, choosing the wrong kind of men. She wondered if she would ever be able to trust her judgment when it came to a relationship.

Tapping her phone, she brought up Remy's message and listened.

Willow, call me back immediately. I don't care what time it is. But call me as soon as you get this.

That was interesting. Usually Remy was up-front when she left a voice mail. Willow could hear the excitement in her agent's voice. She tapped on her favorites and then Remy's name, taking a deep breath as the phone rang in New York.

"Willow. You aren't going to believe this. You have a showing at the Runyon Gallery."

"What?" she squealed. "Please, tell me you aren't joking, Remy. The Runyon Gallery makes or breaks artists' careers!"

"I would not begin to joke about something like that. The good thing? You won't be sharing the stage with anyone else. It's exclusive. And fast. They want to hold it in three weeks."

"Three weeks? That's barely time to select the paintings, much less stage everything," she complained, her head racing with which paintings to select.

"I know that. They know that. But if anyone can do it, it's you. I've already e-mailed you a list of what paintings I have here in New York. The bulk of the show can come from that. You'll need to choose some of your most recent work, however, and ship it over. And get your ass on a plane ASAP."

"Okay." She began to think quickly and then named four paintings in Paris that would need to be shipped, knowing Remy would know which ones she referred to, since Willow always sent photos of her completed work to Remy. "Oh, and the Swiss lake one."

"The countryside on that one is spectacular. We'll definitely include it."

They spoke a few more minutes, discussing what should or shouldn't be included in the show.

"Book yourself on the first flight out tomorrow. Or tonight if you can," her agent urged.

"It's my birthday, Remy. Jean-Luc and I have dinner reservations at a super-fancy place."

"Oh, baby, I forgot! You're thirty today. Happy Birthday!"

"Thanks," she said. "I'll make my flight reservation now and text you the info. I'll also arrange to have the canvases I want sent to New York."

"I can't wait to see you, Willow," Remy said. "You'll stay with me, of course."

"Of course. With Tenley married and living in a tiny one-bedroom, you are my first and only choice."

Remy laughed. "See you tomorrow."

Willow hung up and immediately scanned the Internet for outbound flights tomorrow morning. She made an economy class reservation, ever mindful of money, and then pulled the canvases that would be included in the show. She changed her mind about one and replaced it with a different choice, feeling good about the switch. Then she called Peter, who ran errands for her.

"I have the paintings to ship against the east wall," she told him, explaining about the upcoming exhibition in New York. "See that they go out first thing in the morning. I'll text you the gallery's address."

"Sounds like a big show, Willow," he said.

"It is," she agreed. "The biggest of my life."

"I'll see they're properly crated and shipped. You can count on me," Peter reassured.

"Thank you. I'll see you when I get back. I'll even take you to dinner," she promised.

Willow slipped into her coat and as she locked up

and went down the stairs, she listened to the other voicemails on her cell. Sloane's came up first.

Hey, Willow, I'm in Reykjavik covering an economic summit. Actually wearing heels and makeup for the first time in months, since those don't go over well when I'm on assignment in Africa. Anyway, sorry I missed you. Hope you have a happy birthday. I'll try you again tomorrow once the conference finishes. Maybe I can swing by Paris and we can do dinner. Love you!

She stopped at the bottom of the stairs before going outside and shot Sloane a quick text that she'd be in New York for the next month or so, knowing she'd want to stay for a while once the exhibit began. Since the city was Sloane's nominal home base when she wasn't traveling the globe for her newspaper, she hoped they could manage to meet up if they both were in the States at the same time.

Willow stepped outside into the drab October afternoon. Though it was only three o'clock, it could have been five or later. A soft rain fell, and she immediately raised the hood on her all-weather coat, thinking how chilly it was for this time of year. She listened to Tenley's message as she walked. It was brief and just said to call when she could, so Willow decided to do so now before she arrived home.

The phone rang twice and her old college roommate picked up. "Hello? Willow?"

"Yes, it's me. Walking down a street in the Eighteenth *Arrondissement* and wishing you were here with me."

"Well, happy birthday, sweetie. I'm just sorry Charlie's Angels aren't together to celebrate it. Thirty is a big one."

Willow smiled at the name their landlord in college had given them. The trio had moved from the dorms to a dilapidated house their senior year. The owner of the rental, a guy in his sixties named Charlie, dubbed their trio Charlie's Angels. They'd referred to themselves that way ever since.

"What if I told you I'm flying out tomorrow for New York?"

"Seriously?" Tenley asked, excitement in her voice.

"Yes, I have a show coming up. Remy just told me about it. I have a ton of work to do to get ready for it, but I can always make time for you. Sloane, too. She's in Iceland now."

"Oh, that boring econ conference."

"That's the one. Anyway, I haven't talked to her, but if she makes for home, we definitely need to get together. Even if she doesn't come to New York, I want to see you."

"I'd love that," Tenley declared.

"How's the book coming along?"

"We can talk about that—and your upcoming show—at dinner. They've opened this incredible Italian place in Brooklyn. Not that Brooklyn needed anymore Italian joints, but this one is fabulous. I freelanced and did some of their PR, so they comped me some meals in return. We can go there and eat and drink the night away."

"Sounds heavenly," Willow said. "I'll be jet-lagged tomorrow, especially because I'll head straight to the gallery to see the set up, but I'll text you the day after and we can firm up plans."

"I'm so glad you'll be here, Willow. I miss you."

"I miss you, too, Ten."

By the time she ended the conversation, Willow was only a few blocks from home. The shower turned heavy in an instant, though, and she made a quick decision, ducking into a café to wait out the storm. She ordered a *café au lait* and shrugged out of her coat, placing it across a chair. Looking around, she saw the café was nearly empty, with only one other couple on the far side. As the server set down her coffee, Willow decided to make a quick call to Boo. It was about the time her grandmother got up each day, and she wanted to share her good news about the upcoming show at the Runyon. She would wait to call Jackson. He would already be at his office in LA, most likely with a client, or going over his opening, since he had a big murder trial coming up soon on the docket.

The phone rang seven times before Boo picked up.

"Boo, are you all right?" she asked, instead of saying hello.

"Why wouldn't I be?" was the feisty response.

Her grandmother was eighty-five now and still sharper than most people in their prime. She had visited Willow in both London and Paris, usually bringing along Gillian Roberts, their next-door neighbor, who was like an aunt to Willow.

"You usually answer the phone faster. That's all. I have wonderful news, Boo. Remy has scheduled a showing of my work at the Runyon Gallery in three weeks."

"That's marvelous, Willow."

Though her grandmother's words sounded enthusiastic, all Willow could hear was fatigue in them.

"You sound tired, Boo."

"I am. A little bit, my precious."

"Will you be able to come to my opening? Gillian is also invited, of course."

Boo sighed. "I don't think I'm up for traveling right now, sweetheart. I've had a nasty head cold I've been fighting. Flying and colds don't mix."

"But the exhibit is three weeks away, Boo. And it

will run for a couple of weeks. Surely, you'll be okay by then," Willow pleaded, not being able to imagine such a momentous occasion taking place without her grandmother present.

"We'll see."

She sniffed. "You used to put off Jackson and me with those very words when we were young," she pointed out. "*We'll see* translated to a hard *no* in Boo-speak."

"I did," Boo admitted. "If I'm not feeling up to coming, then I know Gillian can go in my place."

This wasn't like Boo at all. Her grandmother loved everything about New York. Worry filled Willow.

"Is something wrong?" she asked softly.

"Other than Ed Ferguson's poodle peeing all over my flowers on a regular basis, not much," Boo replied. "I need to get some coffee in me, Willow. You know I'm not much for anyone before that happens."

"All right. We'll talk soon. After I land in New York tomorrow."

"Take care, baby."

"I will."

It was only after she hung up that she realized her grandmother hadn't mentioned her birthday. It wasn't like Boo to forget a special occasion, especially the birthday of one of the children she'd raised. Willow sipped her coffee, trying not to fret. After all, Boo was eighty-five. It was probably time she did slow down. Besides, Boo celebrated every day of being Willow's grandmother. She was her grandchildren's most ardent supporter. It didn't matter if a birthday had slipped her mind.

Willow determined that after the exhibition, she would go home to Oregon. Driving cross-country to Oregon after the show might give her time to clear her head. She hadn't been home since her college graduation. It would be good to see Maple Cove and the house she grew up in. Hopefully, Jackson could come up from LA and they could all spend Christmas together.

Finishing her coffee, she saw the torrents of rain had let up and she left the café, walking the remaining two blocks in a fine mist. She entered their building and climbed the five flights to the top floor. When they had found the flat, she had wanted to rent it because of the great light it got, even though it was slightly beyond her and Jean-Luc's budget. Then she sold a few paintings, and somehow she became the one paying the rent. It wasn't as if she wanted to be some little woman whose man took care of her. She only wished Jean-Luc would offer to help out more, especially since he'd sold three pieces over the last two months.

She took out her key, happy to be home earlier than usual. Maybe they could go to their favorite café first and have a glass of wine and catch up before dinner. He had made the reservation to be an early one, so they could come home and celebrate in private.

As she placed the key into the lock, one of her tingles overwhelmed her. She hadn't experienced one in years. Suddenly, she stilled, wondering what awaited her on the other side of the door. Reluctantly, she turned the key in the lock and entered, closing the door behind her. She pushed back the hood and unbuttoned her coat. As she started to hang it on the rack, she stopped.

Another trench coat hung there. A woman's. Dread blanketed her. Instead of calling out a greeting, she slipped off her shoes and padded to the studio, past a beautiful floral arrangement that she assumed was for her birthday. Entering it, she found it empty.

Through the paper-thin wall, she heard a giggle. Then a moan. Followed by the bedsprings squeaking. A sick feeling washed over her.

She had suspected Jean-Luc of stepping out on her before and had confronted him. Both times, he had pleaded his innocence and lavished her with attention in the weeks that followed, lulling her into a sense of false security. This time she had proof of his infidelity.

In their shared bed.

Anger now racing through her, she stormed to the bedroom and flung open the door. As she suspected, her boyfriend was pumping into a naked female who wasn't shy about expressing her delight.

"I hope I'm not interrupting," she called out.

Immediately, Jean-Luc froze. The woman dropped her arms from around his neck and turned toward her. Willow saw it was Laetitia Seydoux, an acquaintance from two floors below, who was a dancer working part-time in a nearby floral shop. Laetitia smiled lazily and then turned back to stroke Jean-Luc's face tenderly.

He rose from the bed, tearing off the sheet and wrapping it about him, his gaze meeting Willow's defiantly. Then he turned to Laetitia.

"Get dressed," he barked.

"But—"

"Now," he commanded, harboring no nonsense from the dancer.

Sullenly, she sat up and swung her legs from the bed. Laetitia took her time putting on her clothes. Jean-Luc turned away from both women. Willow felt her cheeks grow hot as she watched the scene unfold, wondering what lies her lover was currently concocting.

Finally, Laetitia fastened the last button on her blouse. She glared at Willow and said, "I hope you enjoy your flowers. The ones *I* always bring so he can pretend he cares about you."

Laetitia walked past Willow, brushing against her on purpose. She forced herself to keep from snatching a hunk of hair and jerking the woman back.

When the door slammed, Willow said, "Well?"

Jean-Luc sat on the bed, the sheet still draped around him. "What do want me to say?"

"I don't know," she admitted. "I think any apology you offered would be insincere."

"Why should I apologize?" he said angrily. "You are too American," he accused.

Willow resented that he turned the situation to make her appear to be in the wrong. "What's that supposed to mean?"

"Americans are so... moralistic. We French are more open. I need a woman who fulfills my needs."

Fury filled her. "And you're saying I don't?"

He shrugged, that Gallic shrug that could mean a hundred things. "Sometimes you do. Sometimes I need more."

"So, instead of discussing this with me—talking it through as two mature adults who are lovers—you decided to cheat on me?"

"Cheating sounds so... bourgeoisie," he told her. "You are wanting to make something simple complicated."

Willow marched over to him. "And you are making a complicated issue over simplistic." She crossed her arms. "I won't have it, Jean-Luc. You swore you weren't cheating on me before, and yet here I find you in our bed with Laetitia. Was she the only one? Have there been others?"

She could hear her voice rising in hysteria and fought to calm herself.

Again, the shrug. "There may have been a few others."

"That's it. I'm done," she said, stepping back. "I turned a blind eye before, but we're over now. You need to move out."

A part of her felt relief that she had come home and found him cheating. It would save time and pleading. In the long run, she knew she would be better without him.

Hurt filled his eyes. "Where am I to go? You are the one who makes the money, even though you aren't that good an artist."

"What did you say?" she demanded, fury and resentment filling her, knowing he only thought of her as his meal ticket.

His eyes darkened. "You heard me, Willow. You are good—but *I* am *great*. I just need time to be discovered."

"I want you out. Now," she said through gritted teeth and then thought a moment.

Her art had been everything to her ever since she left Maple Cove for college. She had made sacrifices, both large and small, for it. Now, when she was on the eve of her greatest success, nothing but emptiness filled her. She needed more in her life. The people she loved. Jean-Luc had been an itch which she'd scratched. The scratching had gone on too long and created an open wound. She was hurting now. Humiliated. Feeling betrayed. But every wound eventually scabbed over.

When hers did, she didn't want to be in Paris.

She wanted to go home.

"Grab a few things and go to Laetitia's now. You can come back tomorrow night. I'll be out by then. You can keep the flat until the lease ends at the end of the year. I'll contact the leasing agent and make sure he understands it won't be renewed. Are we clear about that?"

He cursed under his breath and then grew braver, cursing aloud as he tossed off the sheet and stepped into his clothes that lay on the floor. As he threw a few things into a duffel bag, he called her names she wouldn't say aloud to her worst enemy. Worse, he accused her of being dull and that he had cheated out of boredom. Willow kept her composure through it all, not wanting to stoop to his level.

What surprised her most was the realization that she felt nothing for him at all. What she did feel was tremendous sadness. Her heart ached from loneliness, something she felt would continue to haunt her the rest of her life. She had never been worthy in the eyes of her various lovers. Any self-confidence she had crumbled in that moment.

When Jean-Luc finally left, she locked the door behind him. Though angry tears coursed down her cheeks, she packed two suitcases for New York with the clothes she favored the most. The rest she would leave behind. She didn't need chipped dishes or old wineglasses or ragged bath towels. Jean-Luc was welcome to it all.

She did text Peter and asked that he ship not only the paintings she'd left out for New York, but she also asked for him to box up her paints and art supplies and send them, along with the canvases she hadn't chosen to be placed in the show. She provided Boo's address in Maple Cove, saying to send the additional items to Oregon. She would go home to Boo and lick her wounds, after she was done in New York.

Boo always made everything better.

"Happy Birthday," Willow said aloud and then slumped to the floor and had a cathartic cry.

CHAPTER 2

MAPLE COVE

D ylan Taylor rolled out of bed and threw on running shorts and a long-sleeved T-shirt. He slipped his phone into his pocket and hit the bathroom before lacing up his shoes. After a few minutes of stretching, he went down the back staircase and out the door to the alley behind Sid's Diner. Sunrise wouldn't be for another three hours, when the polls opened.

The election that would decide if he became the sheriff of Barton County.

He ran down the alley and emerged onto the square. He ran around it, past the diner, Buttercup Bakery, and the Hidden Bear Bar & Grill. He turned south and continued along the square, not paying attention to the places he ran by, trying to clear his head. He cut over to Broad and headed south, still on autopilot.

Dylan had returned to Maple Cove at the request of Walt Willingham. The sheriff had broken the horrible news to Dylan a dozen years ago about the crash that had left him an orphan but at eighteen, a legal adult. Willingham had helped him wade through the next couple of weeks. Dealing with the funeral home. Insurance. Putting the house up for sale. Though he had never seen himself leaving his hometown, the urge to escape it flooded him.

Funny, it had always been Willow who had had the tug of wanderlust pulling at her. Friends since grade school, it had taken until their senior year for them to feel what he joked to be their love connection. Suddenly, he had seen Willow as a woman—and had fallen hard and fast. Still, he agreed with her that after graduation they needed to go their separate ways. They had different goals in life. Different dreams. His had been to put down roots in their hometown. Hers was to live abroad in Europe, in a bohemian lifestyle that he couldn't wrap his head around.

Instead, in a touch of irony, he had probably traveled more places than his former girlfriend had. Walt went with Dylan when he enlisted in the military a month after he earned his high school diploma. Based upon his ASVAB testing, the army saw their new recruit was intelligent, disciplined, organized, and a true problem-solver. After his seven weeks of basic training as a new soldier, he did another fifteen weeks of military police training. The work had taken him to bases around the world, where he investigated crimes and worked in securing military installations. Along the way, he had earned a degree in criminal justice, thanks to the GI Bill and being able to attend online courses, where a huge chunk of his work experience resulted in course credit.

He'd been at a crossroads ten years in, not sure if he wanted to reenlist or if he should return stateside and put his degree and policing experience to use. Dylan had discussed it with Walt, since they had remained close over the years. While he'd toyed with the idea to go to work for the Oregon State Police, Walt had other ideas, convincing Dylan to come home to Maple Cove and Barton County, where a deputy job awaited him. Deciding to take it, he'd come back to the place of his birth and joined the force under Walt's leadership.

It was only after he'd been on the job for a month that Walt confessed he had alternative motives in bringing Dylan home. The longtime sheriff had cancer. A slow-growing kind but cancer all the same. Walt's idea was for Dylan to run for sheriff in his stead when the next election occurred.

Today was election day.

He finished the run and returned to his apartment over the diner. Sid had lived above his place until he married a local teacher. Nancy insisted they move to a house so they could raise a family, and the apartment had been rented out from that time on. Sid had been dead five years now. Nancy quit teaching in order to take over the place. Dylan was the latest in a long line of tenants. With no wife or kids, the small apartment suited his needs.

He showered and dressed in civilian clothes. He had already taken off the day from work so he could be at the polls, greeting voters and pressing the flesh. Since he was on his time, he didn't think it appropriate to be in uniform. Dylan dressed in dark slacks and a sports shirt, running his fingers through his hair as he studied his reflection in the mirror. By this time to-morrow, he would either be sheriff of Barton County or out. His opponent in the race, Rick Mercer, had made that clear.

Making his way downstairs, he saw the diner was already three-quarters full at six in the morning. Walt sat in their usual booth. Dylan slid in across from his friend and noticed the deep, dark circles under Walt's eyes.

"You okay?" he asked.

"When you win today, I will be."

"*If*, Walt. *If* I win."

Walt gazed at him intently. "You will. You have my backing. That means a lot in this community. You've got a stellar military career behind you. You've also done a terrific job as a deputy ever since you've been back. Besides, there's always the football contingency. They'd vote you in for your quarterbacking skills alone."

"Even if that was over a dozen years ago?"

"Especially because it was that long ago. Good sports memories—like that sixty-two-yard touchdown pass your junior year in that one the game with two seconds to go—age like fine wine."

Nancy appeared with two empty cups and poured them both coffee.

"Morning, Nancy," they both said.

"Your food will be right out," she told them, bustling off to another table.

As Dylan doctored his coffee, he noticed Walt's hand shaking. He'd never seen a tremor before.

"Walt, what's wrong? Tell me."

The sheriff glanced around and then leaned in. "They found another tumor yesterday. A big one."

The news hit Dylan hard. Using his best poker face, he asked, "Does that mean chemo? Radiation?"

"Neither," Walt said flatly. "I saw what Janie went through with her breast cancer. How the treatments meant to save her drained the life from her. Her mouth so sore and swollen and her throat so tight that every time she swallowed, it was painful." He shook his head. "I won't go through that. The oncologist said even if I did, I'd only buy myself a few extra months at most. He also admitted they wouldn't be good ones."

The lawman took a sip of coffee. "I'm going to enjoy what time I have left, Dylan. I don't want to fight this any longer. I'll let you take over. Enjoy a little golf and fishing while I can. And then Janie'll be waiting for me when my time is done. Don't try to talk me out of this."

"I won't," Dylan promised, though his heart tore at him.

Walt Willingham had become a second father to him—and then his friend and mentor. The thought of losing Walt, who had always seemed larger than life, cut Dylan to the bone.

"Here you go," Nancy said with a smile, returning with their daily breakfast order. "Good luck today, Dylan," she added. "I'll head to the polls this afternoon after we close."

"Thank you," he said. "I'll need every vote I can get."

She squeezed his shoulder. "You've got this."

He dug into his short stack after pouring plenty of maple syrup atop it and savored the crunchy bacon. He and Walt ate in companionable silence, two long-time friends who could do so without it being awkward. He wished he could ask how long Walt had but didn't want to bring it up. The fact Walt even told him about the new tumor said a lot.

As they finished, his friend said, "Keep this under your hat. I don't want or need sympathy and casseroles. I'd get plenty of both if word got out. This way, I can retire in peace and do my version of riding off into the sunset."

"You know I'll be here for anything you need.

You've always been there for me. You know I'd do anything for you."

Walt smiled. "You were a good boy who had to grow up fast. You've become a good man, Dylan. I will be happy to turn over my office to you."

"I'd better get down to the high school and try to charm a few voters," he said lightly.

"You do that."

Nancy breezed by again "Want coffees to go?" she asked.

"None for me," Dylan said. "I need my hands free to shake hands and kiss babies and do whatever politicians do. I understand being sheriff is as much being a politician as it is being a lawman. Put breakfast on my tab."

"Will do," Nancy said.

He told Walt goodbye and decided to walk the four blocks to the high school. When he arrived, it was five minutes before seven. He went straight for a card table surrounded with *Taylor for Sheriff* signs in red and blue, and a plethora of balloons. His best friend since kindergarten, Carter Clark, stood there with Gage Nelson, a newcomer to Maple Cove. Dylan ran some mornings with Gage, a former Navy SEAL who was now a personal trainer.

"What is all this?" he asked.

Grinning, Carter said, "Mom told me that you need to have a patriotic base of operations today. This is as close as we can get to the gym doors without being in conflict with election rules." He glanced across the drive that led into the high school's parking lot. "Notice your opponent had the same idea."

Dylan looked to see Rick Mercer staring hard at him. He gave the enemy a smile and friendly wave. Mercer turned away.

"Mom helped set things up and then headed to school," Carter continued. "She said she'd be back after cafeteria duty to vote."

He laughed. Dorothy Carter was principal of Maple Cove Elementary. Part mother and part bulldog to both students and staff.

"Did you get in a run this morning?" Gage asked.

"Four to almost six," he replied. "I needed to hit the pavement to calm my nerves."

"No need to be nervous," Gage declared. "This is in the bag. I'm out and about and talk to enough people. Rick Mercer doesn't stand a chance."

"Did you help set things up?"

Gage nodded. "I did whatever Mrs. Carter said. Figured it's easier that way, and it gets done right the first time."

Suddenly, a stream of people appeared, and Dylan focused on talking with as many voters as he could. He'd been at it over two hours and was just shaking the hand of the owner of the town's hardware store when he heard his name called.

Turning, he saw Boo Martin approaching on a walker. That surprised him. Though Boo had to be in her mid-eighties by now, he had always thought of her as a wiry, tough bird, her fingers and arms strong from years of sculpting and her legs muscular from all the miles she hiked.

It's not that he had avoided Boo since his return to Maple Cove two years ago. He'd seen her around town occasionally. He just didn't go out of his way to visit her. Though he'd spent many an hour at her house while growing up, Boo still reminded him of Willow.

The One Who Got Away.

Dylan hadn't really dated during his decade in the army. Instead, he'd had a string of one-night stands over the years with women he came into contact with. He practiced safe sex, but with his job, he wasn't in one place long enough to contemplate having a relationship of any kind. He also didn't like the idea of dating a fellow soldier. Those were the majority of the people he met.

Since his return to Maple Cove, he'd only gone out sporadically, usually when fixed up by some well-meaning acquaintance. No woman appealed to him, and after a while, he'd stopped going out on any dates. He'd buried himself in work, doubting he would ever marry. He was married to the job instead. That would have to be enough.

Dylan asked, "How are you, Boo?" leaning over her walker to give her a hug. Turning, he greeted Gillian Roberts, Boo's next-door neighbor, who wasn't related but still seemed like kin to Boo all the same. Twenty-five years separated the women, but they were thick as thieves after living beside one another for almost forty years.

Looking back to Boo, he asked, "How are you?"

Normally, he would tell her how good she looked for her age and tease her a bit. Today was different. Boo appeared gaunt and leaned heavily on her walker. Her skin seemed sallow. The sparkle in her eyes was missing. The frail woman before him was a stranger.

"I have ovarian cancer," she said quietly.

The second bit of bad news today was another blow. "Do Willow and Jackson know?"

"No. Not gonna tell them," Boo declared. "I'm eighty-five, Dylan. I've lived a good life. Those two don't need to take on my worries. They'll find out soon enough. Jackson's got a huge murder case he's working on. Willow's preparing for a big show in New York.

One that will cement her reputation. Gillian will go to the opening in my place."

"They're not going to like it, Boo," he warned. "Willow and Jackson are as protective of you as you are of them."

The old woman cursed softly and he saw the return of a bit of the feistiness for which she was known.

"I'm here to vote," she proclaimed. "Probably the last time I'll get out, but I want to see you in Walt's place. Rick Mercer is a world-class jerk."

Dylan motioned Gage. "Would you see that Boo and Gillian make it to the gym?" he asked.

Gage gave a rare smile to the two women. "It would be my honor to escort you there. I might even have to show off my muscles and carry you, Boo."

"You do that and I'll slap you to the next county," Boo retorted.

Gage laughed and stood on her right side. Gillian moved to the left. They slowly followed Boo down the sidewalk leading to the gym.

As Dylan watched them, he thought Boo didn't have as long as Walt did. That meant a funeral in the near future. Willow had never returned to Maple Cove since her graduation from UCLA. He'd heard Boo and Gillian had gone to see Willow over the years in the various European cities she'd lived.

He wondered what it would be like, seeing the only girl he'd ever loved, once again.

CHAPTER 3

Willow struggled to keep her focus as she drove the rental toward Maple Cove.

Boo was dead.

Her wonderful grandmother. Lover of pepperoni pizza, Tom Selleck, and anything purple. She would never laugh again. Never take a lump of nothing and mold it into something of great beauty. Never dispense her sage advice, solicited or otherwise.

Emptiness filled her. It had ever since she had received the late-night call from Gillian, telling her Boo had passed away in her sleep. Though Willow pressed, Gillian didn't want to go into detail, telling Willow they would talk when she made it to Maple Cove.

She had left New York this morning, knowing her show was in good hands. The Runyon Gallery had sold all but two paintings and urged her to sign on for another show next summer. She was glad now she hadn't committed, unsure if she would have enough pieces to display by then. With Boo's sudden death, the desire to paint anything had fled. Willow would need time to mourn and then decide where she wanted to live. Europe held no fascination for her.

New York was a possibility, because of Tenley and Sloane's presence there.

Maple Cove, where she had thought to come to lick her wounds, didn't have quite the same appeal with Boo gone. Still, she could stay in her grandmother's house and try to pull herself together before she made any kind of decision.

Salty Point came into sight and she slowed the vehicle, knowing from past experience that the town was a speed trap looking for people to ticket. Being behind the wheel of a car felt foreign to her. In Paris, she walked or took the Metro everywhere, only renting a car on extremely rare occasions. Even trips to the country had been by train, with her and Jean-Luc going together or with another couple for a few days at a time. She would sketch as they picnicked and drank wine.

Thoughts of her ex-lover left a bad taste in her mouth. Willow fumbled with her purse, jamming her hand into it and digging around for a stick of gum. She found it and peeled away the wrapping, popping the gum inside her mouth and chewing furiously, trying to work out her frustrations.

She had chopped the heads off every flower in her birthday bouquet. Knowing Laetitia worked for a florist and remembering the woman's words, she suspected many of the bouquets Jean-Luc bestowed upon her had been ones Laetitia had brought home. Mentally, she kicked herself again, for the millionth time, furious that she'd been so blind to his faults. Being cheated on twice in a row by two different men had her questioning her judgment. One thing she planned to do was stay as far from a relationship as possible. Her emotional state was fragile. She had no business cozying up to anyone male.

One thing she had done for herself was to be tested for STDs when she landed in New York. She had shared a long, weepy dinner with Tenley and Sloane, going into excruciating detail about discovering the two illicit lovers in bed. Her best friends had sympathized with her, urging her to have margarita after margarita to dull the pain. The next day her head almost exploded, but inside, she felt cleansed for the first time since entering her Paris flat.

Sloane had remained in New York another two days, coming by the gallery and lending her critical eye to the paintings Willow had already arranged. They had dinner together once more before Sloane dashed off to Central America on a new story lead. Tenley had remained a constant, as much as she could, being married and needing to spend time with her husband. Willow had a suspicion that the marriage wasn't going well. She had never warmed to Theodore Smith, seeing him as cold and unapproachable, totally wrong for the loveable Tenley. Still, she tried her best to trust her friend's instincts and hoped she merely misread the situation.

Not only had Tenley not wanted to talk about Theodore, she was reluctant to share anything about the novel she was writing. Usually Tenley was full of enthusiasm for her writing. Though she was unpublished, Willow knew once Tenley got that one break, she would soar to the top of the bestseller lists.

She drove through Salty Point, the largest town in Barton County, and then left it behind, continuing on Boxboro Highway toward Maple Cove. It was hard to drive this stretch and not think of Dylan's family doing the same so many years ago, losing their lives to a truck driver who was driving under the influence. All three Taylors had been killed instantly, while the trucker came out of the wreck without a scratch. Fortunately, he'd been convicted of vehicular manslaughter and sent to prison. By then, Willow had already been in college almost two years and Dylan was stationed somewhere on the other side of the world. They hadn't stayed in touch once he joined the army. In fact, he had expressly asked that she not write him. She understood his need to cut all ties with his past. Maple Cove had been a place of happiness for him. After that May night, he wanted nothing to do with the town.

Still, she thought about him every now and then. More during the past few weeks, as she couldn't help but compare the rock-solid, good guy Dylan was to the philandering weasel she'd lived with for two years. What a waste of her life, being tied to a man who was unfaithful, as well as one who had no respect for her talent.

The town limits came into view and Willow passed the sign declaring Maple Cove's population, which had grown by several thousand since she had left to live abroad. She continued to the heart of the town, slowing to a crawl as she reached the square. The speed limit was barely faster than walking and she saw several pedestrians moving along the sidewalks. She spotted a new bakery next to Sid's Diner and grew a little mournful, knowing she had to leave her beloved croissants and eclairs behind. The Hidden Bear Bar and Grill was still open, though, a place she and Jackson had enjoyed eating at when they were growing up.

Then from nowhere, a car backed out just as she reached it. Willow slammed on her brakes but the rental hit the older car with a loud crunch.

"*Merde, merde, merde!*" she cursed, throwing the car

into park and cutting the motor. Just what she needed. A car wreck, when she'd been behind the wheel for the first time in ages.

Opening the driver's door, she got out as a gray-haired man did the same from the vehicle she'd struck. It was ancient. Rusted so badly she couldn't assign any color to it. Its bumper and trunk were covered in faded bumper stickers.

"What the hell were you thinking, lady?" the driver accused.

She heard a dog yapping and glanced to the car. A white poodle stuck its head out and began barking at her. She glanced back at the driver and recognized him.

"Ed Ferguson. Your poodle pees on Boo's flowers all the time."

He squinted at her. "I know you."

"I'm Boo Martin's granddaughter. Willow," she told him. "You pulled out without looking," she declared.

A small crowd had gathered on the sidewalk, watching their exchange.

She looked over at them. "Did anyone witness it?" she called out.

No one said anything, studying her carefully. She knew from growing up in Maple Cove how small town residents stuck together.

And she was no longer one of them.

Just then, a sheriff's county car pulled up beside her.

"Great," she mumbled under her breath.

A deputy with the requisite dark sunglasses and hat stepped from the vehicle and said, "What's going on here?"

"*She* ran into me," Ed declared. "Scared my Pearl to

death. She's accusing me of causing this when everyone saw it was her fault."

The lawman said, "Let me see your driver's license and registration, Ed. And your insurance card. You, too, miss."

Willow returned to the rental and retrieved her purse. With shaking hands, she pulled out her wallet and the rental agreement, having no idea if the registration papers were in the car or not. Then she grabbed her passport, as well, for good measure. She handed the license to the officer.

He frowned. "What's this?"

"My European driving license. It's recognized by all countries who are members of the EU." She had used it more for identification than actual driving but it had allowed her to rent a car when she landed at the Oregon airport.

"Some damn foreigner smashed into me?" Ferguson shouted. "What the hell are you doing driving here? Don't they teach you anything over there, wherever there is?"

Anger surged through her. "I learned to drive here in Maple Cove, Mr. Ferguson. Boo taught me. Remember, I told you I'm her granddaughter?"

He scratched his head, muttering under his breath.

She turned back to the deputy. "Here is my rental agreement. My US passport. I'm a citizen, Officer. I grew up in Maple Cove. Lived on Orchid Road from the time I was three until I left for college."

The deputy opened the passport, studying the picture inside it and then her. He looked over the rental agreement and then walked to the crowd on the sidewalk. Willow couldn't hear what he was saying but saw fingers pointing at her and then Ferguson. Returning to the damaged cars, the deputy studied both.

"Are you going to arrest her?" Ferguson demanded.

"It's your fault," she retorted, her patience running thin and the lack of sleep driving up her irritability level. "You backed out into oncoming traffic. I had the right-of-way."

"I don't need some foreigner telling me what the laws are."

Calmly, she said, "I was born here, Mr. Ferguson. Grew up in Maple Cove. Boo taught me to drive on these very streets."

"I'm not paying for this, Missy. You ran into me. Do something!" he shouted at the deputy.

The deputy touched his shoulder and spoke into the microphone resting there. She supposed he was calling for someone to help out. She fantasized about Ed Ferguson being led away in handcuffs, knowing that would never happen.

"Roger that," the deputy said. "The sheriff is only a few blocks over. We'll let him iron this incident out."

The crowd had now swelled to over two dozen. She felt her face burn with humiliation as they looked at her as if she were some kind of criminal.

"I'll sue you," Ferguson threatened. "And the City of Maple Cove. I'm not paying for this. Why, I report another accident, and my insurance will go sky-high."

Willow remained silent, thanking the heavens her brother was an attorney. He would represent her if push came to shove, though she doubted it would ever go to court. It was an open-and-shut case. She only wished this deputy, who looked so young he probably hadn't been on the job long, would speak up and use the authority he possessed. She also filed away Ferguson's remark about another accident, thinking he had been careless on more than one occasion.

Another county sheriff's car rolled up and stopped. The engine shut off and a tall, uniformed officer in sunglasses and hat emerged. As he walked toward them, her heart began pounding. She recognized the gait. The build. The high cheekbones and sensual mouth.

It was Dylan.

~

DYLAN TOLD Deputy Nolan Wright he would be there in two minutes. It was Wright's second day on the job and he doubts as to whether or not Wright would make for a good lawman. He was shy. Tentative. He was also Mayor Eddie Wright's only son. The mayor could be charming when he chose to be. Most of the time—at least with law enforcement and his staff—he was demanding and uncompromising. Walt had warned Dylan that working with Mayor Wright wouldn't be his favorite part of the job.

The mayor had insisted that Nolan go to work for the Barton County Sheriff's Department. At twenty-four, Nolan had his associate's degree from community college under his belt, earned in four years instead of the usual two. He had tried working for the local sanitation department. The city library. The post office. None of those jobs had lasted. Now he'd been thrust upon the sheriff's department. While Wright had done fairly well during his training, Dylan worried that if confronted with a crisis, the young man would wilt.

As it was, he already wasn't able to handle a minor fender-bender. From what Wright had said, Ed Ferguson had backed out and been hit by some out-of-towner. Ed was pitching a fit, his normal state of being.

It wouldn't surprise Dylan if Ed were already threatening to sue everyone at the scene.

He pulled up in his cruiser and saw Ed flapping his arms, shouting at a woman who had her back to Dylan. Nolan Wright stood passively watching as about two dozen spectators watched with interest. Dylan alighted from the vehicle and made his way toward the accident.

The woman turned. Immediately, his heart slammed hard against his ribs as he recognized Willow. He knew Boo had passed. But he had put out of mind that Willow would show up. It was if he hadn't wanted to acknowledge that fact.

Yet here she was...

The pretty girl he had spent hours kissing had matured into a woman of great beauty. Her auburn hair tumbled about her shoulders, longer than it had been the last time he saw her. She was still tall and thin as a willow tree. As he approached, he saw her lick her lips. His eyes were drawn to them and a sudden rush of desire rippled through him.

This was not good.

He removed his sunglasses. "Willow, it's good to see you," he said, wanting to reach out and wrap his arms about her in a hug but knowing he needed to maintain a professional distance with his current audience.

She swallowed. "Hello, Dylan. I didn't know you were back."

No, Boo wouldn't have told her that, though he was surprised Gillian hadn't mentioned it to Willow.

He turned to Wright. "Deputy Wright, apprise me of the situation, please."

Nolan Wright's body tensed. "Well, it looks as if Mr. Ferguson was—"

"I was minding my own business when she hit me out of nowhere," Ed interrupted. "And she's some damned foreigner."

"You're way off base, Mr. Ferguson," he said formally. "Miss Martin grew up in Maple Cove. We were in the same graduating class."

"Huh." Ferguson looked puzzled by that information.

Dylan looked over the scene and said, "You're at fault, Ed. Plain and simple." He knew Ed was over seventy and impatient. "Drivers along the square have the right-of-way."

"But she hit me," he complained.

"Doesn't matter. You with Porter Williams?" he asked, referring to the insurance agent whose office was on the square.

"Yes," Ed grudgingly said.

"Deputy Wright, please walk Mr. Ferguson over to Porter's office and explain the situation. I'm sure Porter will want to come out and see it for himself. I'll wait here with Miss Martin."

"Yes, Sheriff." Wright motioned to Ed, and the two cut across the square.

"Nothing to see here, folks," he called out. "Go about your business."

The crowd hesitated a moment and then began to disperse.

Dylan went to Willow and saw anger sparking in her eyes. She'd always had a quick temper and what he thought of as being a little moody. He'd always supposed that was part of her artist's temperament.

"Are you okay?" he asked.

"Not really," she admitted, her shoulders slumping. "Hitting Ed's car shook me up. I remember him from years ago. Always yelling at us to stay off his lawn. Boo couldn't stand him and always told me to stay away from him."

Her eyes welled with tears at the mention of her grandmother and he said, "I'm sorry about Boo."

"Do you know what was wrong?" she asked quickly. "Gillian called last night and told me she died in her sleep, but she didn't say much of anything else."

He wondered how much to reveal and simply said, "She was getting old, Willow. Things go wrong as you get older. Your body just doesn't hold up."

"She came to visit me several times. In New York and Europe. I guess I'm just having a hard time coming to terms with thinking she gave out. To me, Boo was immortal."

"Is Jackson arriving soon?" he asked.

"Yes. He should be here late Friday night." She paused. "I didn't know you were here. Or that you were the town's sheriff."

He shrugged. "I've been back a little while. Did a decade in the military in criminal investigation, and then Walt encouraged me to come home. I became one of his deputies and then ran for sheriff in last month's election. Normally I wouldn't have taken office until the first of the year, but Walt decided to retire and let me step in."

"How is Walt? It sounds as if the two of you remained close."

"We did. He's really the only one I kept in touch with," he said apologetically.

She touched his arm and a jolt rushed through him. Her eyes widened as her hand fell away. She said, "Don't be sorry. We always knew we would go our separate ways."

"And now we're both back in Maple Cove," he said

evenly, trying to regain his composure. "Will you be staying long?"

"I don't know," she admitted. "Things are a little up in the air for me right now."

"I saw Boo about a month ago," he shared. "She came out in order to vote for me."

Willow smiled. "That sounds like her."

"She said you had some big show coming up. How was it?"

He only asked to be polite. He'd already Googled it —and her—and knew Willow had received incredible reviews.

"It went well," she said modestly. "Better than I anticipated."

"I'd love to see your work sometime." Once again, he'd already seen several pictures of her paintings online.

"I shipped a few canvases to Boo's before I left Paris."

"Paris. That's where you're living?"

"Not now," she said, her mouth growing hard, telling him something bad had happened there. Willow had always worn her emotions on her sleeve. Or her face.

He saw Deputy Wright escorting Porter and Ed across the square and told her, "Legally, you'll be fine. Ed announces every other day that he's going to sue someone, but he doesn't have a leg to stand on in this case."

"I wish your deputy would have used his authority and stood up to Ed more. He didn't even introduce himself when he arrived at the scene. I only knew his name from the tag on his shirt."

"I'll have a talk with him. He's been on the job two

days now. His dad is the mayor, if that tells you anything."

Willow chuckled. "Small town politics. You're in the thick of it now." She paused. "I'm glad you showed up, Dylan. It's good to see you."

He would do more than show up in the future. He'd walked away from this woman once before.

Dylan swore he wouldn't make the same mistake twice.

CHAPTER 4

Willow arrived at Boo's house, turning into the long driveway and driving its length before cutting the rental's engine. As she got out of the car, Gillian emerged from next door. Her arms opened and Willow stepped into them, tears stinging her eyes. She hadn't allowed any tears since Gillian's call last night and knew they were overdue.

Gillian squeezed her a final time and released Willow. "Can I help you bring in your things?"

"There's not much," she admitted. "I travel pretty light. One suitcase and my backpack."

She had left her other suitcase at Remy's place, not certain of what plans she would make with Boo's death, which had left her drifting and out of sorts.

Gillian claimed the backpack and Willow brought her suitcase inside. The house seemed quiet. Too quiet. She caught the faint smell of brownies, a childhood favorite of hers, one which her grandmother had made with regularity.

"Come sit," Gillian suggested. "I know you have questions."

They went to a plaid sofa. Boo had it recovered

twice that Willow knew of, saying the quality of what lay below the fabric was worth the price of reupholstering the sofa every dozen years or so.

She slipped off her shoes and pulled up her feet under her. "Tell me everything you didn't on the phone last night."

"It was ovarian cancer," Gillian admitted. "It didn't bother her—until it did. By the time she saw her primary care physician and then received a referral to an oncologist, she was in Stage 3."

Willow knew there were four stages of cancer and that ovarian cancer was a beast.

"Why didn't she tell Jackson and me?"

"You know Boo. She always marched to her own drummer. I know she didn't want to worry either of you regarding her health."

"But I would have flown home," she protested. "Taken her to her treatments."

"And that's what she wanted to avoid." Gillian hesitated. "There were no treatments, Willow. Boo chose not to pursue conventional or non-traditional avenues. Her only relief came from her weed-laced brownies. She tried edibles and they left her nauseous, but the brownies hit the spot. They gave her relief and you know she was a chocoholic."

Yes, Boo had passed on her love of chocolate to both Willow and Jackson.

Gillian took Willow's hand. "She knew you would have dropped everything and come if you'd known. It was the very reason she didn't tell either of you. You and Jackson were in her heart. She's still with you, Willow. In your heart. In your soul. In your memories."

"We never talked about her death. Do you know what she wanted for funeral arrangements?"

Gillian nodded and stood, retrieving a folder from a nearby end table and handing it over. "These are her instructions. She wanted to be cremated. No funeral service. Her ashes scattered off the coast. Walt Willingham has agreed to take you out on his boat. Then a party to celebrate her life."

Willow certainly didn't feel like celebrating, but she knew it was what Boo would have wanted.

"You can pick up her ashes tomorrow any time after two o'clock. When does Jackson arrive?"

"Not until tomorrow night. He has a big murder trial about to start. That means he'll just be here for the weekend."

"Then the party better be Saturday night," Gillian declared. "Don't worry. I'll handle the food and beverages, as well as the guest list. A copy of it is in the folder. I'll also call Walt and let him know we need to go out Saturday afternoon so that Jackson can be here for the scattering of Boo's ashes."

Gillian stood. "I'm going to leave you now. I know you have a lot to think about, Willow. But call or come over if you need me, okay?"

She nodded and walked Gillian to the door, hugging her again.

"Thanks for coming to the New York show last week," she said. "I'm sorry I didn't get to spend much time with you."

"You had a lot going on. It looked as if every piece was going to sell."

"It was a very successful show," she said, her throat thickening with unshed tears.

After Gillian left, Willow dumped her backpack and suitcase in what had been her bedroom. Then she went to Boo's bedroom and looked around. Clothes still in the closets and drawers, including the caftans her grandmother had favored in her later years, as well as her usual flannel shirts and jeans. She saw the bottle of Shalimar on the bureau, a scent Boo had always worn. Willow picked up the bottle and squirted a smidgeon on her wrist, holding it up to her nose and inhaling Boo.

Then she went to the bed and curled up on it, bringing the afghan over her as her tears fell. It wasn't just losing Boo. She deliberately had never thought about that, believing her grandmother to be the Energizer Bunny who would outlive them all. At least Boo had gone out on her own terms, having lived a long, fruitful life. She had been an original—an artist, a feminist, and a pacifist. She had instilled her values in her grandchildren, and Boo would live on through her and Jackson.

Willow was at loose ends now. Without her grandmother's sage advice, she was on her own. She was on the brink of incredible financial success with the Runyon show going so well. She had tired of Europe. While it was a wonderful place to have spent her twenties, she didn't realize how a nomadic lifestyle might wear on her. Suddenly, the need to put roots down overpowered her. Whether it would be in New York or here in Maple Cove was the sticking point.

If Dylan hadn't been here, she would instantly have chosen Maple Cove, for its familiarity and the lingering presence of Boo still in this house. But having seen him—and knowing how entrenched he was in the community by recently being elected its sheriff—made her doubt Maple Cove was the place for her to heal from her broken relationship with Jean-Luc. Actually, from all the previous relationships in her life.

Her reaction to seeing Dylan after a dozen years worried her the most. It had been a very physical one. She realized she had never truly gotten over her first love. They had never made love. Never known that sweetness. She was a wreck when it came to choosing men. Very few interested her, and those who did wound up disappointing her. If she did stay in the Cove, she would have to keep her distance from Dylan. After her latest breakup, she was vulnerable and knew she had no business becoming involved with any man.

Much less the one she suspected she still loved.

She forced herself to get up and found sheets to make up the bed in her room. Then she unpacked, hanging clothes in the closet and putting toiletries in the bathroom. She ventured downstairs again and fixed a bowl of cereal and toast for dinner since she didn't feel like cooking.

Her cell buzzed in her pocket and she withdrew it, not recognizing the number. Reading the text, though, she knew exactly who sent it.

Hear you are scattering Boo's ashes. Would like to be there for it—and for you.

Dylan.

She wanted to immediately tell him no but thought better of it. Boo had loved Dylan to pieces and had tried to help put him back together after the senseless death of his family. Dylan had taken off quickly, though, not wanting to remain in the Cove. Boo once slipped, mentioning she had written Dylan a few letters but had never received a reply. Willow had let it pass, knowing Dylan had wanted to cut ties with everything he had known when he entered the military.

Still, he had been someone Boo loved. If Dylan

wanted to be there when Boo was returned to nature, she wouldn't stop him.

Will do so Saturday afternoon before party celebrating Boo's life. Be at the dock at three.

Waiting, she received a thumbs-up from him. Nothing else.

What was she expecting? She didn't want him to come over and comfort her. She didn't want him in her life again. They were completely different people than they had been a dozen years ago. Besides, he probably had married and had a kid or two by now. That was a very sheriff-like thing to do. Willow didn't need Dylan getting into trouble with his wife, spending time with his former girlfriend.

Even if they had been involved a lifetime ago.

JACKSON ARRIVED at ten Friday night, looking haggard. He dropped his bag and enveloped Willow in his arms, no words necessary between them.

"Wine?" she asked, after he released her.

"Sounds good. And a sandwich if you have anything to make one with. I barely made the plane. Was the last one on. No time to grab anything to eat."

"You could've stopped once you landed in Portland," she chided.

"I wanted to get here as soon as I could."

"Go unpack. One sandwich coming right up."

When Jackson returned ten minutes later, Willow had a ham and turkey sandwich made, along with chips and the promised wine. Her brother sat and inhaled the sandwich before he said a word.

"You look tired," she said, once he finished. "You've

got dark circles under your eyes. You look as if you've lost some weight.

"This trial..." His voice trailed off. "It's not good, Willow."

"What's bothering you about it?"

"He's guilty," Jackson said.

"But you've defended plenty of guilty clients before," she pointed out. "After all, you are a defense lawyer. Some of the people you represent are going to actually be guilty. That's just the law of averages."

"This is different," her brother insisted.

"Has he told you he's guilty?" she asked.

"No. I won't let him. But his eyes tell me he is every time we meet. What he's guilty of?" Jackson shivered. "It's vile, Willow. This man is a sick bastard. The crime scene photos turned my stomach."

"Then why did you agree to represent him?"

"I did so as a favor to another client. One I'd successfully defended a couple of years ago. He said he had this friend who needed a really good lawyer. One who was willing to pay all cash. Retainer. Incidentals. The investigator. Trial fees. I make a decent living, but L.A. is an expensive town to live in. I have the people in my office to pay. My paralegal, who doubles as my receptionist. My investigator. Court filing fees. Experts who testify on behalf of my clients. And a partner to split whatever's left."

Jackson raked a hand through his hair. "I said yes before I even knew what the charges were. Rape and murder."

Willow shuddered. "I know this is hard on you. When does the trial start?"

"We're in the middle of jury selection right now." Frustration filled his face. "The thing is, my gut tells me that I'm going to get him off. What scares me is that if I do—he'll do it again."

"You can't think like that," she told him. "Everyone deserves a top-notch defense. You've said so time and again. Do your best job. Then it's in the hands of twelve strangers. They will be the ones who judge him guilty or innocent."

"Guilty or not guilty," he corrected. "Innocence doesn't play into the system."

"Cut ties with him once the case ends," she suggested. "If he's found guilty and wants to appeal the jury's decision, tell him to get himself another lawyer."

Willow placed her hand on his forearm. "Don't take any more murder cases for a while. Maybe you could even take a break after this trial. Why don't you come back up here for Christmas?"

He eyed her with speculation. "Are you staying here?"

She sighed. "I think I am. I can't go back to Paris. I ended things with Jean-Luc. As much as I love my pastries and escargot, I do miss juicy American cheeseburgers."

"But no New York?" he pushed. "I thought if you ever came back, you'd want to live in New York. Your two college roommates and your agent are there. It has lots of galleries to display your work."

"While I would love to see Tenley and Sloane more, Sloane is hardly ever in New York. She's renting a room from a friend's mom. Basically, it's a place to store things she doesn't take on the road. She is always gone covering the latest, hottest story. As far as Tenley goes, you know she's married now." Frowning, she added, "Her husband doesn't like me."

"He told you that?" Jackson asked, surprise in his voice.

"He didn't have to say anything. Theodore can convey most everything he feels with a disdainful look. Frankly, I don't know what Tenley sees in him. She's quieter around him. Not her usual, bubbly self. I'm a little bit worried about her."

"Then stay in touch," her brother advised. "If he's trying to cut you from her life, he'll do it with others, too. Then she'll end up isolated and having no one to turn to." He paused. "So, you think the Cove is for you?"

Willow nodded. "We meet with Boo's attorney tomorrow afternoon. After we scatter her ashes. I'm sure she's left the house to us. I hope you don't mind me living here. I had canvases and art supplies shipped here from Paris and placed them in her studio today. The light in there is amazing. While I'm not exactly chomping at the bit to work just yet, I figure I will eventually."

"You can have the house," he said. "I don't need it. My life is in L.A."

"What if you came back to the Cove?" she proposed. "You could practice law here. I could paint. We might actually have a life and make friends again." She laughed.

Jackson shook his head. "I don't know about that, Willow. That would mean a huge change for me."

"It might be one you need to make," she said. "Once your current trial ends, think about it."

Her advice to Jackson surprised her. Willow knew she would stay for a while in Maple Cove, but living here long-term wasn't in her plans, especially knowing Dylan was here.

Then where was this coming from? Asking Jackson to give up his lucrative law practice in California to practice small-town law wasn't what she had

thought she would suggest. Besides, didn't she want to
leave here after she had licked her wounds and grown
emotionally stronger?

Maybe. Maybe not.

They finished their wine and both headed up to
bed. She had trouble falling asleep, thinking about
her decision to stay in Maple Cove.

And how difficult it might be to avoid Dylan
Taylor.

CHAPTER 5

Dylan had received Gillian's invitation to the celebration of Boo Martin's life. He planned to be there.

But where he really wanted to be was with Willow when she scattered Boo's ashes beforehand.

He had gotten out of Gillian that would happen before the party began. Walt Willingham had a boat and would be taking Willow, Jackson, and Gillian out to sea. Dylan didn't think Walt was in any shape to do so. That would be his in. He had already texted Willow and she had given the okay for him to be present.

It was a start.

Throwing on his all-weather coat, which repelled water, he drove to the dock and headed to Walt's boat slip, finding his mentor similarly outfitted.

"Afternoon, Dylan. What are you doing here?"

"I came to help. You'll need me as second mate when you take the Martins and Gillian Roberts out to scatter Boo's ashes."

The former sheriff frowned. "I don't recall asking for your help."

"You didn't. I'm offering it." He paused and then played his trump card. "I have unfinished business with Willow. I need to be here for her. She agreed for me to come out on the boat with everyone today."

Dylan thought if Walt believed that was why he volunteered his services today, he would accept it. And it was the truth.

He pressed on. "You know Willow and I dated in high school. That night you came to tell me about my parents? It was prom. We were leaving early because... well, we had decided to finally... be together."

He couldn't bring himself to mention sex, which was ridiculous for a man his age.

"That night changed everything," Dylan continued. "You know how shook up I was. How you guided me through what needed to be done. Then I left. Cut all ties with Willow and Maple Cove." He shook his head. "I owed Willow more then. I was too immature and hurting too badly to bring closure to our relationship."

Doubt flickered in his mentor's eyes. "And you think going out with her as she scatters her grandmother's ashes will make up for all that lost time?"

His resolve hardened. "I still love her, Walt. I never stopped. I want to be with her during this trying time and support her. If she'll give me a second chance, I'll take it and never let her go."

Dylan swallowed. He had admitted aloud what he'd held in his heart for far too long. He did love Willow. He had never stopped loving Willow. All these years later, she was still The One.

Walt studied him. "All right. You can come along."

"Thank you," he said humbly, knowing this was the first step to hopefully entering Willow's life again. He had no idea if she planned to return to Europe, where he assumed she had been living, nor how long she might stay in the Cove settling Boo's affairs. Ironically, he had just taken a job that seemed tailor-made for him.

Could he give it up for another chance at love?

And that was if Willow felt the same. A dozen years had passed. She was bound to have had other relationships. Hell, she could be *in* a relationship even now. He hadn't even given that a thought.

First things first. Discover if she was married or seeing someone. Back off if she were, keeping his feelings to himself. If she were free, though, he told himself he had to go slowly. See who Willow was now.

And if they still fit together.

Then he could proceed.

Doubts plagued him. He felt he was being given a second chance with Boo's death and Willow's arrival back in the Cove. But what he thought of as a second chance might be the last thing Willow wanted. She may have moved on from the pure love they had felt for one another. Their lives had taken radically different paths. Who knew what Willow thought now? Who she was. What her goals were.

He only prayed that this was fate—and that he'd not blow it this time.

Dylan climbed aboard the boat and helped Walt get things ready to set sail. Ten minutes later, he spied Willow, Jackson, and Gillian heading toward them. His gaze met Willow's, and he noted she stiffened. Not exactly the reaction he was hoping for, especially after the traffic stop. One touch from her and his pulse had quickened, as she had briefly placed her hand on his forearm. The chemistry still existed between them.

It seemed he would have to convince her to do something about it.

Greetings were exchanged and he shook hands with Jackson, who had been a senior when Dylan was a freshman, a hotshot star athlete in three sports. Dylan had aspired to be like Jackson in every way, from his star turn on the playing fields to his stellar academic career.

"You still in the Cove, Fish?" Jackson asked, calling Dylan by the nickname Jackson had given him when Dylan was a freshman and Jackson a senior assigned to mentor him during football practice.

Obviously, Willow hadn't shared anything about Dylan with her brother.

"Yes. Did a decade in the military police and then came home to play deputy to Walt's sheriff. He recently retired and I took the helm."

"Get ready to cast off," Walt announced.

Jackson helped with the process, saving time, and soon they were underway, sailing from Maple Cove and heading out to sea. Dylan looked longingly at Willow, wanting to talk with her and yet suddenly shy about doing so.

"Let me take over," Jackson said. "Go see Willow."

"All right," he agreed.

Dylan made his way to her. She sat with a bronze urn in her lap, her fingers wrapped tightly about it. He took a seat next to her. Gillian, who sat on her other side, nodded to him and stood, moving toward Walt in order to give them some privacy.

"How are you holding up?" he asked, wanting badly to touch her and refraining from doing so.

She shrugged. "Okay, I guess. I'll admit that I never envisioned a world without Boo in it. The news hit me hard."

She licked her lips, drawing his attention to them. How many hours had his lips been on hers? They must have shared a thousand kisses in those days. A wide gulf of time now stood between them, but he couldn't help but think that, fundamentally, they were the same people they had been then, despite the passage of time. He had known Willow better than anyone. Been closer to her than anyone else in his life, then and now.

"Where are you living?" he asked, wanting to establish that baseline so he could know where he might go from it.

"Nowhere," she said, sadness creeping into her tone. "With Boo's death, it's been a bit of a wake-up call, I guess." She hesitated and then said, "I've spent the last few years in Paris."

"You always wanted to live there," he recalled.

She smiled wistfully. "I did. It was everything— and nothing—like I thought it would be."

"Tell me," he urged, just wanting to hear her voice.

She bit her lip. "I loved the heartbeat of the city. The pace. The cafés and museums. I had a studio I worked in, separate from my apartment."

"That sounds as if you've had a bit of success since you could afford separate workspace."

"I've been selling paintings on a regular basis the past few years. Enough to make a decent living and then some. Out of the blue, I got a call from my agent about an offer to do a show in Manhattan at a very well-known gallery. It would spotlight nothing but my work."

Dylan saw her eyes well with tears and longed to reach for her hand.

"I decided to commit to it and packed up and came to New York several weeks ago in order to help stage it. The show ended just as I got the news of Boo's death."

He swallowed, asking the question that had hung between them. "Will you stay in New York?"

"I don't know," she said softly. "I need time away from the city and all its noise and hustle and bustle." Her gaze met his. "I've decided—for now—to stay in the Cove. For how long? I don't know."

Hope sprang within him. "At Boo's?"

Willow nodded. "I had my assistant ship my art supplies and works-in-progress to Boo's. I don't feel like painting yet, but when I do? Her studio will be ideal." She hugged the urn to her.

Dylan waited until she looked up again, his gaze pinning hers. "I know it's been a long time since we've spoken, but I am here for you, Willow. I want to support you in any way I can."

"Thank you," she said, her voice shaking. "But we can't go back to the way things were between us, Dylan."

"Why not?" he asked, searching her face.

"I am broken," she admitted, shame filling her face. "I am raw and in a world of pain. I just broke up with someone." She hesitated and then added, "I've never had a successful relationship with a man."

"You did. With me," he pointed out.

She smiled ruefully. "We were kids, Dylan. We've both changed in so many ways. If we became involved, it wouldn't last. It would only lead to more heartache. Frankly, I can't stand anymore hurt that what I'm already carrying in my heart. I need to protect myself."

He hated seeing her lack of confidence. Hearing the pain in her voice. He wanted to wrap her in his arms and never let her go.

But now wasn't the time. Willow was grieving. He needed to give her some space. Not too much—or it might drive too large a wedge between them. But for now, he would back off.

"I am here for you," he promised. "If you need a friend to talk with. Someone who can listen without judgment."

"That's... kind of you," she said, her tone already putting distance between them.

Dylan had his work cut out for him.

But his heart told him Willow was the one for him. That together they could have something incredibly special. Stand strong against whatever came their way. It would take a lot to convince her, though. If anything, Willow was stubborn and temperamental. It sounded as if she had already decided there could be nothing between them, and she would stick to that. He would have to wear her down, little by little.

It was the only way they might ever find happiness together.

CHAPTER 6

Willow felt at peace now that Boo's ashes had been scattered in the Pacific and Sheriff Willingham steered them back toward Maple Cove. She headed in his direction as he guided them along the increasingly choppy waters.

"Thank you, Sheriff. I appreciate you taking us out so that Boo could be where she wanted to be."

"Your grandmother always did love the water." He smiled. "I'm not sheriff anymore, Willow. That's Dylan's headache now."

Just the mention of her former love had tingles ripple through her. No, staying in the Cove on a permanent basis would not be a good idea. Especially with Dylan entrenched in his position. It would be hard to avoid him.

And Willow wasn't certain she wanted to avoid him.

She kept thinking of how every relationship she had ever had since Dylan had fallen apart. Was it because she was still in love with her high school sweetheart?

No, that was a dozen years ago. They were completely different people. They probably had zero in common. She knew he had gone into the military. She was a pacifist who didn't really believe in war. Dylan had dedicated himself to serving his country. Now, he would serve the town of Maple Cove and its county in his new role. She didn't need to start up anything with him. Even if he had given off that vibe.

But she still wished they could make love. Only once. Just so she could see if her other relationships had been lacking in that department. They certainly had in every other way, from respect to communication.

No, sleeping with Dylan—even once—would be like playing with fire. She had already been burned numerous times now. She knew better. Temptation might tease her, but she refused to give in to it. As long as she kept her distance from her former sweetheart, she would be good. She couldn't afford any more emotional disasters. Making love with Dylan Taylor would certainly qualify in that category.

"Are you coming to Boo's celebration of life?" she asked Willingham.

"I wouldn't miss it for the world," he told her. "Boo held a special place in the hearts of many people in town." He squeezed her shoulder.

Willow smiled and went to sit next to her brother. "You okay?" she asked.

He raked a hand through his hair. "I guess. I keep thinking Boo will be waiting for us at the house, though. That this all has been some awful mistake."

She laid her head on his shoulder. "I know. I've thought the same."

They sailed into the harbor, and the former and current sheriffs handled tying up the boat. Willow and

Jackson said their goodbyes and joined Gillian, returning to the house.

Gillian said, "I'll be in and out, setting up food and whatnot. Clancy is coming by to discuss Boo's will with you. In fact, there he is now." She waved at the car pulling up.

"Clancy is still practicing law?" Jackson asked, as they got out of the car. "I can't believe he hasn't retired yet."

"He said he's waiting for the right attorney to take over his practice," Gillian informed them. She eyed Jackson. "Know anyone who might be interested?"

"Not me," he informed her.

"Oh, there's the bakery truck," Gillian said. "I need to meet Ainsley."

"Ainsley?" Willow asked. "Ainsley Robinson?"

"Yes," Gillian said. "You remember her? She was a few years behind you."

"I ran into her in Paris. She was attending a pastry chef school. She had big plans."

"Well, she runs the best bakery for a good five counties or more and agreed to cater today's food," Gillian said. "Come say hello to her. Jackson, you go invite Clancy in and get him set up."

"Yes, ma'am." Jackson headed to the blue sedan.

Willow joined Gillian and went to meet Ainsley, who had been a freshman when Willow was a senior in high school. Even then, Ainsley was known for her desserts. Every summer from the time she was eight, Ainsley set up a card table at the high school and Little League baseball games and sold everything from cookies to pastries to whole cakes to spectators who came for games. She expanded and did the same before football and basketball games and also took orders during the Thanksgiving and

Christmas seasons to provide desserts for family gatherings. She had told Willow she made enough during those years to put herself through college and pay for the fancy pastry school she attended in Paris.

Ainsley opened the white panel truck's door and got out. "Willow! Hi!"

Willow ran the last few steps and hugged her friend. "It's been a couple of years."

"Yes, it has," Ainsley said, returning the hug.

"It's so good to see you, Ainsley," Willow said. "We only got to have coffee twice in Paris before you left. I thought you had plans to open a pastry shop in New York."

Ainsley shrugged. "That was my original idea, but I've found throughout my life that plans change. I decided to come back to Maple Cove and open a bakery instead. It's done really well, with strong support from the citizens in the Cove, and even picking up some of the tourist trade along the Oregon coast."

She paused. "I am very sorry to hear about Boo, Willow. She was a wonderful woman, and she always supported me from the time I started selling my baked goods." Ainsley smiled wistfully. "Boo never paid me my asking price. Instead, she would usually double the amount. I never forgot her kindness and generosity. She told me I was an artist in my own right, and she wanted to support my edible art."

Willow's eyes filled with tears. "That sounds just like her. She did have a sweet tooth, you know."

Ainsley chuckled. "She did. Some people are chocoholics, but Boo was a dessert-a-holic. Though chocolate was tops in her book." Ainsley looked to Gillian. "The same with you. You seem to like anything sweet yourself."

Gillian laughed. "Boo and I certainly had that in common. Can I help you bring things in, Ainsley?"

"I can do it myself, but I'd appreciate help setting things up. I worked off the list you gave me, Gillian, and then added a few other items. I quartered the sandwiches so they would be easier to handle and eat. I know there will be a lot of people who come and pay their respects today."

Gillian glanced to Willow. "I'll help Ainsley. You go in and meet with Clancy and Jackson now."

Willow nodded and said, "We'll have to catch up later, Ainsley."

"I'd like that," said the younger woman.

Willow entered Boo's house, thinking she would always think of it as Boo's, and figured Jackson had taken Clancy Nelson to her grandfather's study. She made her way there and found the two men chatting amiably.

Clancy rose and greeted Willow with a firm hug. "Good to see you, Willow. Sorry it's under these circumstances. The whole Cove adored Boo, myself included. She and I were friends nigh on fifty years. If she hadn't have been so devoted to your grandfather's memory, I might have persuaded her to become Mrs. Clancy Nelson. "

The attorney extended a hand. "Have a seat, Willow. We'll get down to business. I know you are expecting a crowd soon for Boo's to-do."

She took a seat next to her brother, and Jackson took her hand, squeezing it in support. Clancy went to sit behind the desk and opened the briefcase sitting atop it, pulling out various file folders and then opening one.

Looking up, he said, "I have copies of everything for each of you. Everything is pretty straightforward.

Jackson, I know you might want to read over the documents, but for now, I'll give you the gist of things. The house and all its contents go to the both of you. The same for Boo's sculptures, with the exception of one which she wanted to go to Dylan Taylor. The sculptures include the ones she has on loan to several museums noted in her will, as well as any completed works within the house itself. I called her agent and have a list of all these pieces for you to use as a reference. As far as her money goes, Boo has made some specific notes of gifts to be awarded to various charities, then the rest will also be divided between the two of you."

Willow listened as Clancy mentioned the numerous charities, both located in the Cove and beyond.

"The last thing Boo wanted done is to set up an endowment for a yearly scholarship to be awarded to a graduating senior from the local high school. Now that she's gone, I'll work on drawing up the paperwork. The applicant must complete an application as well as submit a piece of art, including but not limited to paintings, mixed media, and sculptures."

"What criteria will be used to award the scholarship?" Jackson asked.

"Boo left the details up to you and your sister," Clancy answered. "You can run the contest however you wish, choosing the dates of entry and closing, as well as selecting the recipient yourselves or allowing for a committee of your choosing to do so. Boo supported the arts—from music to dancing and acting, to art itself. She wanted to leave this scholarship as her legacy for the next generation of artists."

"We'll have to think on the details, Clancy," Jackson said, as Willow nodded in agreement. "Can you disperse the funds named in the will, or will we need to do so?"

As her brother and Clancy worked out the details, Willow's mind wandered. She thought it generous of Boo to award an annual scholarship and hoped this would encourage those who might not think majoring in art to be practical to think otherwise. The amount Clancy named for the initial scholarship would cover four years of tuition, room, and board, enabling talented artists to receive the education they deserved and be equipped to enter the art world without debt. Boo had paid for both her grandchildren's educations, including law school for Jackson. The fact both of them started their careers with no debt had made a huge difference. This would be Boo's lasting gift, continuing to give to those talented artists who would become the next generation of crafters.

"I suppose that's it for now," Clancy told them, rising and slipping a folder inside his briefcase before closing it. He indicated the two manila folders on the desk. "One is for each of you. If you need any help discussing the endowment and scholarship, I'd be happy to go over that with you. I'll also speak to Dylan about his sculpture."

"Do you know which one it is, Clancy?" she asked, having gone through the art still in Boo's studio. She couldn't imagine what piece Boo might have wanted Dylan to claim.

"I brought it with me today. It's in the car. Something Boo finished a long time ago." Sadness crossed his face. "She had me hang on to it for her. I think it hurt her to have it around, especially after Dylan left the Cove."

"Boo thought so much of you, Clancy," Willow said, still curious about what Boo had sculpted for Dylan. "I would enjoy having you as a part of the selection committee for this scholarship recipient. At least this first year."

"I would be delighted to serve. It would be an excellent way to honor my longtime friendship with your grandmother. I'll give you two a few minutes to yourselves."

The attorney left the study, his step slow but steady.

Once he exited the room, closing the door, Jackson said, "Clancy wants me to take over his practice here in the Cove."

"Would you consider doing so?" she asked, thinking of their conversation the previous evening.

Jackson sighed. "I don't know, Willow. I always saw myself in a big city, at a large law firm, trying noteworthy cases." He hesitated and then said, "Instead, I find myself at a two-man office. Busy as hell. And almost at my breaking point."

Concern filled her. "Is it this current murder case? Or are you simply burning out because you're a defense attorney and continually see the seamier side of things?"

He nodded. "Probably a little of both. I realize many of my clients are guilty. That doesn't bother me. I know everyone deserves his or her day in court, and I'm willing to represent them. This McInally case, though, has me reconsidering my decision. It's too late to withdraw. We're in the middle of jury selection as it is, and the judge would never go for me exiting now. Besides, you must have a compelling reason to abandon a client. I don't."

"But what about after this case ends, Jackson?" she pushed. "Would you think about coming home and practicing law in the Cove? Last night, you indicated your future was in L.A."

He shrugged. "I told Clancy I would think about it. It wasn't lip service, either. It took a long time to fall asleep last night because I kept thinking about what you'd suggested. Me coming back to the Cove. But I made no promises to Clancy. He did remind me, however, that he is eighty-five and not getting any younger. He said he would give me until next summer before he needed an answer. He turns eighty-six on July Fourth and mentioned he would like to celebrate that day by walking out of his law office and never coming back."

"That gives you time, Jackson. How long do you think this trial will run?"

"We should finish jury selection by the end of next week, if not sooner," he revealed. "However, it's a complicated case. I will be calling a large number of witnesses. With Christmas around the corner, the judge will also give a break to the jury and give them a few days off."

"So, they won't be sequestered?"

"I had thought at one point they would be. These murders have been all over the news. Still, we met in chambers before I came to the Cove, and the judge told both the D.A. and me that he was reluctant to isolate the jury, especially with the upcoming holidays."

"Then with the Christmas break, how long do you see this going?"

Jackson shrugged. "I would say six weeks minimum. Probably eight. Both the prosecution and defense are calling a good number of expert witnesses. That testimony can be tedious and time-consuming, but it does lay the foundation for both of our cases."

"Then you think possibly by the beginning of February the trial would conclude and a verdict would come in?"

"That's my hope. Of course, murder cases usually mean the jury is out a good week or more before they reach a verdict. If they find my client guilty, it will mean an appeals process starts immediately. Going back over the transcript with a fine-toothed comb, trying to see if there's a reason to try it again."

"What about your partner? What's his role in this?"

"Naturally, Bill Watterscheim is my second chair on this case. He also has two upcoming cases he needs to devote time to, though. My paralegal and private investigator are a big help, but the burden of fighting for this defendant mostly falls squarely on my shoulders."

Jackson had spoken to Willow over the years about some of his cases, sometimes with enthusiasm, but she had never witnessed such reluctance on his part. He had told her little, other than this was a case involving rape and murder. She decided instead of asking him about it, she would Google Gerard Mc-Greer and see the particulars about this case and why it seemed to be eating Jackson alive.

If Jackson seriously considered leaving L.A. and returning to the Cove, Willow wanted to stay, too. She had missed the physical closeness of being with her only sibling. She knew also that he was eager to become a father, though none of his relationships had panned out, due to the hundred hours he put in each week at his law practice. Willow could easily see Jackson settled in the Cove, with a wife and children, becoming a leading figure in the community. Her brother was the type who would become involved in Maple Cove, both in its charities and civic affairs. It wouldn't surprise her that if he did return, he might one day run for the school board or even mayor.

If that were the case, she wanted to be here. She wanted to be part of the lives of her nieces and nephews. She had been rootless throughout her twenties. She missed having a family.

The only stumbling block was Dylan Taylor.

Could she live in the Cove with her former love so close? Especially since Dylan seemed bent on picking up where they left off. Willow knew that would be a mistake. She had a feeling that she was destined to spend most of her life alone. Her many failures at a relationship led her to believe so. If that were the case, being close to Jackson's children might be the only way she would ever enjoy young children.

She decided she had time before a decision had to be made. Obviously, Jackson needed to try his case and then give Clancy an idea whether or not he would assume the older lawyer's practice. That meant staying in Maple Cove for at least the next six months or so. Willow decided she could do that. It would take that long for her to figure out what she truly wanted, both professionally and personally. She had a place to stay and time to heal. Already she felt herself itching to hold a brush in her hand. The scenery along the Oregon coast had called out to her as she had driven to Maple Cove, and though she had told Dylan she wasn't ready to begin painting again, she realized she was wrong.

"I suppose we should go out and help Gillian," Jackson said. "Are you going to stay in the Cove for now?"

Willow nodded. "I won't make any decisions about my future until you do," she told her brother.

"Don't hang this on me, Willow," he warned. "You need to live your own life."

"I'm in limbo, Jackson. For now, I wish to take things day by day." She smiled brightly. "Come on. I want to introduce you to Ainsley Robinson. She was a few years behind me in school and we ran into one another in Paris, where she was attending pastry school. Apparently, she is back in the Cove and has opened a successful bakery."

Willow grinned impishly. "You are going to love her chocolate chip cookies."

CHAPTER 7

Willow was overcome with emotion half an hour into Boo's celebration. It amazed her how many lives her grandmother had touched during her eighty-five years.

The turnout had been tremendous, the house filled with people Willow remembered from her childhood and until she left the Cove to head to California and college. She spoke to her former principal and several teachers. The mayor, doctor, and local dentist came, as did the vet, grocer, and members of Boo's book club. Toasts were given and stories shared, letting Willow and Jackson know how Boo had been woven into the very fabric of this coastal community. As she listened to stories of how Boo had touched these people's lives, her eyes met her brother's and they both smiled.

Willow barely recalled coming to Maple Cove after her parents perished in a freak avalanche on the slopes where they were skiing.

Gillian spoke of her deep friendship with Boo, one which had lasted decades.

"Boo was both a mother figure and then friend to

me," their next-door neighbor shared. "I turned to her in good times and in bad. I suppose I will always turn to her and talk things over with her, knowing she is looking down and watching over me and the rest of Maple Cove—and especially Jackson and Willow."

At that point, Jackson accepted the floor and as he spoke of Boo and her influence in his life, Willow openly wept.

Suddenly, a warm hand engulfed hers. Dylan's fingers laced through hers, and she felt warmth and support pouring from him into her. She squeezed his hand, grateful to have him beside her.

He handed her a handkerchief, and she mopped her eyes with it as her brother finished his remarks. Then Jackson looked to her and Willow nodded. She remained where she stood, tightly holding on to Dylan's hand as she began.

"I was only three when I came to the Cove. Jackson and I had lost our parents, and even at such a young age, I remember feeling adrift. Boo became the anchor in my very confused world. With every nightmare that awakened me, Boo was by my side, comforting me. Loving me. She never asked for me to hide my feelings. Instead, I remember her telling me how a good cry could make a person feel better."

Willow smiled ruefully. "I had a lot of those tears, but Boo was right. Tears are cathartic. I am here today mourning the woman who raised Jackson and me and who loved us unconditionally until the day she died. As I look around this room, I see so many of you. People Boo also loved. Lives which Boo touched in ways I may never know. I thank you all for loving Boo as I do. As Jackson does. This town meant the world to her. She instilled the love of Maple Cove in me that I will carry until my own dying day."

Wiping her eyes again, she smiled. "We've re-membered Boo today with a lot of tears, but she would want this occasion to be a happy one, so please lift your glass a final time to my grandmother, Boo Martin, the most remarkable woman I have ever known.

"To Boo," Willow said.

"To Boo," the large crowd echoed.

"Let's have some fun in her memory, shall we?" Willow urged, and the blanket of sadness eased from those gathered. She moved once again from person to person, this time reminiscing with a lighter heart as the music played. All the while, Dylan Taylor re-mained beside her, their fingers woven together. She wasn't going to question it now. She would deal with it later when she had the strength to do so.

They reached Clancy Nelson, and the old lawyer said, "Well done, Willow. Boo was always so proud of you and Jackson. You were the light that always guided her life."

"Thank you for the friendship you offered Boo, Clancy," she said.

"I hope you will consider staying in the Cove, Wil-low," Clancy encouraged. "Jackson, too. I'm sure he told you about my offer."

She nodded. "He mentioned you needed an an-swer by July Fourth. I think it would be good for him, Clancy, but I can't make that kind of decision for him. Jackson will use both his heart and his mind and come to the right conclusion. What's best for him per-sonally and professionally."

"I think he will." Clancy grinned. "I may just have to put him on the prayer chain, though. It wouldn't hurt to have a little divine intervention in his decision-making."

She chuckled. "I can see Boo elbowing God now to give Jackson a nudge to come home to the Cove."

She chuckled but her throat thickened with emotion.

"Dylan, Boo did leave something to you," Clancy continued.

"What?" he asked, and Willow saw his puzzled look. "I don't need anything from Boo."

"You'll want this, son. I guarantee it." Clancy glanced to Willow. "I brought the piece in from my car and placed it in the study. Can we go there?"

"Of course," she replied, and the three of them moved from the large gathering, heading down the hallway until they reached the study.

Clancy held up a hand and they came to a halt. "A little background on this, Dylan. Boo created this sculpture many years ago. She did so to bring you comfort and joy. When you left town, she turned it over to me. I've held on to it all these years. When Boo knew she was dying, she had me make a note in her will. The artwork is now yours. I believe you'll enjoy it."

Clancy turned and left them. Her gaze met Dylan's. "I suppose we should go see what Boo left you."

Dylan turned the handle and pushed the door open, pulling Willow along inside with him. He closed the door behind them and they moved across the room toward the desk. Then Dylan froze in his tracks. Willow saw why.

It was Major.

For the first time in well over an hour, Dylan released Willow's fingers and moved to stroke the statue. It was two feet in height and caught Major as he leaped in the air. The German shepherd had been Dylan's constant companion since the time he was seven, accompanying his master everywhere. Major had run alongside Dylan's bicycle as he delivered newspapers on Sunday mornings. The dog had stood outside the fence, watching Dylan come to bat during baseball games. Boy and dog had slept together each night of Major's life. By the time Willow and Dylan began dating their senior year, the canine had lost a few steps but still was loyal and loving and ever present.

One night in March before their graduation, Dylan awoke and Major didn't. Willow had often thought of the pair as Jackie Paper and Puff the Magic Dragon—except this time it was the animal who left and not the boy. Dylan had mourned the loss of Major deeply, crying in Willow's arms for his friend. Only two short months later, the rest of Dylan's family had perished in a car accident, leaving him alone in the world.

Dylan stroked the sculpture lovingly. "Boo captured every line of Major," he said, his voice breaking.

"The two of you were constants around here our senior year," Willow said softly. "Boo probably loved Major almost as much as she did you."

Dylan smiled, tears brimming in his eyes. "She caught him perfectly in motion, as if I had just tossed a ball to him and he propelled himself in the air, ready to catch it."

"Looking back, I remember she was in her studio more than usual after you lost Major. She must have been working on it all that time."

His hands fell to his sides. "She wrote me, you know. After I left for the military. I had wanted to cut ties with everyone and everything in the Cove. Memories were just too painful. I recall reading her first letter to me and crying like a baby. I knew I couldn't read anymore, much less reply to her."

He glanced up. "I never opened another letter she sent—and she sent plenty. Finally, they stopped coming. I suppose she got tired of me never responding to her." Guilt flashed across his face. "She probably told me about this sculpture in one of those letters, and I was too selfish to read it."

This time it was Willow who reached for Dylan, taking both his hands in hers and squeezing them.

"Boo didn't have a vindictive bone in her body, Dylan. You know that. She wouldn't have blamed you. You were young and hurting."

He gazed steadily into her eyes. "I was young. Immature. I might have made straight A's, but emotionally, I had a long way to go, as far as growing up went. My immaturity hurt people, Willow. Boo, for one. You, as well."

She shook her head. "No, Dylan, I understood. You had a need to move on from the life you had led in the Cove. You knew enough to know that most of the rest of your life lay ahead of you, and you needed to start living that life. It was a good decision for you to join the military."

"It made me the man I am today," he said solemnly.

"I can see that. Besides, we had always talked about ending things between us once I left for UCLA."

He smiled ruefully. "You also had your own life ahead of you, Willow. One that went far beyond the Cove. To college. Europe. Becoming a part of the art world. The only thing is that we never got any closure, did we? We never got to make love that night Walt found us sneaking out of our Senior Prom. Then I was caught up in the haze of everything that had to be done with my family's death. It was overwhelming.

Fortunately, I had Walt by my side to walk me through it all."

His gaze intensified until Willow felt he looked into the depths of her very soul. "But of all the regrets I have in my life, you are the biggest one, Willow," he finished. "We never said a proper goodbye because I didn't think I could walk away from you if we did. I regret having no closure."

"So do I," she whispered, her heart hammering against her ribs, those tingles filling her, the ones which always did whenever Dylan touched her.

"We both had a lot of growing up to do, Dylan," she added. "Thankfully, we've done so. We made it through the rest of our teen years and our twenties. We still have many years in our future to look forward to."

"*Our* future? Do you think we have one together, Willow?" he asked.

Willow wanted to tell him no. She didn't want to start something up with the boy she had loved, who had become this imposing man. Yet words escaped her, and she looked at him helplessly.

She knew at that moment that Dylan was going to kiss her.

And she wanted him to. Desperately...

CHAPTER 8

When Dylan's lips met hers, Willow believed she had finally come home. No kiss had ever been sweeter.

She had only kissed five men in the past dozen years. Two had been men she dated at college. The other three men she had kissed had been ones she had lived with. One in Berlin. Another in London. And finally, Jean-Luc in Paris. Every one of these men had wounded her. Betrayed her. Made her feel unworthy and insignificant.

Would Dylan do the same?

Even as he kissed her, Willow held back a part of herself, unwilling to totally let go and live in this moment.

He broke the kiss. "Why aren't you kissing me back?"

She saw the confusion in the gray eyes she had loved so much. And hurt. Hurt that she had put there.

Touching her fingers to his cheek, she said, "I'm no good at this, Dylan."

"Kissing? I beg to differ, Bear." He framed her face

in his large hands. "You have always been spectacular at kissing."

A blush heated her cheeks, both from his compliment and the fact he had called her Bear. When they had first started dating, Dylan told Willow she was cuddly like a teddy bear—unless she was pissed about something. Then he said she could be a bear about whatever bothered her. She had forgotten he called her that term of endearment.

Until now.

"Dylan, I—"

"You don't trust me yet." Hope shone in his eyes. "But you will, Willow. I promise you that."

He pushed his fingers into her hair, kneading her scalp, making her go weak-kneed and tingly at the same time. She fought the feelings building inside her. Old feelings for the boy she had loved. The boy who had become this man.

One she didn't really know.

"It's been a dozen years since we were together, Dylan. Since we kissed."

His thumbs moved to smooth her eyebrows and lingered at her temples. "We both still remember how to kiss, Willow."

"Kissing just leads to... messy things," she said, realizing she was being vague.

"I get it," he said softly. "You've had relationships which didn't work out. Tell me this—are you involved with anyone at this moment?"

"No," she admitted.

"Then I'm not stepping on any other fellow's toes. I just want to enjoy kissing you. It can lead to as much or as little as you choose, Willow. I won't rush you." He paused. "You said you were no good at this. What did you mean?"

She took a deep breath and expelled it. "Relationships. I fail miserably at them."

Dylan chuckled. "And I succeed at never having them," he quipped. "Oh, we are a pair, Bear."

His hands cradled her face again. "But maybe it's because we were meant to be together. Did you ever think of that? Maybe that's why nothing has ever worked out for us with someone else?"

Still fighting him, she said, "We aren't the same people we were at eighteen," she protested.

"I sure hope we aren't," he said, a teasing smile playing about his sensual lips.

Lips she really wanted to kiss.

Why the hell not?

She was a grown woman. Kissing this man didn't mean they would be in a committed relationship. It would be a kiss. That's all.

Just a kiss.

This time, Willow took the lead. She fisted her hands, snagging his shirt, jerking him to her. Her mouth landed on his and she became the aggressor for a moment. Then Dylan answered her call. Soon, their tongues warred, the spice of his subtle cologne filling her with giddiness. He gentled the kiss, which had been demanding and greedy, and explored her leisurely, one hand cradling her nape, the other resting against her throat, his fingers sensually stroking it.

Willow wanted him to caress more than her throat.

She wanted to make love with Dylan Taylor.

Easing away from him, she forced her lips and her body to step back. She trembled, wishing she could fall into his arms again.

"I think I need to get back to the others," she said,

her chest heaving as she tried to get her emotions under control.

"We're not finished yet," he told her, his eyes dark with desire.

"I agree."

His eyes widened. "You do?" He cursed low, under his breath.

"I've never heard you curse before," she said.

Shrugging, he said, "Picked it up in the military."

"I'd like to hear about those years," she told him. "Maybe over pizza?"

"How about we go for a hike tomorrow?" he suggested, taking her hand, his thumb caressing her knuckles. "Then pizza and beer after. And whatever else we feel like doing."

"All right. What time?"

"Eight too early for you?" he asked.

"No. I'm still an early bird in search of that proverbial worm."

He squeezed her hand. "I remember you used to get up early and catch the morning light when you painted."

"I still do."

She looked at him wistfully, wondering if spending time with him was wise. But she was an adult. One who had never gotten Dylan Taylor out of her system. She would make love with him once and satisfy her curiosity and then move on. Willow didn't know if that would happen tomorrow or not, but she would be open to the idea.

Suddenly, he yanked her toward him, slipping his arms around her and giving her a lengthy kiss. He broke it and grinned.

"Just in case you think you might forget me between now and then. Think about that kiss."

Oh, Willow would definitely be thinking about that kiss. And the hard, muscled body that went along with those lips.

WILLOW WAS UP BY SIX, combing through the clothes she had left years ago, and finding a flannel shirt she had loved in a drawer. She paired it with the jeans she now wore and then searched the bottom of the closet and found the hiking boots she had left behind. She hadn't hiked in many years and regretted that, having gotten some of her greatest inspiration from those times in nature. She still was a walker, though, and had done that in the streets of the cities she had lived in over the past decade. But it felt good to be back in Oregon, a place where outdoor activities were encouraged year-round. It was time to dedicate herself again to her painting. Hikes would be the first step. She had always drawn her greatest inspiration from being out in nature.

She went downstairs, finding Jackson in the kitchen.

"Coffee's already on," he told her.

"Do you have time for a quick breakfast?" she asked.

"Cereal and toast for me," he said. "I need to get the rental back and make my flight. I have a ton of work to do."

She watched him get cereal bowls for both of them as she peeled a banana, slicing half into each of their bowls. Jackson put bread in the toaster and collected jam from the refrigerator.

He smiled. "I have missed Boo's blackberry jam. I

wonder if she has any jars I could take back to L.A. with me."

"I'll check the pantry," Willow told him, finding not only blackberry but three other types of jams.

She grabbed a jar of blackberry and one of strawberry and set them on the table. "These should last you for a while. But I mean it, Jackson. I want you to come back here for Christmas."

He poured coffee for them and set the mugs on the table. "It'll depend upon the trial, Willow. Jury selection will be done by then. I don't know if we will have gotten far into the actual trial, though. I don't know if the judge will sequester the jury, especially with it being holiday time. A hostile jury not getting to see their families at Christmas is never a good thing for a defendant. Particularly one accused of a heinous crime."

The toast popped up and he put the slices on plates, bringing those to the table, and they sat.

"I do hope you'll give Clancy's idea consideration."

He studied her a long moment. "I might—if you stay in the Cove, that is. Speaking of that, I saw you disappeared with Dylan for a while yesterday."

Her cheeks warmed as she said, "Clancy had a sculpture which Boo had done for Dylan years ago. It was of Major."

"His dog?"

She nodded. "That dog was like family to Dylan. They were inseparable for over ten years. To lose Major and then his entire family such a short time after was a hard blow."

"I vaguely recall hearing that Dylan went into the military. Funny, I thought one of the reasons you two broke up was because he wanted to stay in the Cove, while you wanted to travel the world. Instead, it seems as if he left before you did."

Jackson sipped his coffee thoughtfully and then asked, "Is there anything still between you?"

"Honestly? I don't know. He seems to think so."

Her brother put his hand over hers. "What about you and Jean-Luc?"

"That's over," she said brusquely. "Another of my doomed relationships where my significant other cheated on me in spectacular fashion."

He squeezed her hand and released it. "I'm sorry, Willow. It seems neither of us has had much success in the romance department. I put in so many hours that the idea of having a relationship with a woman is laughable."

"If you practiced in the Cove, I don't think you would be nearly as busy," she reminded him. "Of course, it would not be as profitable either, I suppose."

"You'd be surprised," he said. "Cost of living in L.A. is through the roof. Even when I have clients who can pay well, the retainer is eaten up quickly. Rent for the offices. Paying staff, including the investigators. It adds up quickly. Right now, we're barely keeping our heads above water."

Willow decided she had nudged Jackson enough. If he were ready to come back to the Cove, he would need to make that decision on his own.

"If you stayed here, that would be a good reason for me to close shop in L.A. and return here."

"I can't make any promises now, Jackson. Boo's death has thrown me for a loop. I don't want to return to Europe, but I'm not sure I want to stay in the Cove full-time. That's for me to figure out over the next few months. I'll keep you apprised of any decision I make."

"Same."

They finished eating and rinsed the dishes, putting them in the dishwasher.

Jackson enveloped her in a long embrace. He pulled away. "Let's talk more often," he suggested. "I think I may need some of your sunshine to help get me through this murder trial."

She walked him out to his rental and kissed his cheek. "Text me to let me know you got back all right."

He got into the car and pulled out of the long driveway. Willow returned to the house and wandered restlessly from room to room. She knew at some point she would need to clean out Boo's things. Donate her clothes, hopefully to a women's shelter in Portland. If she were to stay permanently in Maple Cove, she would also have to tackle a few repairs and updates around the house. It was obvious Boo had let things go in her last years. The kitchen could use new appliances and countertops. The inside and outside of the house also needed to be painted. It looked like new gutters might also be in order. If Jackson chose to remain in California, they might need to sell this house if she moved on. It would sell more quickly if those updates had been done. If they kept the house and she stayed, the changes would make for more pleasant living. She would talk with Dylan about who might be available to help her with any construction.

The doorbell rang and anticipation flooded her. She tried to tamp down the wild emotions and get them under control as she walked to the door. She didn't like the fact she felt giddy as a schoolgirl at the mere thought of Dylan Taylor.

"You are an adult, Willow Martin," she reminded herself as she reached the front door and opened it. "You aren't eighteen anymore."

All thoughts of trying to control her excitement went out the window when she saw him standing on the porch. Dylan had been a good-looking teenager, his frame athletic because of the multiple sports he played, but in the years since then? He had filled out in all the right ways. Physically, he appealed to her.

Very much.

He wore a flannel shirt of gray and blue, bringing out the gray in his eyes. She yearned to run her fingers through his thick, coal-black hair. More than anything, she longed to kiss his sensual lips again.

"Good morning," he said, giving her an admiring glance. "Ready to go?"

"Let me grab some waters."

"No need. I have everything in the car. Waters. Snacks." He grinned. "Even a pizza coupon for later."

"My, aren't you the Boy Scout, being all prepared?"

"That's one thing the military taught me," he shared. "I learned to be organized. To think critically. To be decisive in my actions.

"Like this."

He took a step toward her, his hands settling on her waist as his lips brushed against hers softly. Her hands went to his shoulders, clasping them tightly, as the soft kiss became more. Much more. For several minutes, Dylan greedily explored her mouth. Willow reveled in the sensations of his tongue gliding against hers. His teeth softly sank into her bottom lip, pinning it, sucking on it hungrily. Then he kissed her a final time, gently, and broke the kiss.

He gave her a disarming smile. "Ready to hike?"

CHAPTER 9

Dylan knew he had taken a huge risk kissing Willow so early, but he couldn't help himself. He had tossed and turned in bed last night, finding it hard to fall asleep because thoughts of her danced through his head.

This was the woman for him.

She was fighting that notion, however. It was up to him to convince her they belonged together. Permanently. It would be a fine dance as he did so. He didn't want to prod her too hard. Willow had a stubborn streak a mile wide, and if she thought he pushed too hard and fast, she would step away and never look back. He didn't want to chase her from the Cove—much less his life—and told himself to keep his hands off her this entire hike. She would need to make the next move, whether she did so today or another time.

At the heart of the matter was trust. He wanted her to trust him again. Once, long ago, she had. He had broken that trust when he fled the Cove, signing up for the military without even going to tell her good-bye. If he had been more mature, he might have handled things differently, but grief had swallowed him whole, and all he could think of was escape.

He had had more than a dozen years now without Willow. He wasn't willing to spend another lifetime without her. Dylan realized her trust had to be earned. He would do everything in his power to help her regain her trust in him.

He led her out to his SUV and opened the passenger door for her. She climbed in, her long legs in those tight jeans tantalizing him. He pictured them wrapped around his waist and willed the thought away.

Dylan slid behind the wheel and as he pulled out of the driveway, shared where they would be hiking this morning—a spot he'd discovered shortly after he returned to Maple Cove, and one he and Willow had never been to together.

"I don't think we'll run in to many people," he said. "Several other places have become more popular with the local hiking crowd."

"I was happy to find Boo hadn't thrown out my hiking boots. I found them in the closet of my old room."

"Guess you didn't have many opportunities to hike in Paris," he chuckled.

"No, but Paris is definitely a walking city. Parisians stay in such good shape because they walk so much. It also allows them to splurge on those morning croissants and afternoon pastries."

"How long did you live in Paris?" he asked, curious about her life. "I know that had always been a goal of yours."

"The first time was when I spent a semester abroad my junior year. It was the spring semester, and I'll admit it—there *is* nothing like Paris in springtime.

Anyone who lives there during that time falls in love with the city.

"And the second time? After I graduated, I moved to Berlin first, in order to study privately with a renowned artist who had been a visiting professor at UCLA. She encouraged me to come and spend time with her in Berlin. I learned quite a bit from her, brush techniques that I use to this day."

Dylan listened as Willow recounted her time in Germany and then her move to London.

Finally, "I wound up in Paris as I always dreamed of doing. I had my first true success there, albeit on a small scale."

By now, they had arrived at the state park and the trooper at the gate waved them through, seeing Dylan's annual pass stuck to the windshield. He parked at his favorite spot. They got out and he handed her a small hiking pack, slipping a water and trail mix into it and then doing the same for himself. They shrugged into the trail packs and set out.

"I've dominated our conversation, Dylan. Why don't you tell me a little about your time in the army?"

He wanted to know much more about her in the years they'd been apart. Willow had done nothing but speak about surface matters, talking about her art and things she had learned. Paintings she had created and sold. Yet she had not mentioned a single friend or relationship. He would have to dig deeper later. For now, he would allow her some privacy.

"The first thing I had to do was take the ASVAB. You remember that test from high school?"

"No," she said, chuckling. "You know I wasn't much of a student. I was all about art. Although I have found I do have a knack regarding numbers."

"I had done well on the ASVAB in high school, but

they had me take it again at the recruiting office. I blew the roof off that puppy. Apparently my scores indicated that I would be good if I served in the military police. The MPs."

He elaborated some on his basic training, telling her a few stories to make her laugh as they hiked, and then mentioned some of the places he had been stationed around the world over the years.

"Here I thought *I* was the world traveler. You have been many more places than I have. Did you have a favorite post?"

He shrugged. "My favorite place was always where I was stationed. I tried to get to know the local cuisine. See the sights tourists did and go beyond that to where the locals hung out and ate." He stopped. "But the lure of home was always there. I tried not to think about it often, but I did miss the US. The Cove, in particular. Yes, I saw a lot of the world and many beautiful places, but the Oregon Coast is embedded in my DNA, I suppose."

"What was the catalyst that had you return here?"

He began walking again, turning to go up a switchback as they headed uphill. "I was coming to an end of my most recent enlistment and got a letter from Walt. He said there was a place on the Cove's force for me if I wanted it. That the training and experience I had being an MP would be invaluable. So I came home. I haven't regretted it."

"Walt didn't look good to me," Willow noted. "Is he ill?"

"I think he had an inkling of it when he wrote to me. Janie had just passed away. I realize now he was thinking long-term, looking for his replacement. Yes, he has cancer. At the time I came home, I was just happy to be back in the Cove as a member of the police department."

"What kind of crimes did you deal with as an MP? Did you have special training?"

"After basic training, I went with others in the army and marines to do a special course in criminal investigations at Fort Leonard Wood in Missouri. It involved course work in crime scene investigation and interrogation, among other things. I learned how to think analytically. How to pay attention to details. It also helped me with my people skills. A lot of investigations involve gaining the trust of those involved with or even on the periphery of the crime.

"I've investigated things from property loss and destruction to criminal activities, injuries, and deaths."

"That doesn't seem all that different from things you might find in Maple Cove," Willow observed.

"You're right about that. Citizens here become drunk and disorderly. Smack their wives around. Set things on fire."

"Do you miss being in the military?"

"Not really. I miss the friendships I made, but MPs are transferred with some regularity. I got used to leaving friends behind and making new ones. I keep in touch with a few of them. A text here. An e-mail there. I prefer a steadier kind of life, though. I ran from the Cove because I was hurting."

He gazed steadily into her eyes, stopping on the trail once again, clasping her elbow. "I ran from you. I'm sorry about that, Willow. I might have been book smart, but I had a lot of growing up to do. I did that during my army years. It gave me a purpose. It provided me with leadership skills. I also communicate better now. I'm not so closed off."

He released her elbow, because all he wanted to do

was move closer and kiss her again. He wanted to keep his promise to himself and remain aware that the ball was still in Willow's court, and she had yet to send it back his way.

"I've put roots down in the Cove, thanks to winning the election for sheriff. I'm in it for the long haul."

"I envy you," Willow said wistfully. "It seems you know exactly who you are and what you want. You're ready to build a life in the Cove and help the people here."

Once again, he stopped and forced her gaze to meet his. "You know exactly who *you* are, Willow. Your art has always grounded you. It doesn't matter where you've gone in the world. You are talented and dedicated to it. Would I like you to stay in the Cove and paint here? Sure, I would. But I believe your heart will tell you where you need to be. Just listen to it."

Dylan fervently believed her heart would tell her to stay here.

"I feel guilty," she said, starting down the trail again.

"Why?"

"Because Boo was so sick and I didn't know about it. I should have come home. I never did after I moved to Europe. I hope this guilt won't eat me alive."

He wheeled, stopping directly in front of her, halting her progress. "Don't you *ever* feel guilty for following your dreams, carving your own path. Boo was the bravest, boldest woman I ever knew. She blazed her own path and marched to her own drummer, all the while caring for you and Jackson. She would be the first to tell you to shake this off and get on with your life. Boo Martin would not want you to feel sorry for yourself."

He saw his words getting through to her as a slow smile turned the corners of her mouth up.

"You're right," she told him. "Boo encouraged me to always walk my own path. She may not be here physically with me, but her spirit will be what guides me the rest of my life."

"Good."

He turned and continued along the path. They hiked in amiable silence until they reached a small clearing that had a beautiful view of the water.

"Let's stop here," he suggested. "I love this spot."

And I love you...

The thought jolted her. Frightened her. Surprised her. Feelings she thought had been buried long ago suddenly rose to the surface, demanding to be dealt with. Willow buried them, not wanting to acknowledge them. They were friends. On a hike. That was all.

She sat, her back leaning against a fallen log, and he joined her. They opened their waters and drank deeply and then snacked on the trail mix he had put together. He caught her up on some of the gossip of the town. Boo, though an intricate part of the Cove, had never spent much time sharing these things with Willow. They had a tendency to talk about their art. What pieces they worked on. What was inspiring them. Or they discussed books they read and things in the news. Now, Dylan caught her up on who had married and divorced. Who had moved away. Who had died and who had started new businesses. It seemed very comfortable between them, like slipping your foot into a well-worn boot. He hoped she felt the same way. Then from the corner of his eye he saw movement and the bushes stirred slightly. Protectively, he stretched an arm out across her.

"What is it?" she asked quietly.

"I'm not sure."

Then from the brush emerged an animal. It took Dylan a moment to realize it was a dog. Actually, a very young one, somewhere between puppy and adulthood. Its coat was tangled, and the animal was filthy, as if it had been locked up somewhere and forgotten. He assumed the dog was starving and didn't know if it would attack or not. He sat warily until Willow pushed his arm aside.

"Come here, baby," she cooed.

Immediately, the dog's ears pricked up and he limped toward them. As he got closer, Dylan could see why the dog was limping. One front leg was about an inch shorter than the other, giving him a lopsided gait.

"I figure he was abandoned," he said quietly.

"I think so, too." Her attention still focused on the dog, she added, "That's right, baby. Come here. We won't hurt you."

The dog approached cautiously, his ears now pinned back until he stood two feet in front of them. Then he seemed to relax as Willow held out a hand for him to sniff.

"You've been out here a long time, haven't you, sweetheart," she said, her voice soft and reassuring. "I know it's hard to trust, baby. I know that more than most."

The dog hesitated a moment and then licked her fingers.

"That's it," she encouraged. "Dylan, pour some of the trail mix into my hand."

She held up her right hand to him as the dog continued licking the fingers of her left.

He did as she asked, sprinkling some into her upturned palm. Slowly, she moved the hand toward the dog. He stiffened and then looked at her longingly.

"Go ahead, baby. It's for you. I know it may not be what you normally eat, but we have to get something in you."

Tentatively, the dog placed his lips near her hand and then daintily nibbled the trail mix. When he finished it, Dylan saw that Willow's left hand was still stroking the animal.

"He seems friendly enough," he said. "Just scared. Who knows how long he's been out in these woods? Here, let's feed him a little more. Not too much, though. We don't want him to get sick."

Willow held up her hand to him, and Dylan refilled her palm with a little more of the trail mix. She fed it to the pup, all the while cooing to him as she petted him.

"He has to be thirsty," she said. "I'm going to cup my hands together. Pour some water into them if you would."

She turned slightly toward him and he did as she asked. The dog, in the meantime, had backed up a few feet, still uncertain.

Then Willow slowly faced the dog, the water resting in her hands. "Come drink, baby," she urged.

This time the dog needed no more encouragement. He came closer, lapping up the water in her palms. Dylan was ready and poured more water into them, and the dog drank again, until her hands were empty. He repeated it twice more.

"That's probably enough," he said. "What do you think we should do?"

Willow smiled at the dirty mutt. "Why, I'm going to take him home with me."

Dylan smiled at her. If anything could keep Willow in Maple Cove, it just might be this forgotten pup.

CHAPTER 10

W illow surprised herself by saying she would take the dog with them. She decided to correct any wrong impression Dylan may have gotten. She didn't need or want a dog.

"I mean, I just want to take him back to town with us. We can't leave him out here all alone. He needs to see a vet. Make sure he's not sick. Get him cleaned up. Hopefully someone will adopt him then."

Dylan chuckled. "You don't mean that. I can already tell that this is a case of love at first sight. The only thing now is to determine if we've got a boy or girl on our hands so you'll have a better idea what to name him—or her."

She petted the dog and Dylan joined in as they both tried to gain the animal's trust.

"You think someone abandoned him because of his leg, don't you?" she asked.

"Yes, I do. I think underneath all the dirt and matted fur, he's probably a pretty pup. But there are too many people in this world that only want perfection."

"I know," she said softly. "I've tried to be perfect in the relationships I've had, and it's only brought a lot of heartache."

Dylan's palm touched the side of her face, his thumb caressing her cheek. "Bear, you don't need to be anyone but yourself. If there were men foolish enough not to want you just as you are, then they were the fools. Not you."

By now, the dog had crawled into her lap and fallen asleep.

"How can he trust me so much?"

Dylan's thumb slowly swiped over her bottom lip. "Because he knows how good you are. How good you'll be to him. If anything, Willow Martin, you have always been loyal to your friends and family. This pup knows he's just found himself a home with you. He's already family, and you'll do whatever it takes to protect him—and love him."

Willow had tried for years to pour love into her relationships with men. "Maybe all I've needed is a dog," she mused aloud. She looked to Dylan. "Have you ever gotten a dog since Major?"

"No. It wasn't possible while I was in the army, especially moving around as much as I did. So many countries have strict laws in regard to bringing in pets. They make you quarantine them for months. I couldn't do that to a fur buddy. Then when I came back to the Cove, I was too busy to think about it. I don't even have a house," he told her. "I rent a couple of rooms above the diner. A dog needs a yard to run around and play in."

"If you are truly putting roots down as you say you are, then you should buy a house, Dylan. That will show the community that you are investing in them and the town."

"I really haven't given that much thought. I suppose you're right. Maybe you can help me find something. You've always had excellent taste."

"I'd like to do that," she told him, wanting for him to be more settled. Willow told herself it was something she would do for any friend. If anything, surely she and Dylan were still friends.

They sat and talked until the dog began to stir in her lap.

"We should head back," he told her. "It's a long way, though, and I don't if this little guy can manage to go that far. Do you think he would let me carry him some?"

"I guess we'll have to see," she said, as the dog moved from her lap and looked up eagerly at her, as if to ask, '*What now?*'

"We're going home," she said to the dog.

Dylan rose and gave her a hand, helping her stand. Willow ignored the tingles from that small touch and focused all her attention on her new dog. Yes, Dylan was right. This dog needed her as much as she needed it. She definitely wanted to have the dog looked over by a vet and cleaned up, but she would enjoy the companionship he would bring.

"Ready to go home?" she asked.

The dog woofed in reply, and she and Dylan laughed.

They walked at a slower pace than they had on the way up the trail, the dog staying close to her. He seemed to move well, despite the difference in the length of his front legs.

"He is dogging every step you take. Closer than your own shadow," Dylan remarked.

She smiled at him. "That's it. Shadow." She looked at the dog. "Hey, Shadow."

His ears perked up and he barked again.

"Great name, Bear. Whether it's a boy or girl, Shadow is a gender-neutral name."

They walked another few minutes and then Dylan said, "He's starting to fall behind. I think he's tired. Despite a few bites of trail mix, he has to be starving. I'm going to see if he'll let me pick him up."

Dylan squatted, looking at Shadow. "Hey, Shadow, I know you're getting tired, boy. Do you think I could carry you?"

He held out his hand and the dog came and sniffed it once before licking it. Dylan petted him several times and then said, "I'm going to pick you up now. It's going to be all right."

His arms went under the dog's belly, and he lifted it, rising and holding the animal close to his chest. Willow saw not panic in Shadow's eyes—but trust.

"I think we'll be fine," Dylan told her, starting down the trail again.

She envied Shadow. He possibly had been abused and most likely dumped, yet the dog had opened his heart and trusted her. And now Dylan.

Could she do the same and open her heart to the man she had once loved?

They reached the car, and he said, "Can you fish the keys from my right pocket?"

She stepped close to him, petting Shadow with one hand and slipping her other hand into Dylan's pocket, retrieving the keys. She caught a whiff of his cologne and wished she could bury her lips against his throat.

As she unlocked the car, he said, "Open the back. I've got a blanket in there. You can put that across your lap and wrap Shadow in it. He needs every bit of reassurance. He's trembling now. He may be remembering the last time he was in a car and how he was left."

Willow got the blanket and opened the passenger door, slipping inside the vehicle. She draped the blanket across her lap and chest and Dylan leaned down, placing Shadow in her lap. He then pulled the blanket up around the dog, tucking it in snugly.

"I figure it's like swaddling a baby," he said. "It gives them comfort. Maybe it will for Shadow, too."

"Since when do you know anything about babies?" she asked.

He grinned. "You'd be amazed what military police training teaches a guy."

They headed into town, and as they did so, Dylan called the local vet.

"I know it's a Sunday, Stan, but I was out hiking with Willow Martin. We came across an abandoned young dog. Willow wants to keep him. For my peace of mind, I was hoping you could check him out."

The vet agreed and said he would meet them at his office within half an hour.

Dylan ended the call. "That's a small town for you."

Willow knew what he meant. Growing up, she had always thought the Cove was special, but she had come to appreciate that more in the big cities she had lived in—first when she went to UCLA, and later when she moved abroad. Berlin, London, and Paris were all cities which offered so much, yet none of them had ever had the feel of Maple Cove. Perhaps that's why she longed to come—and stay—home now. Because she missed that feeling of belonging somewhere. Of walking down the street and knowing most everyone she passed. Just as Dylan had called up Stan Shorter and asked a favor of him, she knew the vet would not expect that favor to be returned. People in the Cove simply helped out one another, lending a helping hand when it was needed.

She bent and buried her face in Shadow's fur and whispered to him, "You're home now, Shadow. We both are."

They reached Maple Cove and Dylan drove straight to the vet's office, which was a couple of blocks from the town square. Stan Shorter met them and had Willow set Shadow on an examination table. Both she and Dylan stood near, one on each side of the table, stroking Shadow as the vet stood at the head.

Dr. Shorter examined Shadow thoroughly, confirming the dog was a male.

"I would place his age at nine months," the vet said. "He's underweight, obviously, but it won't take him much time to put on the needed weight." Shorter scratched Shadow between his ears. "He's mostly a Labrador, with maybe a little border collie in him."

Shadow sat patiently as the vet ran his fingers over the dog's coat, feeling his throat, chest, legs, and tail.

"His eyes are clear. His lungs sound good," he added, listening with his stethoscope. "I would like to get a blood and stool sample from him. You said you found him while out hiking?"

"Yes," Willow confirmed. "Dylan and I think someone dumped him. Probably because of his right leg."

Shorter ran his fingers along the leg she spoke of. "No deformities in it. Shadow just got shortchanged by nature. He seems to be a sweet boy, though."

"He was shy at first but friendly," Dylan confirmed. "We gave him water and a little trail mix. It was all we had with us."

"I'm going to put him on a high protein diet for now," Shorter told them. "I have the prescription food here. He's going to need shots, but I think we can wait on that. Today has already brought a lot of changes for him, and he's been through enough trauma by the looks of him. Let's give him a week to adjust to his new life, Willow, then you can bring him in for tests and shots. Make sure you have a fresh stool sample when you arrive. In the meantime, keep him away from other animals as a precaution."

"I can do that."

"Other than the food and a much-needed bath?" The vet smiled at her. "I would recommend lots of love and attention." He stepped back.

She wrapped her arms about Shadow's neck. "That will not be a problem, Doctor."

"I know it'll be a challenge, but try and keep him away from table scraps. He's probably been scrounging like crazy, trying to get enough to stay alive, and who knows what he's put inside himself. He should like the pet food I'm recommending, though. Two scoops a day. One in the morning and one around dinnertime. Fresh water whenever he wants it. Let me get that food for you. I'll be right back."

Shorter left, and Willow held her cheek close to Shadow as Dylan rubbed the dog's belly.

When the vet returned with a twenty-pound bag of food and some dog shampoo, she thanked him profusely for seeing Shadow on a Sunday.

"Not a problem. Boo was always good to my wife and me. She even did a piece for my wife when her cat died. Streaky was just over twenty years old—and she may have loved him slightly more than me. She really missed him. Boo was in her book club, and they got to talking about it. Boo asked to see pictures of Streaky and the next thing we knew, your grandmother brought over a small sculpture of the cat. Both of us broke down in tears." He shook his head. "Boo wouldn't take a cent for it."

He placed a hand on Willow's shoulder. "I'm the one who should be thanking you for sharing Boo with us. With the entire Cove, actually. Now, take this mangy beast home and get him a bath. Doctor's orders."

Dylan scooped up the food and shampoo, and Willow wrapped Shadow back in the blanket and picked him up.

"What do we owe you, Stan?" Dylan asked.

"Not a thing," Shorter replied. "This first visit and bag of food are on the house. Just be sure to call tomorrow and set up an appointment in a week."

"Thank you again," Willow said.

They returned to Dylan's SUV and Willow kept Shadow in her lap the entire way back to Boo's. When they arrived, Dylan helped her from the vehicle.

"Head straight for the bathroom," he advised. "Close the door and run a warm bath. I'll gather up towels and the shampoo and also set out bowls of food and water." He scratched Shadow's head. "I know you'd rather eat, boy, but if you want the run of the house, you need to be clean—especially if you're gonna sleep in this lady's bed."

"Oh. I thought I'd get a crate for him."

Dylan's brows arched. "Seriously? Nope. Shadow needs to snuggle with you. I slept with Major every night of his life. Best bed buddy I ever had."

His gaze was intense as he studied her. Willow wondered what kind of bed buddy Dylan might be and found her cheeks heating at the thought.

"Okay. I'll go upstairs and run the water. Let's go, Shadow," she said, carrying the dog up the stairs.

She brought him inside what had been Boo's bathroom, since it had a large, claw foot tub. She shut the door, turning on the faucet and letting the water grow hot before adding cold water. By the time the tub filled, Dylan had slipped inside the room.

Shadow didn't look very happy as Dylan scooped him up and set him inside the tub. Both of them knelt, with Dylan scooping warm water into a plastic bowl he'd brought and pouring it over Shadow until his coat was entirely wet.

"It may take more than one soap and rinse," he told her.

He was right. They drained the tub three different times and ran new water, each time soaping up Shadow and rinsing him. The final time, no dirt remained. Though Shadow still looked reluctant at being bathed, he had sat without protest in the tub.

"When the weather's warmer, you can bathe him outside. Right now, it's too cold to do so. I wonder if we should blow-dry him?" he asked.

"I think a dryer might frighten him. Let's just towel him off really well."

Dylan lifted Shadow from the tub and they went to work on him, drying him thoroughly.

"I'll clean up in here," Dylan said. "Take him downstairs. Bowls of food and water are waiting."

Willow wanted to carry the dog but knew it would be good for him to get his bearings and move around on his own.

"Come on, Shadow," she said, patting her hip lightly and then leaving the bathroom.

The dog followed, sticking closely to her. She found the bowls on the floor in the kitchen, slipping a placemat under them. She would need to go to the store tomorrow and pick up doggy supplies, including a mat to place under the bowls, a leash, and a few toys for Shadow to play with.

Her new pet approached the bowls carefully and glanced up at her.

"It's for you," she explained. "No one but you. Go ahead."

He took a few tentative bites and then gobbled the food, washing it down with the water. Willow refilled the water bowl and Shadow took a few more drinks before backing away.

Dylan stood watching from the doorway. "He was hungry. He'll probably need to nap now. Why don't you go sit on the couch with him? I placed a blanket there."

She led the dog into the den and sat next to where the blanket had been opened. Patting beside her, she encouraged the dog to jump up on it. He did and after circling a few times, he sat, placing his chin on his front paws, his eyes closing.

"I know you're hungry, too," Dylan said. "Would it be okay if I went and picked up that pizza?"

Willow realized she was famished. "That sounds heavenly."

"Okay. Be back in a few."

She watched him leave and then sat absently stroking her new fur friend. Today had been full of big changes. She had left the house being on her own and returned with a pet who would be dependent on her. Before the hike, she had wanted to have sex with Dylan more out of curiosity.

Now, she wanted to do so because he was a good man. She wanted to trust him. If anything, Shadow was beginning to teach her about trust. If she opened her heart to the dog, maybe she could also do the same with Dylan.

Willow rested her head against the back of the sofa and closed her eyes.

Tomorrow. She would ask Dylan to make love with her then.

CHAPTER 11

Dylan let himself into Boo's house. No, it was Willow's now. Hers and Jackson's. They owned the big, rambling house.

But would that be enough to keep Willow here?

Dylan had never felt so emotionally fragile, and that included the time after he had lost his parents and Grace in the car accident. That had been devastating.

But to lose Willow again would crush his soul.

He brought the pizza into the den and caught sight of her asleep on the sofa, Shadow curled up next to her. The dog, though underweight, was a fine looking one, now that he'd been cleaned up, and he would be a good companion to her, friendly yet protective. He drank in the woman who had been the girl he loved so many years ago, knowing he still loved her and always would, no matter what happened between them now. He came closer and bent, pressing a soft kiss on her brow.

She began to stir and then opened her eyes, giving him a sleepy smile.

"Hey."

"Hey, yourself. I'm sorry I woke you."

Her stomach grumbled loudly. "It's a good thing you did. The pizza smells divine. Where is it from?" she asked as she stood, petting Shadow once. The dog didn't stir.

"Let's go into the kitchen," he suggested. "Despite what Stan Shorter said, it would be hard for me to turn down giving Shadow bits of pepperoni if he begged for them."

He walked ahead of her into the kitchen and set the pizza box on the table, opening the lid as she gathered napkins and plates. Dylan moved to the refrigerator and found a pitcher of iced tea inside, removing it and pouring them both glasses.

They sat at the table, and Willow began telling him about what she thought needed to be done to fix up the house.

"I would appreciate you walking through it with me to see if you can think of anything else you see that might need repairing or updating."

"I'd be happy to do so when we finish."

"I also would like an idea of who might be able to do the work for me," she continued. "I know I could do some of it on my own, but I'm actually ready to get back to painting again. The hike today definitely inspired me."

He took her hand and threaded his fingers through hers. "You always did like to get out in nature and put on canvas what you'd seen."

He squeezed her fingers and then released them, once again wanting her to make the next move.

"There's a new guy that came to town about seven or eight years ago," Dylan told her. "Pete Pulaski. He can do everything—plumbing, electricity, painting. He works on his own some days, and on others he employs off-duty firemen, like Gage."

"I spoke with Gage briefly yesterday, but I would like to catch up with him. It surprised me that Emily wasn't with him. I know Boo told me they got married."

Sadness filled him. "They did after Emily graduated from Oregon State and came back here to teach. She died about five years ago."

"What? I didn't know that." She frowned. "I'm afraid there's a lot Boo didn't tell me."

"Maybe she knew there was nothing you could have done to help. Emily had a sudden aneurysm. The doctor told Gage nothing could have been done to prevent it. I hated being half a world away when Gage was in so much pain." He hesitated and then said, "Emily had just found out she was pregnant."

Tears welled in Willow's eyes. "How tragic. To lose Emily and the baby. I'm so sorry I didn't know."

"Only a handful of people knew about the baby. Their folks. Me. If I were you, I wouldn't bring it up to him. It's still something hard for him to talk about."

"I won't," she promised, wiping away a tear.

They had a last slice of pizza, and Dylan told her he was stuffed.

Willow closed the box and put it inside the refrigerator, telling him, "You can take it with you when you leave. Right now, I'd appreciate you walking the house with me."

"Then let's start outside while it's still light."

They moved about the perimeter of the house. Dylan agreed new gutters were in order but thought the roof was fine.

"Pete can get up there and check it out for you. He'll let you know if you need to replace it or not. I would shore up the chimney, though. You could also clean up the landscaping around the house some. It looks a little neglected. Let's go back inside."

When they reached the door, Shadow stood waiting for them, his tail wagging. Dylan thought that a good sign. They lavished attention on the pup and then started the tour of the inside of the house. He thought the floors could use a good sanding and agreed with her that the kitchen needed several updates. He also thought new fixtures would be nice in the bathrooms and help spruce things up.

"Thanks for your suggestions. I'll call Pete tomorrow and have him come out and take a look at things. One idea just came to me," Willow said. "I might want to knock down the wall between the kitchen and den so it would be a little more open."

"As long as it's not a load-bearing wall, you could do it. You might sacrifice some cabinet space, but the kitchen already has plenty as it is. Besides, you've also got that butler's pantry off the kitchen. I'm sure it has storage you could use."

Dylan ran a hand through his hair. "I'm going to take your advice and call Shayla Newton tomorrow morning. I don't know what's listed now in the area, other than two houses I've seen when I've gone out on patrol."

"You do that? I thought that's what your officers were for."

He shrugged. "I like to be out and about. In a place like the Cove, it doesn't hurt to be seen."

"What are you looking for in a house?" she asked.

"That's a good question. One I'm sure Shayla will ask me. I don't know. I'd have to think about it. What do you think?"

"It won't be my house, Dylan. It'll be yours."

A little of his hope died within him with her comment. Even if Willow did stay in Maple Cove, it would be hard for her to leave Boo's house. Where Dylan had dreams of marrying this woman, her casual remark made him think that she hadn't given that a single thought. Perhaps he might put the real estate idea on hold for now.

"I guess I'll have to mull it over. Check my finances. It may not even be a good time to buy. Properties don't go up for sale often in the Cove. It would have to be just the right place for me to commit. Still, I'll give Shayla a call."

He would follow through in case Willow asked but let Shayla know it was merely a fishing expedition for now.

"I should be heading out," he said. "Keep the pizza. Thanks for hiking with me today."

"Thank you for taking me." She grinned. "If we hadn't gone, Shadow wouldn't be here now."

Dylan leaned down and scratched the dog between his ears and saw the look of contentment on the animal's face.

"Maybe we can do it again another time," he said, hoping to plant that seed in her mind of them spending more time together.

"Maybe so."

Willow's violet eyes were large and luminous as she stared at him. Her palm went to his chest, flattening directly against his heart. He knew she could feel how it beat rapidly from her touch.

"It was good to be with you today, Dylan. I hope we can do this again. Hiking. Dinner."

Then her other hand reached out and curled about his nape, pulling his face close to hers. Her lips brushed softly against his for a moment and then she broke the kiss. Leaning her forehead against his.

Dylan stayed for a moment, drinking in the scent of her floral perfume, and then raised his head. Her hands fell from him.

"Goodbye, Willow."

As he left the house and walked to his SUV, he was pleased she had made the effort to kiss him. It hadn't been a kiss of passion. It might have been one of friendship.

He wondered where their relationship might be headed.

"Wait!"

Dylan turned, surprised to see Willow running toward him. Before he could speak, she leaped at him. He caught her, her legs going around his waist, her arms entwining about his neck.

And her mouth crashing into his.

The kiss sizzled from the start, nothing meek about it. It was demanding. Possessive. Reckless. Passionate.

He turned, taking a few steps toward his SUV, placing her bottom on the hood. Her limbs stayed wrapped about him as the kiss continued. Their tongues warred with one another. His heart slammed violently against his ribs. His pulse raced in double-time. His cock hardened.

Willow began leaning back, taking Dylan with her. He broke the kiss, moving his lips to her throat, burying his face in its softness. In her floral scent. He licked and nipped at her pulse point, hearing her moan, turning him on like nothing previously.

Taking her wrists, he peeled them from behind his head and moved them to the hood of the car, pinning them by her head, his mouth drawn back to hers. He sank his teeth into her lower lip and heard her gasp. He sucked on it hard, knowing he was bruising her but consumed by need.

He forced himself to release her lip and trailed his down the column of her throat, nudging her shirt aside with his cheek so his tongue could trace her collarbone.

"Yes," she whispered, sending a ripple of desire through him.

Dylan found the curve of her breast, his tongue following it, her skin so smooth and sweet. Frustrated, he released one of her wrists and unbuttoned two buttons on her flannel shirt and slipped to the front enclosure on her bra. She had always worn that type in the past and he was grateful in the moment that she still did. He undid the clasp and then captured her free wrist again. Using his teeth, he pulled back each side of the black bra, exposing her breasts, their rosy tips crying out for his touch.

He grazed his teeth over one nipple and then softly nipped it, hearing Willow's gasp. He sucked hard on it, remembering this taste from so long ago. She began writhing beneath him as he slowly licked around the nipple, circling it again and again before taking it in his mouth and sucking once more. By now, she was pleading with him, wriggling, firing his blood. He moved to her other breast, giving it the same consideration, wondering how he had lived as long as he had without being able to touch her this way.

In the haze of desire, though, he realized he wanted more from her. More than sex.

He wanted commitment.

He needed it—as much as he needed her. Once with Willow would never be enough.

Slowly, Dylan kissed his way back up to her mouth

and continued kissing it, long, drugging kisses that had her crying out. Then he released her wrists and framed her beautiful face, breaking the kiss and staring deeply into her eyes.

"Why did you stop?" she asked, her eyes glazed with passion, her chest heaving. "I need more, Dylan."

"I want more than you can give me now, Willow."

He refastened her bra and buttoned her shirt again, stepping back from the vehicle's hood, seeing confusion in her eyes.

Willow pushed herself up and slid from the car's hood. "What do you think you need?"

"Commitment."

She flinched, as if he'd slapped her. "What?"

"You heard me. The last time we did something like that, we were committed to one another."

"But we were going to let each other go," she reminded him, anger now sparking in her eyes.

"True. We'd decided to make love once and then go off and see if we could fulfill the destiny we hungered for. Well, I went out and lived. A lot. I became more than I thought I could be. I grew up. But I still find that I want you, Willow. And I'm not willing to have just a part of you.

"I want all of you."

She shook her head. "I can't give you that kind of commitment, Dylan. I keep telling you we've both changed."

"I know we have," he said, not bothering to hide his impatience. "But I also know deep down, we are basically the same people we were. Yes, we've matured. Yes, we've had other relationships. But fate has led us back to one another. I don't want a part of you, Willow. I want all of you."

"I can't give you that," she said flatly. "I told you I'm terrible at relationships."

"And I told you it's because the road needed to lead you back to me."

Dylan leaned toward her and kissed her softly. "When you're ready, I'll be here."

He moved quickly to the driver's door and stood by it, his heart racing. He might have totally blown it. She wasn't ready to agree to be with him.

Willow turned and faced him. "Why can't we just have sex? Don't tell me you don't want me, Dylan. I know you do."

Frustration filled him. "Of course, I do, Bear. Having sex with you would be fantastic. But I want— no, need—more than sex. I don't just need your body. I need your heart and soul. I need a commitment from you. I want to make love to you, Willow, in the worst way. But settling for sex won't cut it for me."

He paused, trying to sweeten the pot. "I'm not asking you to marry me. I'm just asking for you to make a promise to me that you'll let us see where this goes. That we won't see anyone else while we do. I need you to be all in, not with one foot out the door before we begin." He paused. "Let me know when you're ready for that."

Dylan climbed behind the wheel and started up the vehicle, his eyes on Willow the entire time he backed away. She shouted an expletive at him which sounded French and stormed away.

That was his Bear.

At least he'd said his piece. Ball in her court.

And he would be ready when she returned his serve.

CHAPTER 12

Willow was furious.

She watched Dylan's SUV pull away and screamed in frustration after he turned and was out of sight.

How could he stir her up as he had, her blood to a boiling point, need filling her—only to walk away?

She couldn't commit to him. She refused to commit to him. He was not going to back her into a corner. If she had a sexual itch that needed to be scratched, she could find someone else to fulfill it.

Deep her heart, she knew no one could ever fill the emptiness inside her.

Except Dylan.

She began walking, trying to get her feelings under control.

"Be rational, Willow," she told herself. "What is Dylan asking for?"

She tried to look at it from his point of view. He was thirty years old. He had traveled the world. Now, he had come back to Maple Cove and had settled into a position of authority. He would want to settle down, not only professionally but personally. By this age, a person had a better grasp on to what he or she wanted in life. Obviously, Dylan wanted stability in a relationship with a woman.

But what did she want?

He had asked her for *a* commitment. Not commitment. *A* commitment, she emphasized to herself. Even he had come out and said he wasn't proposing marriage, which would have been extremely foolish. But he did want her to commit to an exclusive relationship with him. Would the possibility of marriage be at the end of it? Willow was almost certain that the answer to that question would be *yes*.

She did want this man, though. More than she had wanted to be with her previous live-in lovers. Men who had all cheated on her and undervalued her.

Her heart told her that Dylan would do neither.

If anything, Dylan was a good man. One that she was immensely attracted to. One who had more depth and compassion and understanding in his smallest finger than anyone she had ever slept with.

She slowed her pace and then stopped. Why not? Why not have sex with Dylan and explore the possibilities of a relationship with him? If she had to begin to trust anyone, Dylan would be her obvious choice. He had never let her down. Ever. Despite the fact that he thought he had. She had understood when he left the Cove without a proper goodbye to her that he was devastated by what had happened to his family. It changed the trajectory of his life. Willow had not judged him in any way because of that. Instead, she had willingly let him go, not forcing anything between them by trying to contact him. When he made no attempt to contact her during her UCLA years, she had respected that.

They were adults now. They could enter a consensual relationship with no promises of what the final outcome would be. Willow couldn't say she trusted Dylan 100 percent at this point, but she knew he would never deliberately hurt her as other men had. She figured the sex would be phenomenal. It was about time she enjoyed some good sex. When it came to the other men she had been with, she felt she had always been the one who gave more in the relationship. She worked harder to please the other person, both in and out of bed. Instinct told her that Dylan would be different. That he would make sure she was feeling fulfilled before he did.

It was settled. She would let him know she was willing to go to bat with him. But she didn't want to fold right away. It wouldn't hurt to give him a few days before she capitulated.

Returning to the house, she saw Shadow waiting at the door for her again. She opened it and let the dog out in order for him to do his business. He sniffed around some of the bushes and found a suitable one to mark as his territory.

"Come on, boy," she called, heading back to the house and letting them both inside.

She locked up for the night, something Boo had never done since Maple Cove was a small town, but Willow had lived in large cities and had it ingrained upon her to be safe.

Going to the kitchen, she poured herself a glass of wine, and while it was breathing, went upstairs for a long, hot shower. She slipped into her pajamas and puttered downstairs, reclaiming the glass of wine and going to sit on the sofa. She picked up her phone, which she had left on the coffee table and saw she had a text from Tenley. It asked if she would like to Face-Time. It had come in ten minutes ago. Doing the math, she figured it was after ten Tenley's time. Willow decided to text her back first to see if she were still up for some conversation.

Tenley replied immediately. Not by text, but by calling Willow. She tapped her phone to accept the call and said, "Hey, you," as her friend appeared on the screen.

Tenley smiled back, looking tired to Willow. "Hey, yourself. I wanted to give you a little time after yesterday's remembrance of Boo. Are you up for talking about it? Or anything else?"

Tenley walked as she spoke. Willow wondered where she might be heading.

"It went really well," she told her friend. "Jackson and I, along with Gillian, went out on Sheriff Willingham's boat in order to scatter Boo's ashes as she requested."

"I'm sure that was emotional," Tenley said, taking a seat in what looked like the stairwell to her condo. "I'm glad both Jackson and Gillian were there for you. I adore Gillian."

"There was someone else on board," she added. "Dylan. Dylan Taylor."

"Your Dylan? *The* Dylan?" Tenley asked. "So, he's back in Maple Cove then. From the army, is that right?"

"Yes. He did several tours and then came back to the Cove and joined the police force recently. In fact, he is the new town sheriff. Walt Willingham is sick and handpicked Dylan to run and be his successor."

"Hmm. Does that change your plans, as far as staying? The way you've talked about Dylan over the years —and it hasn't been often—I've always had a feeling that he was the one who got away. Maybe this could be your chance to find out. Make a fresh start."

"I am pretty confused right now," Willow admitted. "Yes, Boo's remembrance went well. A lot of townspeople turned out for it. Dylan was very supportive of me throughout. Never left my side. Then we went hiking today."

"Ooh, romantic."

She laughed. "It was a pretty momentous day because of this." Willow turned the phone from her so that Tenley could see Shadow sleeping on the sofa beside her. Then she moved the camera back to her. "We found him out on the trail."

"You brought him home?" Tenley asked, a slow smile spreading across her face. "Good for you, Willow. Dogs are wonderful companions. I would have one, but Theodore doesn't like them. He says they are too high maintenance and we're too busy to have one."

Willow caught something in Tenley's tone but didn't press, figuring her friend wasn't ready to talk about it yet. Tenley could be a little prickly and private. Willow had learned just to be there for her friend. When Tenley was ready to share what was wrong, they would talk.

"His name is Shadow. He's about nine months old and a mix of mostly Labrador and a little retriever. That's the vet's best guess. His right front paw is a little shorter than his left, but it doesn't keep him from doing what he wants. We believe someone abandoned him because of his abnormality."

She stroked the dog. "But I think he's just perfect, flaws and all."

"If anything will keep you in Maple Cove, it will be Shadow," Tenley predicted. "Unless... it might be a handsome sheriff. How has Dylan aged over the years?"

"He could be *People's* Sexiest Man Alive," Willow said.

She and Tenley burst out laughing.

"We kissed, Tenley. And it was better than I remembered."

"Better than Jean-Luc? As I recall, you seemed to like the way he kissed."

"I did. But Jean-Luc was a pretty selfish lover. He was all about what I could do for him instead of what he could do for me."

"And Dylan wouldn't be like that," Tenley observed.

"No," Willow confirmed. "I am curious about what sex with him would be like," she admitted. "We... kissed a lot before he left tonight. He also gave me an ultimatum."

Tenley sat up. "Do tell."

"He wants a commitment from me," she told her friend.

"What kind of commitment?"

"He thinks we still belong together. That's why neither of us have ever had a relationship that lasted."

"Do you believe the same thing?"

"I don't... know. But Dylan wants us to give things a chance. He told me he wasn't proposing to me, but he would like a commitment between us. That we wouldn't see other people. That we try to explore if there's truly anything left between us."

"I think that's reasonable," Tenley said. "Obviously, the sexual chemistry is still there."

Willow chuckled. "The sexual chemistry is off the charts. I thought I would ignite in flames just kissing him."

"All right. That box is checked. I think you should give him a chance, Willow. Give you both a chance to see if anything could come of this. You owe it to your-self. You had a string of choosing the wrong men. Maybe Dylan has been the right one all along. Maybe it took being apart all these years for you both to learn and grow and then come back together."

"You sound exactly like him," she accused lightly.

"It makes sense to me," her friend said. "If it works out, it was meant to be. And if it doesn't? Then at least you will have had some mind-blowing sex. And I will need a few details about that," Tenley teased. "Not a full-blown account. Just enough to keep me interested. So, what else is going on with you?"

Willow spent a few minutes telling her friend about some of the changes she wanted to make at the house, explaining that it would make it more comfort-able to live in, and if she did decide to leave the Cove, more attractive for a buyer.

"How does Jackson figure in all of this? You haven't mentioned him yet."

She sighed. "My brother is in a bad place right now."

"How so?"

"He is in jury selection for a murder trial. He knows his client did it and has most likely committed more murders. Jackson's good, Tenley. If anyone could get Gerard McGreer off, it would be my brother. But it's like the guy has gotten in Jackson's head. He's wor-ried if he does persuade the jury not to convict, Mc-Greer will go out and do it all over again."

"That's awful. At least you're in the same time zone now, Willow. Just be sure to stay in touch with him and keep an eye on his state of mind. Maybe he's not meant to be a defense attorney, after all. I know he and his partner have built a successful practice, but he might need to go in a different direction."

"Funny you should mention that. Clancy Nelson, the Cove's resident attorney for decades, wants to retire finally. He's eighty-five years old and asked Jackson if he would like to take over his law practice. He's even given him a deadline. Fourth of July. That's Clancy's birthday."

"Interesting twist," Tenley observed. "I know you would appreciate living in the same town your brother does."

"It will all depend upon the next few months," Willow said. "If this thing goes south with Dylan and me, I may not want to remain in the Cove. It also depends upon the outcome of Jackson's trial and how he's feeling. Whether he would want to move here and take over Clancy's practice. A lot of what-ifs hang in the air."

"Well, you know I'm always here for you," Tenley told her. "I'm just sorry I was tied up this weekend. I wanted to be there for you and Boo."

"I understand you had that event at Theodore's firm. New York is an entirely different universe from the Oregon coast. I understand the politics of you showing up at something like that Christmas party and how it could help Theodore's career."

Tenley bit her lip in thought. That was Willow's clue that something wasn't quite right in her friend's marriage. She wondered if she should say anything.

"I would like to fly out some weekend if you wouldn't mind hosting me," Tenley said. "There are... things we need to talk about."

"Like why you're sitting in a stairwell having a conversation with me?"

"Yes," Tenley said softly. "I may have made the mistake of my life, Willow."

CHAPTER 13

W illow awoke and for a moment, she had to think where she was. She looked about her childhood bedroom and decided maybe it was time she moved into Boo's bedroom. She would tackle Boo's closet and drawers later today, after she got in touch with Pete Pulaski.

She looked beside her to Shadow, who snuggled against her and had kept her warm throughout the night. She was already in love with this beautiful fur friend.

"Want to go outside, Shadow?" she asked.

The dog's ears perked up and his eyes opened, nothing but love reflected in them. Once again, she was astounded at how open and trusting the lab was, even after the untold misery he'd been through.

She took the dog outside and let him do his business then brought him inside, giving him a scoop of the food Stan Shorter had provided, as well as fresh water. Instead of putting on coffee, she went upstairs and got ready for the day, thinking she would go into town and run some errands. She had looked at Pete's website after her conversation with Tenley last night.

Tenley's words hadn't shocked Willow. She had known something was very wrong with her friend and had suspected it might be her marriage. When pressed, though, Tenley refused to talk about it, saying a public stairwell three thousand miles away wasn't the place to unload. She also said she had a lot of processing to do before she spoke aloud about her problems. Tenley said it was a conversation they should have in person, and she promised to do her best to try and come out to Oregon sometime early in the new year.

Willow backed off after that, respecting Tenley's feelings and understanding her needing to mull over her situation, since Willow had done much of the same in recent weeks. They had ended their conversation shortly after Tenley's declaration of making the mistake of her life.

She knew from the website where Pete Pulaski's small office was located, just off the Maple Cove square. Deciding to drop by Ainsley's bakery for coffee and a Danish, she would then head over to see Pulaski.

Going to Shadow, she petted the dog. "I have to leave and run some errands, boy. I will be back. You can count on me. Always."

Her new pet seemed to look sad that she was leaving but resigned to the fact. He ran and jumped onto the sofa, resting his head on crossed paws.

She went out to her rental and decided a new car was also something she would have to consider. Rental fees would rack up quickly, and she would rather be making a car payment than see her money swirling down the drain, with nothing to show for it. Since she had no plans to return to Europe, the investment made sense. Even if she left the Cove, the car would go with her.

On the way to town, Willow dialed Pulaski's number, wanting to leave a message to see if he could see her sometime today. Surprise filled her when he picked up since it was only a quarter till seven.

"Pulaski Contracting. Pete speaking. How may I help you?"

"Good morning, Pete. My name is Willow Martin, and I am Boo Martin's granddaughter. Dylan Taylor recommended you to me."

"Boo was considered royalty in the Cove. I'm sorry for your loss, Willow. I met Boo a few times, and she was definitely a spitfire."

She chuckled. "That's an apt description, Pete. I'm calling because my brother Jackson and I have inherited Boo's house. I'll be living in it for a few months, if not permanently. There are some things that need to be fixed up, and some ideas I have to modernize it a bit. I was hoping to make an appointment with you if you have any free time today and discuss is with you."

"You've caught me at the right time, Willow. I'm actually in between jobs and was going to catch up on paperwork this morning. Paperwork is not my cup of tea. I'd much rather meet with a client or be out working on a job site. What's your schedule look like this morning?"

"I'm actually driving into town right now. Stopping for coffee and something to eat."

"Then I hope you're headed to Buttercup Bakery. Ainsley Robinson makes the best pastries and scones in town, not to mention her pies and cakes."

"That's exactly where I'm going. If you'd like, I can pick up coffee and something for us to eat and head over to your office."

"That's the best offer I've had all day," Pete teased. "Coffee black for me and anything sweet. Get here when you can. The door will be open. Looking forward to visiting with you."

"Same here," Willow told him, ending the call.

By now she had reached town and drove to the square, cruising around it until she found a parking spot close to the bakery. She got out and studied all four sides of the square, noting places she was familiar with and new ones which had cropped up in the years since she had been away.

She walked across the street and entered Buttercup Bakery, finding a line. It moved quickly, however, thanks to the efficiency of the two clerks filling orders.

As Willow reached the front, Ainsley breezed in with a new tray of freshly-baked scones.

"Willow, it's so good to see you. "I've been thinking about you. I think we need to do a girls' night."

"That would be wonderful, Ainsley," she responded, excited for a chance to socialize.

"Would you mind if my cousin Rylie came along? She owns Antiques and Mystiques, which is two doors down. She used to spend summers in the Cove with my family."

Willow vaguely remembered a brunette with the same periwinkle eyes as Ainsley, sitting with Ainsley at summer ball games, helping to sell baked goods.

"I'd like that. Just let me know what night you're both free."

"How about tonight?"

"Why not?" Willow agreed. "Where would you like to go?"

"Let's meet at six at Hidden Bear Bar & Grill. It's right next to Antiques and Mystiques."

"I'm familiar with it. I'll see you and Rylie there tonight at six. Casual clothing?"

"Is there any other kind?" Ainsley joked.

Willow placed her order for two coffees to go and two of the new scones which Ainsley had just brought out. She carried breakfast the two blocks to Pete's, thinking it easier to walk than getting back in her car and driving.

She realized Pete must work out of his house since the street was residential. The bungalow was neat and had beautiful landscaping. She knocked to let him know she was coming inside and then opened the door. He met her and she handed him his coffee.

"Good to meet you, Willow," he told her. "Let's go into the kitchen. I'm pretty informal and usually meet with clients there. I do have a room set aside with various samples that we can look at if you decide to hire me."

She followed him and they sat at the large table. Willow told the contractor not to worry about plates and placed his scone on a napkin, using the paper bag as a plate for her scone.

"I haven't been by Boo's house, but I know the general area where it is since I've done a few jobs nearby. Tell me what you're thinking about."

Willow did so, and Pete nodded, taking notes as she spoke.

When she finished, he said, "I would like to see the place as soon as possible and firm up the jobs you wish for me to complete in order to give you a detailed estimate."

"I'm happy for you to come out anytime today if you're available."

"Why don't we finish up here, and I'll follow you home," he suggested.

She agreed and he dropped her at her car on the square. Once they arrived at Boo's, Willow walked him through the inside and outside of the house, much as she had Dylan. Pete took a ladder from his truck and climbed onto the roof to inspect it. When they finished, they went inside and sat at her kitchen table. Shadow joined them, perching on Willow's feet.

They discussed the paint job inside and out, and Pete gave her a solid estimate for that. It would include the entire exterior and every room except the art studio inside. The wall she wanted knocked down wasn't load-bearing, and so that would be easily accomplished. He also suggested several other projects that would spruce up the place, things she hadn't considered but ones that made sense once she heard them.

"I'll have to go back and work up a full estimate for you. I can have that to you by the end of the day. You can approve whatever jobs you wish and let me know when you'd like to get started."

"You said you were between jobs, so the sooner you can move on this, the better. Dylan told me sometimes you employ off-duty firemen."

Pete nodded. "Yes, a lot of firemen have their own businesses, which they run in their free time. Fencing. Installing garage doors and sprinklers. Painting. I give them the opportunity to work for me, and they don't have to worry about keeping the books or paying taxes or doing any advertising."

"I was friends with Carter Clark in high school," she told him. "If you can use Carter on any of these jobs, I'd appreciate it."

"Carter is a hard worker who's become a good friend. I'll throw as much his way as possible."

Pete asked for her e-mail address in order to send

the estimate, as well as her cell number. "I'll text you a heads-up when I send the e-mail," he promised. "I'm looking forward to working on this house if you go with me. It has great bones."

"It was a wonderful place to grow up, but I do know nothing has been done to it for a good long while. Thanks for considering this project. I'll forward what you send to me to my brother, who's now the co-owner of the house with me. He's agreed to give me the lead on this, though. If your prices look right, I'll be comfortable moving ahead with you. Thanks for your time today, Pete. You've had some really thoughtful suggestions."

"Happy to help."

After the contractor left, Willow was itching to paint before she did anything else. She went to the room designated as Boo's art studio. A long row of windows on two sides let in a good deal of natural light. She would have to set aside Boo's art supplies at some point since she did no sculpting and thought she might donate them to the local high school. For now, she unpacked her own, preparing and setting up a blank canvas, and then taking out some of the oil paints and a few treasured brushes. She slipped into one of Boo's smocks and caught the scent of Shalimar on it, her grandmother's signature scent. Tears sprang to Willow's eyes as she missed Boo anew. Still, she felt Boo's spirt with her as she picked up her brush and began.

Usually, she liked to do a few sketches before committing anything to a canvas. This time, however, she knew exactly what she wished to paint.

The clearing from yesterday.

Even as she had sat talking with Dylan about the town and its citizens, her eyes had been roaming across the area. She understood why it had become a favorite spot of Dylan's, because of its beauty. The trees, the hills, the water in the distance. The scene had burned itself into her soul, and she painted with speed and ferocity.

Two hours later, she stepped back and admired her work. She believed she had captured the essence of the place and decided this painting would be for Dylan. She would offer it to him—and herself, as well.

She cleaned her brushes and washed up. Shadow padded after her as she left the studio, determined to make some headway with the things on her to-do list. She drove back into town and stocked up on groceries and pet supplies, something she had intended on doing this morning until Pete had wanted to come to the house after their initial meeting.

Once the refrigerator and pantry were stocked and expired items trashed, she took a box of garbage bags to Boo's bedroom. For the next two hours, she sorted clothes from the drawers and closet, and made several trips downstairs, carting full trash bags filled with clothes to the car. She would drive into Portland tomorrow and drop the items off at a women's shelter she had found online. Then she would go to a car dealership and see about buying a car. Her recent art showing in New York had left her with a healthy bank account. She might decide to buy a new vehicle instead of a used one. She would ask Ainsley and Rylie tonight what they drove and where they'd purchased their vehicles. Hopefully, she could return the rental and drive back to the Cove in a car of her own, something she'd never had.

She was tired and sweaty by the time she brought the last sack to the car and decided she better get cleaned up for her girls' night. She looked forward to this. Tenley and Sloane would always be her closest friends, but they were usually a few thousand miles apart from wherever she was. It would be nice to make female friends in the Cove. She realized now that in her three previous relationships, she had isolated herself from others, focusing on work and the man in her life, and really didn't have outside friends. She had become acquainted with people who worked in the galleries showing her paintings and with a few fellow artists, but she had been lacking in seeing friends on a regular basis. Hopefully that would change in the Cove.

Her phone dinged, and Shadow's ears perked up. The dog had followed her everywhere in the house, truly identifying with his new name.

The text was from Pete, and she took a moment to open her e-mail on her tablet so she could see the estimate on a screen larger than her phone's. It was meticulous, broken down by job, and very thorough. Pete had already explained many of the costs to her, and she thought his prices more than reasonable. She also knew Dylan would not have recommend the contractor if he did shoddy work. Willow forwarded the e-mail to Jackson, telling her brother she had met with a local contractor and wanting him to look over the details of the estimate. Boo had left not only the house to them, but the money in her checking and savings accounts, as well. It would easily cover these costs, but she wanted to make sure Jackson had a say in this, even if he had told her to hire whomever she wanted.

She texted Pete and told him she had forwarded his notes to her brother and that she hoped to get back to him within twenty-four hours.

She would have to hurry now in order to get ready for her night out. She placed a pair of black leggings and a long-sleeved, purple wool tunic on the bed, hoping she would appear stylish yet comfortable.

Willow jumped into the shower and then dressed again before applying a bit of makeup and blow-drying her hair. She applied a new lipstick she had bought in New York, since it claimed to have staying power.

Taking Shadow downstairs and outside, he peed on a new shrub this time. She fed the dog and left a few lights on before locking up and heading into town.

Once more, she parked on the square, this time directly in front of Hidden Bear Bar and Grill.

"Willow?" a voice called.

She turned and saw a woman coming toward her, wearing a slim-fitting white shirt and dark pants with an open black jacket over the shirt. As she approached, Willow saw the periwinkle eyes.

"You must be Rylie." She offered her hand. "I'm sure we met a long time ago."

"We did. You were two years older, and I thought you were so glamorous with your red hair and violet eyes. Ainsley and I talked about how you were the most beautiful girl in the Cove."

She felt the blush on her cheeks. "Thank you. You certainly are gorgeous yourself. You have beautiful skin, and I envy all that thick, dark hair. My hair is so fine, I can't do much with it other than pull it back into a ponytail or let it hang naturally."

"Let's go inside. Ainsley just texted me that she grabbed a table. It's Monday night, and *Monday Night Football* will have the place hopping."

They entered and Ainsley waved them over. "Sorry. I forgot it was football night. I literally got the last booth. It's going to be impossible to talk here.

Should we order it as takeout and head to my place?"

"Why don't we just take it to my shop?" Rylie suggested. "It's right next door. The food will still be hot that way. No need to microwave anything."

"I'm game," Willow said. "They'll probably be happy for the table being freed up."

A server came and they asked for a moment. She quickly scanned the menu and decided what she wanted, as did Ainsley and Rylie. Willow motioned for the server to return and they placed their order, asking for it to be to-go.

"Any drinks with that?" the server asked.

They all asked for iced teas and chatted for a few minutes, with each filling in a few of the blanks as to what they had been doing since high school. Willow learned that Rylie had worked for her dad's furniture store in Seattle after graduating from college with a degree in marketing.

"But my real love was antiquing," Rylie explained. "Hitting up flea markets on the weekends. Seeking out great finds on antiques or finding things to repurpose. Dad died from a heart attack just as Ainsley decided to put down roots in Maple Cove, I decided to follow a crazy dream and start my own antique store. I still scour places like crazy, hitting garage and estate sales. I also do most of the repurposing myself. I also take furniture on consignment."

"I'm happy we decided to take dinner to your store," she said. "We can eat and then I want to wander around. I'm redoing some of Boo's house. I may have some furniture to place with you, and then I'll want some new pieces, as well, once Pete Pulaski finishes up his various jobs."

"What are you having done?" Ainsley asked.

Their server appeared with bags. "Here you go, ladies."

Ainsley handed him a credit card. "Place it on my card if you would. My treat tonight."

When Willow protested, Ainsley said, "You can pay next time out."

They gathered up the bags and Ainsley said, "I'll wait for the server to return and pay. Why don't you go ahead and take the food to Antiques and Mystiques? I'll be right behind you."

Willow and Rylie moved toward the door when suddenly their progress was halted. An angry, blond woman stood in front of Willow. She looked vaguely familiar and then it came to her.

Missy Newton.

She had been a year behind Willow in school and one of the worst gossips in the Cove. She also had a thing for Dylan, but he had never asked Missy out, telling Willow even before they ever dated that he thought Missy was trouble.

"Don't think just because you're back in the Cove that Dylan is going to fall all over you, Willow Martin. You may think your shit doesn't stink, but I know better. You were the reason Dylan would never ask me out in high school. I'm telling you now—stay out of my way. This time, I want him all to myself. I intend to be in his bed by Christmas."

CHAPTER 14

Dylan closed the file and placed it in a small stack of files he'd already dealt with today. He had buried himself in paperwork, some of it tedious, hoping to keep his thoughts on his work instead of Willow.

He had failed miserably.

Chewing on the end of his pen, he thought how the same thing had occurred during his senior year, after he and Willow had begun dating. They had run in the same crowd for years and gone together to various places, having similar experiences. Yet when they finally paired off, he had discovered she was much more than the kind, loyal girl who occasionally came up with a clever zinger. He had found she possessed true depth, both in her dedication to her art and the way she saw the world. Willow might not have lit the academic world on fire with her mediocre grades, but she had insight and was clever and challenging to be around.

God, how he had missed her.

He supposed he had put his memories of her on a back burner in his mind, one which remained simmering all these years. Now, the temperature had been raised and things had come to a boiling point. The kisses they'd shared already had him restless, filled with an unnamed yearning.

Was she as affected as he was?

If so, she was playing her cards close to the vest.

True, he had angered her by his proposition that they see each other exclusively for a while and allow things to run their natural course. He believed if she agreed to do so, it was only a matter of time before she realized they belonged together permanently. He hoped it would be here in the Cove, but if she needed more than the small coastal town could offer, Dylan was willing to follow her anywhere in the world.

He raked a hand through his hair, knowing he'd gotten all the work done that he could. He needed to blow off a little steam. Reaching for his phone, he decided to text Carter when his cell dinged with a message from his friend.

You up for MNF at HB? Gage & I just grabbed a table. It's Seahawks & Cowboys.

Dylan still enjoyed watching football. He preferred college over pro but needed to hang with his friends and have a little fun.

Willow is here if that'll get you here quicker. And first round is on Gage.

Dylan grinned. He texted a thumbs-up and stood, pulling his jacket from the back of his chair. He stepped outside his office and told Deputy Raymond Garcia the watch was his. Then he bid goodnight to Pam Warner, his dispatcher, and left the station. Within two minutes, he'd reached the Hidden Bear Bar and Grill and stepped inside, seeing the place was full.

Then he caught sight of Willow and Rylie Robin-son. Rylie looked worried.

Willow looked pissed.

He saw why. Missy Newton stood in front of them. The hair stylist had a huge crush on him in high school and had made it clear to Dylan when he re-turned to the Cove that she was still interested. Missy had two divorces behind her and while still attractive, she had a hard edge to her. Dylan suspected she drank a little too much, which was playing havoc with her looks. She had brought cookies to the station twice and donuts on another occasion. She had even left him a coupon for a free haircut, which he had passed up, choosing to go to the barbershop he and his dad had frequented. Dylan had made it plain to Missy that he wasn't up for dating her, but it seemed she hadn't gotten the message yet—or was choosing to ignore it.

As he moved toward the trio, he saw Ainsley also headed in their direction and figured the three women had come in for a bite to eat before Missy confronted Willow.

Dylan got there just as Willow said, "Dylan always asked out who he wanted to, Missy. He didn't need me telling him whom to date. Dylan is the kind of man who lets a woman know if he's interested in her. I'll give you a heads-up, though, so you'll know where you stand—Dylan and I have decided to start seeing each other again. Exclusively."

"Bitch!" Missy cried, raising her hand to strike Willow.

He caught her wrist and spun her around, seeing her bloodshot eyes and knowing it was the alcohol doing a lot of the talking.

"I think you've had a few too many, Missy. You don't want to be arrested for public intoxication, much less assault. Are you here with anyone? If not, I can arrange for you to have a ride home."

"I'm not drunk, Dylan," she said, her words slurring slightly. "And what does she have that I don't?"

He leaned close. "Willow has my heart, Missy," he said, so softly only Missy would be able to hear. He raised his head and looked to Willow and her companions. "Everything all right, ladies?"

"Yes," Rylie said. "We just stopped by for some takeout and are leaving."

His gaze met Willow's and she nodded. "Everything is fine, Sheriff."

"Then I'll wish you a good night."

He watched the trio pass him, his eyes steady on Willow as they left the bar. He still had Missy's wrist and turned back to her, saying, "Let me radio for a ride home."

"I'll take her," a voice said. "We came together."

Dylan saw it belonged to Rick Mercer, his opponent in the sheriff's race. Rick had quit the department after losing the election. Dylan had no idea what Rick was up to since.

He released Missy, and Rick slipped an arm about her waist.

"Let's leave," Rick told her. "You've already embarrassed yourself enough."

"Rick," she whined, but he strode from the bar with her in tow.

Dylan watched them leave and turned, realizing all eyes in the place were on him.

"Show's over, folks. What's the score?" He glanced up and saw the game was at commercial.

"Cowboys leading by three," Carter called out. "But the Seahawks are in the red zone."

He moved to join his friends, and conversations

picked up again. Sitting, he grabbed Carter's mug and washed down the final third of it, wiping his mouth with the back of his hand.

"I'll get us another round," Gage volunteered, rising and heading toward the bar.

Carter grinned. "Glad to hear you and Willow are seeing each other again." His friend punched him in the arm. "That didn't take long." He glanced around. "And it won't take long for that news to get out. Half the bar and grill is talking about that little scene that just played out, while the other half looks to be texting the gossip to anyone who's not here."

Dylan shook his head. "I guess I need to catch you up on things."

Gage rejoined them. "Beers are coming. I also put in for an order of nachos and wings."

"Good," he replied, remembering he hadn't eaten anything all day.

Gage said, "Carter pointed Willow out to me. She's a looker. When did you two hook up?"

"We haven't," he told his friends. "We did go hiking yesterday. Found a dog in the woods and Willow adopted him. Named him Shadow." He paused. "There might have been some kissing involved."

"I heard—pardon me—the entire bar heard that you two are now dating," Gage said. "Only each other. How did that come about?"

He chuckled. "Beats me. I told her that's how I wanted it between us. She muttered something nasty in French. That's where we left it between us last night."

"Sounds like she changed her mind," Carter said, accepting a beer from their server and placing it on the table.

"It was the first I'd heard of it." He took a sip of his

beer. "But I'm extremely happy that's the decision she arrived at."

Gage shook his head. "Women."

"Women," Dylan and Carter agreed, holding up their beer mugs and clinking them together.

Their food arrived and he turned his attention to the game.

Wondering when Willow would make her next move.

~

"SO, YOU AND DYLAN ARE DATING?" Ainsley asked, and then bit into her cheeseburger.

Willow nodded. "I think we are." She dipped a fry into her ketchup.

"You *think*?" Rylie quizzed. "You seemed pretty sure back there when you told Missy Newton off."

She waved the fry in the air. "Missy is just a pain in the ass. She was crazy for Dylan back in high school, but she was a vicious gossip and had a reputation for mean-girl behavior. Dylan was pretty much a straight arrow. A good athlete with terrific grades. He steered clear of Missy. What's her story?"

"She's a hairstylist now," Ainsley shared. "Has a chair at Serenity Salon. Most of the women in town patronize it. I never let her cut my hair, though. She was mean to me in middle school. I was a sixth grader and she was in seventh grade." She shuddered. "Let's just say I told on her and she got into a lot of trouble. I've steered clear of her ever since."

"I did let her cut my hair once when I first moved to the Cove," Rylie revealed. "She didn't listen to a thing I said. Cut it shorter than I asked for, and then she bullied me into some henna rinse. It made my dark brunette hair have a reddish-purple tint to it. Thankfully it washed out after a couple of weeks. And my hair does grow fairly fast, so while I wasn't happy with the length, it was back where I wanted it after about six months. But I couldn't trust her after that."

"I wonder how she keeps any clients," Willow mused.

"Oh, she does give a good cut," Rylie said. "Most women don't know what they want and love that she tells them exactly what they need. I look on my stylist as a partner, not my boss."

"Let's get back to Dylan," Ainsley said. "Yes, I think half the Cove knows Missy has been coming on to him. She's even taken cookies by the sheriff's office. *My* cookies, I might add. Putting them on one of her plates and covering them with foil and claiming she baked them."

They laughed and Rylie said, "No one fell for it, Ains. They know your cookies are the real deal. Missy Newton couldn't come close to your recipes."

"Still, she's shown her interest in Dylan, even if he hasn't reciprocated it. Missy has two divorces behind her." Ainsley gave Willow the particulars. "Both guys are gone from Maple Cove now. I don't think they could stand to be around her and didn't want to cross paths with her." She paused. "So... Dylan?" she prompted.

"He really was supportive during Boo's remembrance. He also went out on Walt's boat when we scattered Boo's ashes. And we went hiking yesterday. We found a dog. Actually, he's my dog now."

Quickly, she told them about Shadow, and both women said they were eager to come see him.

Then Rylie redirected them. "Dylan?" she asked.

"It feels really good being around him again,"

Willow admitted. "Even though a lot of time has passed, we're comfortable around each other."

"And?" Rylie pushed.

"We've kissed. Quite a bit." She felt her cheeks begin to flame. "Dylan is by far the best kisser I've locked lips with."

"Rylie and I hang with Dylan and his friends some," Ainsley said. "Kind of that group thing people did in high school. Him, Carter, and Gage Nelson. He's new to the Cove. A former Navy SEAL turned personal trainer. We've watched some football and basketball on TV. Had a few game nights. I've only been back in Maple Cove about a year. Rylie came not too long after that."

"You mentioned your dad passing away. Where is your mom?" she asked Rylie.

"Mom died from cancer when I was four. That's why Dad dumped me in the Cove with my aunt and uncle every summer. I don't really mean it like that. I loved my aunt and uncle, and Ainsley's always been more sister than cousin to me. But I was never close with my dad. I think I reminded him too much of my mother. He died right after Ainsley came back from Paris and opened up Buttercup Bakery."

"I told her she should move here permanently," Ainsley said, picking up the story. "That lots of people travel to the Oregon Coast. Specialty stores seem to do well. Maple Cove didn't have an antique store."

"Ainsley convinced me to come," Rylie continued. "I sold the Portland store and more than half its inventory to a competitor. Brought the rest with me after I rented out space on the square." She looked around the store. "You can see a lot of what I have is antique furniture, but then I started carrying a few more modern items, along with the consignments. It puts money in my pocket and keeps people from going all the way into Portland to shop."

Rylie sipped her iced tea. "What about you, Willow? I know Ainsley said she ran into you while she was in Paris. What have you done since you left the Cove? That must have been over ten years ago."

"Graduated from UCLA with my art degree. I took courses in painting and drawing. Photography and sculpture. Ceramics. Art theory. Then I moved to Berlin to study. I'd always longed to live abroad. I eventually lived in London, and finally Paris before I came home."

"Any marriages?" Ainsley asked. "I know you were living with a guy in Paris when we ran into each other."

"No. Three serious relationships. At least they were on my part. Not on theirs. I finally broke up with Jean-Luc, another artist, just before I came to New York for an exclusive show last month. My first ever."

She provided details about the show and some of the paintings that had sold. The conversation was so easy and natural, Willow knew she was going to be good friends with both these women.

"With Boo's death, I came back to Maple Cove to regroup," she shared. "I felt I was at a crossroads."

"And now you're seeing Dylan," Ainsley said, approval in her voice. "He's a good one, Willow. I'd think twice before letting him go."

She laughed. "I'm going to have to let him know we're seeing one another. Where we left things last night? I was a little perturbed by his insistence that we see one another—and only one another."

"Yet you spoke up quite clearly about that at the Hidden Bear," Rylie pointed out.

"I have a bit of a temper. Missy Newton pushed a few of my buttons."

"Well, everyone inside the bar and grill heard what you said," Ainsley told her. "Which means all those patrons will be telling everyone else in the Cove."

"I guess that means I'm seeing Dylan Taylor and only Dylan Taylor," Willow said. "So much for scratching my itch with another man."

Rylie grinned. "I think Dylan will excel at scratching, Willow."

They burst out laughing.

CHAPTER 15

Willow was up by five the next morning. Girls' night hadn't lasted as long as she had suspected. By eight-thirty, Ainsley was yawning, telling Willow she was at the bakery each morning by three to put on the first of her doughnuts, pastries, and scones. She usually went to bed at nine each night. Willow had told Ainsley not to apologize and thanked her and Rylie for a wonderful evening.

Both women had been funny and charming, and Willow could see herself becoming good friends with both of them. Ainsley was much more outgoing than her cousin, but Rylie admitted she did better in a small group of people, saying she had to force herself to put on a smile each time a customer entered her store and then she relaxed after meeting them, once they began talking about antiques. She laughed, saying she was more comfortable with furniture than people. They agreed to get together again soon.

She had asked them about the cars they drove and where they purchased them. Both said they went to the same Portland dealership, and Rylie had even gone to college with one of their salesmen. She had told Willow she would text him tonight and tell him to look for Willow tomorrow morning.

She decided to go for a run, getting back into a habit she had developed during college when the freshmen fifteen threatened to overtake her. Her lovers in Europe laughed at this practice, especially Jean-Luc. He told her Parisians got plenty of exercise as they walked everywhere, and he even made fun of her for her daily runs.

But Willow knew the runs did more for her than exercise her limbs and help keep a bit of weight off. They were an escape. A time to plan her day. A way to spend time within herself and visualize whatever painting she would be working on later that day. Her runs helped keep her stress level low. Being back in Oregon now, it would be a natural addition to her day.

She decided to take Shadow with her. It would probably be more of a jog with the dog along because of his shorter front leg, but Willow thought Shadow might enjoy the time spent together. She got into running clothes and slipped into her sneakers before stretching for a few minutes.

"Come on, boy," she said to her dog, going downstairs, Shadow being her literal shadow.

She gave him fresh water but decided to wait and feed him after their outing. She heated a cup of water in the microwave slightly, squeezing some lemon juice into it, and then drank it quickly to hydrate herself.

The dog surprised her, easily keeping up as he loped along with his odd but endearing gait. She increased her speed, and he was able to stay with her pace.

Willow didn't push herself or the dog too much,

returning to the house after half an hour. It had been a good two weeks since she had last run in New York, and she decided she needed to ease back into the habit. Shadow gulped the rest of his water and she re-filled that bowl and fed him, as well. She went upstairs for a quick shower and dressed, coming downstairs and putting on the coffee while toasting two slices of bread. She would take the coffee with her but eat the toast now.

She poured the coffee into a thermos and tight-ened the lid before slathering Boo's homemade rasp-berry jam on her toast. She sipped on some orange juice as she ate and wasn't surprised when her phone rang.

"Hey, Jackson," she greeted. "I guess you looked over Pete Pulaski's proposal."

"I was hoping to catch you," he said.

"I just got in from a run and showered. I'm going into Portland today. What about you?"

"I just finished the same. Run and shower. Ready to conquer the day now and thought I'd touch base with you. I think Pulaski's estimates are generous and thorough. If you feel he's the man to do the work, then I say go for it."

"Dylan recommended him, and he has his finger on the pulse of the community. I like Pete. He walked the property with me and pointed out a few things both inside and outside that I hadn't noticed. He also employs off-duty firemen for the painting and con-struction and promised me he'd put Carter on as many jobs as he could."

"I noticed the estimate included a few things we hadn't discussed, but they made sense."

"I'll give him a call this morning on my way to

Portland and see when he can start the work. How about the trial?"

"Opening arguments are this morning. They should take most of the morning if not all of it," he said neutrally.

"How are you?" she asked. "I know this case hasn't set well with you."

"I ran my opening by Bill and our paralegal. They both suggested a couple of changes, and I reworked it some. I think it will be good. Very good." He paused and added, "Listen, I need to get going. Just wanted to touch base with you about the construction."

"Thanks for doing so. And Jackson? Remember, I'm in your time zone now. Call or text anytime," she reminded.

"Will do."

She finished eating her toast and let Shadow out one more time for good measure before grabbing her purse and heading toward the car. It usually took a little over an hour from Maple Cove to Portland, but she would hit some morning traffic outside the city and definitely once she arrived in it.

She was on the road by a quarter after six and waited until seven before dialing Pete's number.

He answered after the first ring, and she said, "Hi, Pete. It's Willow Martin. I just spoke with my brother, and we're both comfortable with you taking on every job listed on your proposal."

"That's great news, Willow. Usually before I start a job—especially one this extensive—I meet with my client and explain everything in detail. I feel I've already done so with you. I can start today unless you have reservations and want me to go over everything with you again."

"No, today is fine. But I'm on my way into Portland

right now. I didn't think about leaving a key for you. I'll be sure to have one cut and give it to you. In the meantime, could you start outside?"

"Will do. I can work on replacing the gutters and painting. No, I can't. You haven't selected the colors you'd like me to use. I know you're an artist and color is important to you. I'll do gutters and begin on the landscaping today. Would you have time to meet with me about paint colors while I'm there?"

"I should be home by early afternoon," she told him. "Bring samples with you, and we can go through each room inside and also talk about the outside."

"Then I'll see you when I see you," Pete said.

Willow reached the women's shelter she had discovered online, drawn to its mission statement. Not only did the place feed, clothe, and house women and their children, it also set up job training opportunities for those women, including helping them get their GEDs if they needed one. Unfortunately, she had forgotten to note the hours. The shelter did not open until eight. With the half-hour she had to wait, she dug inside her purse and pulled out the small notepad she always carried with her. She began sketching a few things she had passed on her run. By the time the shelter opened, she had ideas for three different paintings.

Approaching the door a few minutes after eight, she found it still locked. Knocking on it, she immediately heard a voice speak to her.

"How may I help you?"

She glanced up and saw the camera overhead. Looking into it, she said, "My name is Willow Martin, and I live in Maple Cove, which is about an hour away from here on the Oregon Coast. My grandmother recently passed away, and I have numerous bags of her things to share with you."

"Could you please remove a form of ID and hold it up for me to see?"

She didn't mind doing so, thinking the people who ran the shelter were smart to be so careful. Domestic abuse victims were often pursued by their abusers after they left their horrifying situations.

She removed her passport and held it up high, explaining, "I've been living abroad in Paris and recently returned after my grandmother's death. I don't have an Oregon driver's license yet, so I hope my passport will suffice."

"It looks good, Miss Martin."

She heard a lock being thrown electronically, and a moment later, a tall woman with graying hair pushed open the door.

"I'm Eliza. Can I help you bring in your grand-mother's items?"

"Only if you want a good workout," she teased. "My car and trunk are packed to the gills. And please, call me Willow."

With two of them working, they brought in the garbage bags within five minutes, leaving them on the floor in the reception area.

When the last one was inside, Eliza said, "Thank you very much, Willow. The women here appreciate your generosity. Your grandmother's things will be put to good use."

"I'd also like to make a donation," she said spontaneously.

"We make it easy," Eliza told her. "You can donate online with the click of a few buttons. The site takes credit cards or you can use PayPal."

"That's convenient. I will do so once I get home later today. It was pleasure meeting you, Eliza."

"Thank you again for your donation, Willow."

She returned to the now-empty rental, feeling good about what she had just done. She tapped a reminder on her phone about making the donation so she wouldn't forget.

She sipped the last of her coffee and plugged in directions to the car dealership on her phone. Portland traffic was heavy on her way there. She didn't arrive at the dealership until after nine. Once again, she found it didn't open until ten. Disappointed, she decided to make lemonade from the lemons and indulge in one of her favorite things about Portland, driving to Voodoo Donuts and joining the long line which came out the store's door.

When she arrived at the front, she ordered her favorite, a maple bacon bar, rectangular in shape, a pillowy delight of sugar with the salty bacon balancing the sweetness. She took it to her car and savored every bite of it. France might have its croissants, but Portland would always reign supreme with Voodoo Donuts.

She arrived back at the car dealership and entered, immediately greeted by a salesman in his late twenties, with dark hair and a ready smile.

"I'm Tom Presley. Might you be Willow?" he asked.

"How did you know?"

"Because Rylie described you to a T, and told me—and I am directly quoting—'You better take care of my girl Willow, or you'll lose Ainsley's and my business.'"

They both laughed.

"Come into my office before we even look. I want to talk about what you want in a car. Rylie said you've been abroad a good many years, and I'd like to not only hear about your needs but tell you a little about what cars offer today. Can I get you coffee? Water?"

"No, thank you," she said, following Tom into his office and taking a seat.

He took out a yellow legal pad and jotted her name at the top. "Off the top of your head, what do you wish for in a vehicle?"

"I believe an SUV would be my best bet," she told him. "I'm an artist, and I might be bringing paintings into Portland at some point to ship to New York. I need something with a roomy back, or at least a back seat that folds down and gives me enough room to place and secure my canvases. That would be my number one priority. Other than that, I'm open to suggestions. Of course, I'd like the basics. Air conditioning and heating. Four-wheel drive would be nice. So would a sun roof. You tell me what you think I might need, living in Oregon."

Tom talked for several minutes, pulling up images on his tablet and walking her through various features from different models. He was right. Cars had evolved quite a bit since she had graduated from college. Although Willow had never owned a car of her own, she had ridden places with friends. Their cars had not had heated seats or Bluetooth and GPS. The few times she had rented cars in Europe, they were basically boxes, with none of these bells and whistles that Americans wanted as standard in their cars. She wanted to get her Oregon driver's license, and as they spoke, she jotted another note on her phone to look into how to study for the test and where she could take it.

Tom stood. "I have a few things to show you now, Willow. The only question I have left is would you prefer a new or used vehicle? New is always fun because of that new car smell and the few miles on it.

Used, you don't know who drove it or how hard it was driven before it arrived here. We do guarantee, though, that our used cars have been thoroughly vetted and are in terrific running condition, especially the gently used ones. Those are a year or less in age."

"Let's look at new vehicles first," she said. "Then maybe gently used."

They moved onto the showroom floor, Tom pointing out various features as Willow climbed behind the wheel to see how the car sat. He took her outside, and she really didn't find anything among the used cars that excited her. She decided to drive two of the new SUV models, one a mid-range size and one large.

They took out the mid-size first, and she drove the streets around the dealership before Tom encouraged her to get onto the freeway.

"You need to see about the pickup and how it handles at a greater speed," he explained.

Willow liked how thorough the salesman had been and enjoyed driving this model a few exits on the freeway before doubling back to the dealership.

They traded vehicles and left the lot with her behind the wheel of the larger SUV. She didn't feel as comfortable driving it.

"Though it handles well, it seems too long and wide," she told him. "I don't think I need to even drive it on the highway. I like the other one better."

"Then let's head back. If you're ready, we can write up a deal."

They returned to Tom's office, and she looked at few brochures to see various interior and exterior colors available. She decided on a hunter green exterior with a dark gray interior.

The salesman punched a few keys on his computer, saying, "I'll see if we have your choice in stock."

Moments later, he smiled. "We do. Do you want to take it out?"

"I don't think that's necessary. If it's the same make and model of what I test drove, I'll be happy."

Willow was happy her agent had encouraged her to set up an American bank account while she lived abroad. Remy had told her it would be easier to have one. They had chosen a national bank, which had branches in over forty states, including a few in Portland. When she left France for good, she had closed her checking account there, doing a wire transfer of her funds to her US bank account.

"I'm not interested in financing," she told Tom. "I'd like to pay cash for the car."

"There actually is a slight discount if you pay all cash," he told her. "Let me go talk with my manager and update him on our transaction. After that, we'll get your bank on the phone and see if we can close this deal."

She was glad Dylan had reminded her to arrange for automobile insurance with Porter Williams before she came to Portland today. He had told her once she had selected a vehicle to be sure and call him so he could get the make, model, and VIN number.

Tom was gone less than five minutes and returned. "We're all set."

He named a figure, which she had seen on the window sticker, and then told her his manager would take five percent off it for the cash payment. They contacted the closest branch of her bank and ironed out the details over speakerphone. Tom printed out some paperwork for her to sign and then told her the SUV was hers. He went to have it washed and then brought up to the front, even claiming her rental car's keys and telling him a junior salesman would return the car for her.

By a little before one, she was on the road heading back to Maple Cove again. Traffic was light for a weekday and she pulled up Boo's long driveway just after two o'clock, seeing Pete's truck.

Willow took one more whiff, drinking in the heady new-car smell, and then got out of her vehicle. Glancing up, she saw the gutters had been changed out. Much of the scraggly shrubbery which had surrounded the house had been removed, and new ones had replaced them. Two men were planting flowers in the front beds. She recognized purple pansies, winter heath, and ornamental cabbage and kale

Pete was one of them and he stood, coming to greet her. "We hadn't talked about what you wanted planted, but I hope you'll be pleased with what we've done today."

"I'm very pleased," she told him. "I love the spot of color."

He introduced her to the other worker, a fireman who worked with Carter, and then Pete went to his truck, bringing out sample cards with various shades of paint on them.

"Let look at these in the light and decide upon what you want on the outside first," he suggested.

After several minutes of debating pros and cons, Willow decided on a slate blue and cream, with a dark navy to be used as an accent color.

"We can start on the exterior tomorrow," Pete said. "Carter and two other firemen are on the schedule, and I'll be joining them. We'll have the entire outside painted by the end of tomorrow. Ready to discuss the inside colors?"

They walked through each room inside the house, discussing the neutral palette Willow wanted to run throughout the house. She liked both cool and warm beiges, some darker browns, and a lighter and darker sage. Pete took notes on her choices for each room and told her they could start the interior the day after tomorrow.

"We'll need three days on the inside. Baseboards and trim work slow us down. So do these high ceilings. We'll also sand the floors after we've painted. Now that I think about it, we need to knock out that wall in the kitchen that you wanted down. We should do that before we paint." He paused. "We can work around you, but I'd suggest moving out for five or six days. After that, you can return. The rest of the work is small stuff, such as changing out the faucet fixtures and putting new handles on drawers in the kitchen and bathrooms. What would you like to do—stay or go?"

"I'll move out. I don't want to be in your way." She gave him an extra key which she remembered Boo kept in a kitchen drawer. "Now that I think about it, the art studio is the only room we're not touching. Do you think I could come work every day? I promise to stay out of your way."

"I don't think that would be a problem. Feel free to come and work whenever you want." He placed the key on his key ring. I'll head back outside and help finish up with the plants."

Willow was glad she would be able to continue to work throughout the renovations but didn't know where she would stay at night. It should be fairly easy to book herself into a B&B, but she didn't know if they would take Shadow. There was a small inn between here and Salty Point. Maybe they would take pets.

Then she decided that it would be the perfect time to test if she and Dylan really were compatible. Nothing like living with a man for a week in close quarters to see if they might have a chance at the long run.

Before she lost her courage, Willow dialed Dylan's number.

CHAPTER 16

Dylan sat brooding in his office, wondering if—or when—he might hear from Willow. It was obvious the way his staff tiptoed around him at the station today that everyone had heard what Willow had told Missy Newton at the Hungry Bear last night.

He only wished Willow would confirm it to his face. That they were now seeing each other.

A knock sounded at his closed door and he growled, "What is it?"

Slowly, the door opened and for a moment, he thought it might be Willow.

Wrong.

Instead, Missy Newton entered, holding a basket in her hand and wearing a sheepish grin.

"May I come in, Dylan?" she asked.

He sat straighter. "What can I do for you, Missy?"

She stepped tentatively into the office and held up the basket. "Peace offering? They're blueberry muffins."

"From what I can tell, you don't need to be making peace with me," he said flatly. "I think you should be offering those muffins to Willow."

A pinched look appeared on her face, and she snapped, "Well, I suppose if I give these to you, Willow Martin will still wind up eating them, won't she?"

Dylan raked a hand through his hair in frustration. "Missy, you're a nice girl, but—"

"But I'm not the one for you, am I, Dylan? Oh, I know how Willow turned your head in high school. It's obvious she's still doing the same. But women like her are always out for themselves. Why, she left the Cove for years and years. Didn't care what happened here or to her grandmother."

Anger surged through him. "Leave Boo out of this, Missy."

She gave him her prettiest pout. "All I'm saying, Dylan, is that I have always been around. I would be so loyal to you. I would love you like no one ever has. Or ever will. Especially Willow Martin. Sure, she may be here now, but she's not the kind that would stay. You need someone like me in your bed."

Missy fanned the flames of all the doubts Dylan had about Willow and him. He had given his heart to her years ago and knew she had continued to hold a piece of it ever since. His greatest fear was that she would worm her way totally into his heart. That they would make love and it would be the best experience of his life. Then she would walk away—and never come back—leaving him forever broken.

"Missy, you have a lot going for you if you lay off the booze." He rose and went to stand in front of her. "I see a lot of good in you. I know others do, too, but it would never work between us. I think you're still hung up on the popular boy from high school, that golden athlete who younger kids idolized. I'm just a man, like any other, and I have plenty of flaws of my own. But I have to be honest with you. There is no chance of anything happening between us. Not short-term. Not long-term."

Tears welled in her eyes, but Dylan also saw the anger that sparked there. He reached for the basket and claimed it from her.

"Thank you for the blueberry muffins. I'll share them with the rest of the department. Go on, Missy, and leave. I'll be cordial when we see one another in public, but you need to stop dropping by the station. I don't want to give you any false hopes. Are we clear?"

"She's blinded you, Dylan Taylor," Missy said, venom in her voice. "She's not who you think she is. Willow Martin is selfish and not the right woman for you. When you finally figure that out, you know where to find me."

Missy wheeled and stormed from his office. Dylan gave her a couple of minutes to get out of the building before he ambled in and said to no one in particular, "Fresh blueberry muffins if anyone's hungry."

He set the basket on a table, knowing his deputies would pounce upon it the moment his back was turned. Turning to Pam, he said, "I'll be out on patrol. Call if you need me."

He strode from the station to his cruiser and got inside, collecting himself before he started the engine. He drove around the square and then went west on Orchid Lane, turning on Sea Coast Road.

He had been cruising a good half-hour along the coast when his phone rang. Reaching for it, he knew it wouldn't be his dispatcher, because Pam would have raised him on the radio. Surprised filled him when he saw Willow's name and he answered.

"Sheriff Taylor."

After a slight pause, she said, "Dylan, it's me."

He swallowed down the emotion thickening his throat at the sound of her voice and said, "Hey, Willow. How are you? Have you met with Pete Pulaski yet?"

"Funny you should ask that. Pete came out yesterday morning and worked up an estimate for me. I ran it by Jackson, and we've given Pete the green light for several projects, which includes painting the inside of the house and some construction work. He started this morning."

"That's good news. Pete could use the business, as well as the off-duty firemen he employs."

She was silent a moment and then said, "I guess we need to talk. In person."

"You're right. We do."

"Could we have dinner tonight?" she asked. "At your place?"

Hope filled him. "Sure, I'd like that. Seven okay?"

"Seven would be fine," she confirmed. "Could I bring Shadow along?"

"I'd be happy to host the both of you. I'll pick up something from the diner. Any requests?"

"No, you know what I like. Pretty much anything that isn't liver and onions."

He chuckled, remembering how it was one of Boo's favorite meals to prepare and that Willow couldn't stand the smell or taste of liver.

"Liver and onions are off the table then," he told her. "Anything else will be fair game."

"Then I guess I'll see you at seven. Where do you live again? I remember you told me you rented a couple of rooms."

"I'm actually above Sid's Diner. Since it's on the corner of the square, there's an outside staircase leading up to the second-floor entrance." He hesitated a moment and then said, "I'm glad you called, Willow. I'm happy that I'll see you tonight."

"See you later." She ended the call.

He slipped his phone back into the tray under the dashboard. Elation filled him. Willow could be stubborn and set in her ways. For her to have reached out to him, especially after her last words to him had been angry ones, meant a great deal. He hoped tonight would be the fresh start they needed to move forward. Having dinner alone would be an intimate experience. He couldn't help but wonder if it might lead to intimacy of a different kind.

"Don't get ahead of yourself," he told himself.

As far as sex went, he wanted Willow to be the one to speak up first and initiate it. He didn't want to sway her and then have her think he manipulated her into making love. No, she would definitely have to show—and tell—him she was an interested party before he would participate.

For now, however, he would relish the time spent with her and Shadow. He wondered why she was bringing the dog along, and if the pup might be used as a buffer between them.

Dylan headed back toward town, his mood considerably lighter now. He returned to his office and put in another few hours' work, leaving at five-thirty, which was early for him. No one said a word to him about his early departure. He decided to straighten up his rooms when he went home. Life as a bachelor meant leaving things strewn about, and he made quick work of making certain no dirty clothes were on the floor and clean ones were hung in the closet or put away in drawers.

Fortunately, the army had instilled in him a love of neatness which had carried over into his tiny kitchen.

It was tidy, with no dishes in the sink and the counter-tops clean. He jumped in the shower to wash off the smell of work and then dressed in a blue button-down shirt and jeans. He called Sid's Diner and placed an order for two and was told it would be ready in ten minutes. Giving the apartment one last glance, he locked up and headed down the stairs to the diner.

When he arrived, Nancy Mayfield, the owner, said, "I forgot to ask if you wanted rolls, cornbread, or both."

"Both," he said, thinking it would have been a long time since Willow had eaten cornbread, something he remembered she loved.

"Your order should be out in a minute, Dylan," Nancy said, heading toward the kitchen.

She returned two minutes later and said, "I'll add it to your tab. I suppose you're having company?"

Dylan frequented the diner since it was close and he wasn't much of a cook, ordering dinner from it several nights a week and then paying at the end of the month for all his meals, along with his rent.

"What if I told you I was merely extra hungry tonight?" he teased. "Or that I decided to order for tonight and tomorrow night at the same time?"

Nancy gave him a motherly smile. "Then I would say you're a bald-faced liar. Tell Willow I said hi."

He gave her a grin. "Will do."

Dylan carried the takeout back upstairs to his rooms, setting the Styrofoam boxes on the counter before removing two plates from the cabinet. He had nowhere for them to sit and eat dinner, other than on the well-worn sofa, and so he took napkins and silverware and placed them on the scarred coffee table in front of the couch. Then he opened a bottle of wine in order to let it breathe, not knowing Willow's taste in that area. With her having lived in Paris, he figured she was a connoisseur of good wine and hoped his selection from Costco would pass muster.

A knock sounded on the door, and he moved toward it.

~

WILLOW STOOD NERVOUSLY at Dylan's door. She held Shadow's leash in one hand and the painting she had done for Dylan in the other. She made sure it faced her, not ready to share it with him just yet.

She had changed her mind at the last moment, deciding she should ask Dylan in person if she could stay with him, rather than over the phone. She thought it important to see his reaction to her request.

Gathering her courage, she knocked on the door, her heart racing. Moments later, Dylan opened the door, and her heart slammed against her ribs.

How could she have ever looked at another man when she had loved this one for so many years?

He wore his favorite color of blue, which brought out his gray eyes. The shirt fit him snugly, showing off his broad shoulders. She itched to see was underneath that shirt and hoped tonight she would be able to do so.

"Hi," he said softly.

"Hi," she repeated.

They stood drinking one another in for a moment and then he said, "I'm not being much of a host, am I? Please, come in."

He stepped aside and she entered the apartment. It looked to be two rooms, with the living and kitchen space flowing together, and a door leading to what she supposed was the bedroom. The carpet was worn, as was the furniture, and she supposed it had come furnished, since she saw nothing of Dylan's personality reflected in the room's furnishings.

He closed the door and then knelt before Shadow, holding his hand out for the dog to sniff.

"Remember me, boy? I'm the one who was with this pretty lady when we found you."

Shadow eagerly licked Dylan's fingers, and he scratched the Lab between his ears.

Looking up at her, he asked, "Shall I undo the leash from his collar?"

She nodded, and once Shadow was free, she turned and placed the painting against the wall.

"You brought me a painting?"

"Yes. But I'd rather you look at it later," she told him. "After we talk." Her stomach grumbled. "I guess that's our cue for dinner," she joked.

She placed her purse beside the painting and slipped the leash inside it before following him to the small kitchenette.

Dylan opened the first box, and the smell of meat loaf wafted toward her.

"Ah, that looks and smells heavenly. I haven't had corn on the cob in ages, much less fresh broccoli."

He opened the lid of the other, and she saw roast beef covered in gravy, along with mashed potatoes and baby carrots.

"Which is mine?" she asked.

"You can have either. You're the guest."

"I don't think I would be able to decide. Mind if we split? That way, we could both have a little of everything."

"That's easy to do."

Dylan took a knife and halved both entrees,

placing them on the nearby plates. Then he divided and spooned the vegetables onto the plates as well.

"I'll apologize in advance. I have no table for us to sit at. I usually come home and crash on the couch, eating and watching TV."

"I'm fine sitting there as long as you keep the TV off."

"Would you like the wine now? Or later?"

"Let's save it for after dinner."

They carried their plates to the sofa. Conversation was easy between them. She told Dylan about her day, dropping off the clothes at the shelter and then purchasing her very first vehicle, as well as what Pete had worked on.

"That's a lot for one day," he said. "I'll have to go down and see the new SUV. I know you're proud to finally own your own car."

"I will say it's a cut above that old Ford junker you drove in high school."

He laughed. "I put a lot of hours into working on that sedan. With Dad. He was really mechanical. I miss him. I miss all of them."

Willow reached for his hand and squeezed his fingers. "I know you do." She looked to the lone painting he had hung. "Is that one Grace did?"

He nodded. "I put a few things in storage before I left for basic training. This was one you helped her with, and she had just finished it before the accident."

"I thought I recognized it. Grace had a lot of talent. She would have been a wonderful artist."

"I think so, too."

She hated seeing him hurt, even after so many years. Boo and Jackson may have lived half a world away from her, but they had always been there for one another. Dylan had not had anyone all those years in the army.

"Why don't we try that wine?" she suggested.

He took both their plates and rinsed them, leaving them in the sink, before returning with the wine and two goblets.

As Dylan poured the bold red, he said, "Don't break that glass. I only have two."

She giggled. "The life of a bachelor. I wouldn't worry if I were you. I used to drink wine in jam jars. Boo would ship a few over each year, filled with whatever she had made, and I collected them. Drinking my wine out of one made me feel a little closer to home."

Willow took a sip. "Yum. This is good. Cabernets are my favorites."

"I didn't know what you might like," he admitted. "Or if you even drink wine. I figured living abroad, though—especially in Paris—you had to like wine."

"I do. I developed a real taste for it."

"Oregon has a lot of vineyards. Maybe we could check a few out. Most are dog-friendly. You can bring in a picnic or buy food and wine at the vineyard. Have a picnic."

She smiled. "I'd like that. How about this weekend?"

Willow stifled a laugh seeing the surprise on his face.

"Yeah. That would be great."

"Are you surprised that I want to make plans with you?"

"A little," he admitted. "Are we at the part where you're ready to talk? About us?"

She drained her wine glass and set it down, then took his glass from his hand and placed it beside hers.

"Sometimes talk can be overrated," she told him.

From the moment she had entered his apartment, it had been a struggle not to kiss Dylan. Willow leaned toward him, her palm going to his chest. His hand cradled her nape as his lips touched hers.

Heaven...

CHAPTER 17

As much as Willow knew they should talk, she needed this more. The feel of Dylan's lips on hers. His scent overwhelming her senses. Her body had been in a state of anticipation ever since he had pinned her to the hood of his car, desperate for his touch.

His hand on the back of her neck almost scalded her. Dylan had always radiated heat, and it seemed he did even more so, now that they were adults.

Though she was the one who initiated the kiss, he quickly took control. His arm went about her waist, drawing her near as he leisurely explored every crevice of her mouth. She could taste the rich wine on his tongue, which had already given her a slight buzz because she had downed her glass so fast. She had needed a bit of liquid courage to make the first move.

But she was so glad she had.

Dylan deepened the kiss, causing her heart to skip a few beats and then pound madly within her chest. Everything about this moment felt incredibly right. His mouth on hers. His arm securing her to him. The heady experience of kissing a mature Dylan. Yes, his kisses had been potent when they were teenagers, but now he possessed a skill he hadn't before.

Her body responded to the sizzling kisses, heating as an inferno. Her breasts grew heavy, aching for his touch. Her limbs grew languid. Her core began to throb, longing for him to touch her there.

He pulled her into his lap, and Willow brought her arms around his neck, pressing her breasts into him. Hearing his low growl, she smiled. He broke the kiss, breathing heavily, as his lips trailed along her cheek and went to her ear.

"Your ears always were your weakness," he murmured, as his teeth caught her earlobe and tugged. A surge of desire spread through her. She pushed her fingers into his thick hair, tightening her grip as his breath grew warm against her ear. His tongue outlined the shell of her ear, bringing quick shivers. His mouth moved back to her throat, caressing it, as his hands framed her face. He held her in place as he kissed her deeply.

But it wasn't enough.

"Touch me," she said against his mouth.

"Where?" he asked.

"Anywhere. Everywhere."

Dylan continued the drugging kisses as his hands moved to her breasts. The touch was like a jolt of electricity rippling through her, cranking her need to Defcon 5. He massaged them. Kneaded them. Tweaked her nipples playfully, all while he continued savaging her mouth.

Then he broke the kiss and his lips hovered at her jaw, nibbling it as his fingers worked the buttons of her blouse, parting it when the last one slipped through its buttonhole.

He helped her shrug out of it, continuing to kiss

her jaw and neck. Then he moved lower, his lips pressed to the pulse point of her throat. It beat wildly as he pulled the shirt from her shoulders and managed to get it off her. Hot fingers grazed her chest as he unhooked her bra and removed it, leaving her bare to the waist.

This was as far as they had gone in high school. A few times in his car she had allowed him to remove both her shirt and bra, and Dylan had feasted on her breasts. Need pulsed through her, though, and she knew she was ready for more.

She only hoped he was willing to satisfy her need for him.

"You are so damned beautiful," he murmured, his admiring gaze causing her to blush.

He brushed her nipples with the back of his fingers, teasing her.

"I need more room than a couch for what I want to do to you," he told her, his voice low and rough. Waiting a beat, he asked, "Can we move to the bedroom?"

"Yes," she whispered, her throat closing with emotion.

Dylan rose, carrying her with him as he did so. Willow entwined her arms around his neck and he moved through an open door.

A single lamp burned next to the bed. He placed her on it and gazed at her, the corners of his mouth curling up in a smile.

"Ooh-la-la," he quipped, causing her to giggle.

He removed her shoes and then his and climbed on to the bed, hovering over her, his knees against her hips. Then his mouth went to her breast and he began a slow, torturous dance of teasing, licking, and sucking that drove her wild. She reached up and unbuttoned his shirt, pulling the tail from his jeans.

"Take it off," she commanded.

"With pleasure."

He stripped it from him, tossing the shirt to the floor. Willow's gaze lingered over the muscular chest with its light dusting of hair and flat abs, the ridges forming a six-pack.

Her fingers danced along his ribs. "So sexy," she said, watching the muscles bunch at her touch.

A growl emerged from him and he captured her wrists in one hand, bringing them over her head and pinning them to the pillow. With his free hand, he caressed one breast as he devoured the other. She found her hips rising, pushing against his pelvis as she strained to brush her body against his. He laved and sucked and had her frantic, her breath coming in short spurts. Then he moved to the other breast and repeated his performance, whipping her into a frenzy.

"Dylan!" she cried in desperation, struggling to free her wrists.

He lifted his head, his gray eyes dark with desire. "Yes?"

"I want to touch you," she pouted.

Releasing her wrists, he allowed her to push him to his side and then onto his back. Willow straddled him, her hands grasping his shoulders as her mouth moved to one of his nipples. She toyed with him as he had her, enjoying the low groans and movement of his hips. She could feel his cock hardening beneath her.

And wanted him inside her.

She pushed up and eased off the bed, ready to remove her leggings.

"What are you doing?" he asked.

"Taking the rest off," she said smartly.

"No." He sat up. "That's my job to enjoy."

His hand shot out and latched on to her wrist, jerking her so she fell back on to the bed. Her legs dangled from it and Dylan stood, slipping his fingers beneath the band around her waist and slowly peeling the leggings and her underwear down her hips and thighs. He took his time, watching as new flesh was exposed. She could feel the blush heating her cheeks.

He pulled the leggings over her feet and discarded them and the thick socks she wore. Her legs still dangled from the bed and Dylan knelt, gripping her knees and inching her legs wider. Willow felt exposed as he knelt in front of her.

"I've wanted to do this for as long as I can remember," he said, raw need in his voice.

Then he kissed her knee. His lips traveled up the inside of her thigh, so sensitive to his touch. He reached her nest of curls and grinned.

"Red. Just as I thought."

His hands slipped under her butt, pulling her closer to him. Then his lips were touching her, his tongue gliding up and down the seam of her sex. She shivered.

"Oh, Bear, you're already so wet for me."

His mouth moved higher, kissing her belly, as his finger teased her. He pushed it inside her and stroked her deeply, causing her to shudder. Another finger joined it and the caresses nearly drove her out of her mind. Then he pressed hard against her clitoris, rubbing in a circular motion. Her orgasm built and erupted violently. Willow cried out as her body trembled.

Dylan's mouth returned to hers and she clung to him, riding out the waves of ultimate pleasure that seemed to go on forever. Finally her body stilled.

"That... I never felt that so strong before," she told him.

She rarely experienced an orgasm during sex and when she did, it was short in duration. None of her lovers had enjoyed foreplay and she hardly ever felt satisfied during or after sex.

"Let's see what else I can do for you." Dylan gave her a lazy smile.

Then his mouth traveled down the length of her body again, stopping where his fingers had been. Without warning, he plunged his tongue inside her, almost causing a new orgasm to erupt. He anchored her hips, holding her in place, licking, sucking, plunging his tongue deep inside her. She bunched the comforter in her hands as the feelings built and then exploded again, causing her to call out his name again and again.

When it ended, she went limp.

He rose and hoisted her fully onto the bed, tucking a pillow under her head, and then lying next to her, his lips caressing her throat, his palm flat on her belly.

"I want to reciprocate—but I literally cannot move," she told him.

"I don't need anything from you now, Bear. Just lie here with me."

Dylan continued to lie beside her, nuzzling her neck.

And Willow felt loved.

He hadn't uttered the words. No, her man was too smart for that. He knew if he did so, it might cause her to panic and run. But she felt the love pouring from him, all the same.

She placed her hand atop his. "I don't know if I would have been ready for that at seventeen," she admitted. "I don't know if at thirty I can wrap my head around it."

He pushed his fingers into her hair, pulling them through her long locks. "Come on. You act like you never had an orgasm before."

"This was special, Dylan. I know you felt it. You had to," she pressed.

He turned her head so their eyes met. "It was special. Because it was you, babe. It's always been you."

He kissed her softly, so tenderly that tears sprang to her eyes.

"Could I have some more?" she asked.

"Baby, I'll give you as much as you can take."

"I want you inside me, Dylan. Now."

"No. It's too soon. You've only been back a few days. We can wait."

She pushed up on her elbow. "You're wrong. It's been too long. We planned on it years ago."

He gazed at her steadily. "But you're the one who keeps saying we're different people now. I agree. And I think we should wait."

Willow huffed. "So, my opinion doesn't matter?"

"I didn't say that. I just don't want to rush you into anything."

"You're not rushing me. If anything, I'm rushing you." She touched his cheek. "I want this, Dylan. More than I thought possible. You've made me feel better about myself in a few minutes than I have in ten years."

He shook his head. "I don't believe you."

"You should. I told you I was shitty at relationships. I picked the wrong men every time. There weren't many—but they were all selfish and only cared about their needs. Not one of them paid as much attention to me in the time we were together as you did right now.

"Please," she pleaded. "I want to make love with you, Dylan. I want to see how good it can be between us."

She watched him consider it.

"Could we take a little break? Sip some wine. Talk. Then see if you feel the same."

Willow knew she would and didn't see the point of delaying the inevitable, but for some reason, it seemed important to him for them to delay things for a bit.

"All right," she agreed.

She rolled off the bed and found his shirt, slipping into it and buttoning a couple of the buttons. It was barely long enough to cover her butt. She padded into the other room and poured herself a glass of wine and then topped off his glass.

Shadow looked up from where he lay on the floor.

"All is okay," she reassured the pup, and he settled back down.

Willow sat on the sagging sofa, thinking Dylan certainly could use a new one. He joined her, reaching for his glass as he slipped an arm around her shoulders. She rested her cheek against his bare chest.

"I'd love to get you out of those jeans," she told him, her fingers toying with the hair on his chest.

"All in good time," he told her. "Let's talk."

She decided she couldn't delay any longer. "You heard what I told Missy last night. That we're seeing each other—and only each other. Everyone in the Hungry Bear heard me—and I'm sure by now ninety-eight percent of the Cove knows, as well."

"Did you mean it?" he asked. "Or were you simply trying to put Missy in her place?"

"Fair question." She took a deep breath. "I meant

it." She was not telling him how the thought of Missy with him made her incredibly jealous.

"You were pretty upset when I left Sunday night," Dylan pointed out. "When I told you I wanted a relationship with you, and that it needed to be one where we were only seeing each other."

"Upset? A little. Angry is more like it. But I calmed down after you left. I saw your point. I decided that we were both adults. That there was no reason for me not to give this—us—a chance."

"And you didn't call and tell me this yesterday?"

Willow smiled. "I'll admit I wanted to wait a few days. I didn't want you to think I'd capitulated that easily. But I meant what I told Missy, Dylan."

She raised her head and met his gaze. "Even after all these years apart, I still have strong feelings for you. I think now that we're both back in Maple Cove and free to see one another, we should give this a chance to play out and see where it goes."

A smile lit his face. "You really mean that, don't you?"

"I do." She leaned over to pick up her wine glass and swallowed a healthy portion. "In fact, I have a suggestion to make. The only room not being touched in the house is the art studio. Pete doesn't mind me being upstairs painting during the day, but because of the chaos, he thought it would be a good idea if I moved out for a week while he and his crew completed the work. The dust. The paint."

Willow looked at him hopefully. "I thought this might be a good idea to test things between us by having me stay with you."

"Ah, it makes sense now. Why you brought Shadow with you. You want to stay tonight. And the

nights to follow." His lips pressed against her brow
tenderly.

"Yes. What do you think of the idea?"

He framed her face in his large hands. "I like it. I
like having you to myself. Coming home to you.
Seeing the spark between us being fanned into a
bright flame."

Dylan stood and pulled Willow to her feet.

"Yes."

"*Yes* to what?" she asked.

"Yes—I think I'd better take advantage of every
moment I have you here." He kissed her softly.
"Willow Martin, will you allow me to make love to you
now?"

Warmth filled her. "How about we make love together?" she countered.

"You're on."

With that, Dylan swept her off her feet and carried
Willow back into the bedroom.

CHAPTER 18

Dylan gently deposited Willow on her feet. He pulled back the comforter and sheet and then reached for her, pressing his body against hers. He couldn't get over how they fit together as puzzle pieces meant to be side-by-side.

Willow took the lead on the kiss and he let her, wanting her to be a full participant in this act. From the little she had said, she felt like a failure in her past relationships. To him, it sounded as if she had tried to be something she wasn't in order to please her lovers —and that they were selfish assholes who hadn't taken care of her the way they should have.

Their kiss grew more urgent, full of fire and heat. Dylan slipped his hands beneath the shirt she wore, caressing her rounded ass. She murmured something he didn't understand but then she reached for his belt and unbuckled it. He knew she wanted him stripped down.

Breaking the kiss, he stepped back and pulled the jeans over his hips, turning to sit on the bed to remove them. Willow beat him to it, grabbing the bottom of both pants legs and yanking them off. She gave him a mischievous grin and tossed the jeans over her shoulders.

"Stand up," she ordered.

He did as she instructed, her eyes roaming up and down his body. She moved to him, slipping her fingers inside his boxer briefs and slowly inching them downward, moving her body lower as she did. When they got to his ankles, he stepped out of them.

But Willow remained on her knees. She took him into her mouth, working his rod with teeth and tongue and lips. He gripped her shoulders, unable to contain his groans. Everything she did made him feel like a god. He feared ejaculating too soon, though, and that was not going to happen. Not when he yearned to make love to this woman.

Easing her away, he said, "We've got more to do, Bear. Remember, I was a Boy Scout. I like to be prepared—and I want you prepared for the ride of your life."

He stood and kissed her hard, holding her tightly to him, wishing this moment could go on forever and that he never had to let her go. He tasted hope. Desire. *And love...*

Dylan had never known love with any woman besides this one. His infrequent, one-night stands over the years kept him from becoming involved emotionally. But just in these few minutes together tonight, he understood intimacy wasn't just physical. What was about to happen between them wasn't simply sex. Instead, he and Willow would create a special bond. They would share themselves both physically and emotionally. Forge connections. Sex with Willow would mean something deeper than anything he had experienced before.

He unbuttoned the shirt, ridding her of it before

placing her on the bed. Then he thought he better get a condom out now so that he wouldn't lose his head in the heat of the moment. Leaning toward the nightstand, he opened the drawer and removed a silver packet.

"You don't need that."

"Are you on the pill?"

She laughed. "Not a chance. I tried it and was a hormonal mess. You think I have a temper sometimes? My gosh, you should have seen my mood swings on the pill. I was an irritable mess. No, I have an implant."

She held up her left arm and indicated a spot. "It's under the skin. Long-term. No muss, no fuss. And easy to remove."

Dylan tossed the condom back into the drawer. "Good to know."

He spent the next half hour exploring every inch of her beautiful body. The curves of her breasts and hips. The sensitive place behind her knee. He touched and stroked and tasted her everywhere. By the time he was ready to enter her, he thought he might explode.

"Please," she begged. "I need you inside me now. I'm half mad with want and need."

He straddled her, her body between his knees, kissing her a final time. His fingers found her ready for him and he stroked her a few times, her hips rising as she moaned.

Then he changed his mind. As much as he wanted to plunge deep inside her, he wanted Willow to have all the control.

Dylan captured her waist and spun so his back was on the bed and lifted her onto him.

"What are you doing?" she asked, panic in her voice.

"I'm making love *with* you, Bear."

Confusion filled her face and he realized although she may have had prior relationships, most likely she had never been given the opportunity to be placed in this position.

He looked at her, love pouring from him, and said, "You are going to set our pace, love. You will ride this train for all it's worth."

Understanding spread across her face—as did the most beautiful smile he had ever seen.

"Thank you for trusting me," she said, sincerity shining in her eyes. "I may need a little guidance," she added.

He cupped her cheek. "We're in this together, Bear."

He hoped forever...

Taking her waist once more, he lifted and eased her down onto his cock, letting her take the length of him in, then she sat for a moment before moving tentatively.

"Oh, that feels so good." Wonder sounded in her voice.

"You bet it does."

For the next several minutes, Dylan enjoyed watching Willow's face as she experimented, moving in different ways and at different speeds. Then they both became caught up in the dance of love and moved as one, wringing joy from one another. For the first time in his experience, he climaxed the same time as his partner, and they both shouted out their pleasure.

Willow collapsed atop him, her cheek against his beating heart. He stroked her long, slender, sweat-slicked back. His hand moved up and down the smooth skin, from her back to her buttocks and back up. He loved being inside her. He loved having her this close. Dylan vowed to never let this woman go.

She stacked her hands and placed her chin atop them, gazing adoringly at him. "Dylan, was that good for you?"

He heard doubt tinged in her voice and cradled her face with his hands. "Bear, it was the best I've ever had."

"Me, too," she said solemnly. "I rarely have an orgasm during sex. Being on top was... delicious."

He smiled up at her. "You are the delicious one."

They gazed into one another's eyes, and it was as if he not only saw their history together, but the future they could build with one another.

"I'm sorry in a way that we didn't do this years ago." She hesitated. "But if we had? I don't think I could have ever let you go."

"I agree. It would've kept us from going off, though, and having the experiences we did." His thumb caressed her cheek. "But we're bringing our life experiences to the table now. I hope you want to be in this for the long run, Willow."

She frowned slightly. "I don't know what kind of commitment I can make to you now, Dylan."

He knew doubts lingered within her. "Then let's start with this one week being together."

She nodded. "One week." Then she smiled. "It's going to be a fantastic week, Dylan."

"I think so, too."

Willow said, "I packed a bag just in case you were willing to have me stay. I also brought food for Shadow."

"Let me get dressed, and I'll go down and get it," he told her.

Dylan eased Willow off him and rose from the bed. He dressed quickly under her admiring glances. He couldn't help but think how right she looked in his bed.

"I'll take Shadow out with me."

He left the bedroom and retrieved the dog's leash and her keys, which were sitting next to her purse, and went downstairs. Shadow pulled on the leash, and Dylan crossed the square to the center, where a large gazebo stood, surrounded by plenty of grass and shrubbery. The Lab peed on three different bushes before they returned to Willow's new SUV. It was easy to spot since the square only had a few cars parked on it. The paper license tag was the dead giveaway which vehicle was hers.

He unlocked the car and lifted her suitcase and the bag of food the vet had sent home with the dog. Climbing the stairs to his apartment, he entered and filled one bowl with water and a second with a scoop of Shadow's food. He removed the leash as the dog dug into his late dinner. As he started back toward the bedroom, his eye fell upon the painting Willow had brought with her. Curiosity filled him as to what she had painted, but he would wait until the time was right to see it.

Entering the bedroom, he placed her suitcase next to the bed. By now, she was sitting up, the sheet pulled to her waist, her beautiful breasts still bare. All he wanted was another taste of them.

"You kept my painting," she observed, as he undressed and climbed under the sheet, bringing an arm about her.

"Yes," he said, as he looked across from the bed to the only picture hanging on the wall in the room.

It was a cove close to where Boo's house stood.

They had spent many hours on that beach. Walking. Talking. Kissing endlessly.

"That was a special place," he said softly. "A special time in our lives. I look at it, and the painting takes me back."

"I'd love to go down to the beach again and see this cove. Maybe once all the work is finished at Boo's house we could go together if you like."

"It's a date. You know, I haven't been down there since I left Maple Cove."

"You haven't? Why?"

"Because it reminded me too much of you, Willow."

She threaded her fingers through his. "Yet you hung this painting so you could see it every morning when you awoke."

"Yes, I did that deliberately. I guess I wanted to think of you each morning when I rose and every night before I went to sleep."

"I missed you, Dylan," Willow said quietly. "I went for long periods of time when I deliberately didn't think about you, but you always lingered in my mind. And my heart."

He lifted their joined hands and kissed hers. "Same. Wherever I was in the world, a part of you was with me."

"I have a new painting I brought for you."

She released his hand and slipped from the bed, padding from the room. Dylan enjoyed the view of her backside as she left.

Willow returned moments later. "I painted this after our hike."

She turned the painting so that it faced him, and he saw it was of the clearing they had stopped in, where they had found Shadow. As he studied it, Dylan was amazed by her attention to detail.

His gaze met hers. "This is the best gift I have ever received."

He tossed back the sheet and climbed from the bed, framing her face as he kissed her. Then he broke the kiss.

"No, it's not the best gift I've gotten."

Disappointment flashed across her face.

"*You* coming back to the Cove—back to me—that is the best gift possible."

He kissed her again, a sweet kiss that soon grew needy. He broke it only to take the painting from her hands and prop it against the wall.

"Come back to bed, Willow. I want to make a few more new memories with you."

CHAPTER 19

W illow opened her eyes, blanketed by Dylan's warmth. Last night had gone even better than she had imagined possible. They had made love twice, the first time in a very different position for her. She had never been the one in control during sex and to have that power—and the amazing orgasm that accompanied it—had been nothing short of eye-opening. Then again, she had known making love with her first love would be an incredible experience.

Dylan had not rushed either time, exploring her as if she were something new and wonderful, making her feel desired and cherished at the same time. She felt the ice melting about her encased heart and wondered if she could trust enough to let this man fully back into her life.

He stirred and she felt his lips grazing her shoulder. She stroked his forearm, which held her to him.

"Good morning," he said huskily. "I like waking up to you in my arms."

"It is pretty nice to wake up with you nearby," she admitted. "I didn't even need a blanket last night," she teased. "I had my own personal one draped about me."

He chuckled. "The scent of your floral perfume makes me feel as if I have a garden in my bed."

He turned her so she faced him and he gave her a thorough good-morning kiss. Willow had never wanted to kiss anyone first thing before brushing her teeth, but it didn't seem to stop Dylan and she didn't mind. Soon their heated kisses stirred her into a frenzy, and the sex was quick and scorching hot.

Dylan came and collapsed atop her, burying his lips against her throat. Willow liked making love with this man. Each time it seemed to be a new and different experience. Then worry filled her. Sooner or later, Dylan would tire of her, just like her lovers had.

"What's wrong?" he asked.

This was dangerous. He was so in tune with her body and her feelings. She felt as if she needed to distance herself from him.

"Nothing," she responded brightly. "I suppose you need to get up and get going."

He reached for his phone on the nightstand and checked the time. "I'm good. But I do need to get into the shower."

"I'll make some breakfast while you're showering."

"Are you sure you don't want to join me?" he asked, a wicked grin crossing his face.

She laughed. "I don't think so. I saw your shower last night. It's smaller than the ones in Europe. I have no idea how you fit into it, much less how I could with you in there."

He laughed. "True."

He climbed from the bed and she admired his broad shoulders and muscular back as he padded toward the bathroom. She had touched and kissed a good deal of his body last night. She had always been tentative when touching her partners. She knew now they had rushed her in order to get quick satisfaction for themselves. If anything, Dylan had taught her making love was a process. That foreplay could be lengthy and an important part of coming together.

She slipped into his shirt again, buttoning it and seeing Shadow sitting beside the bed.

"I better rethink this," she told him, removing the shirt and redressing in her own clothes.

She clipped the leash to his collar and took Shadow down the stairs and to the nearby grass. Once he finished, she returned to Dylan's apartment, glad she hadn't seen anyone on the square since it was so early. Although the small town would soon know she was staying with him. Someone would note her getting out of the new SUV and that it stayed on the square overnight. Then the gossip would begin. Willow pushed aside that thought, not wanting it to matter to her. She had agreed to give Dylan this week, and he was what she would focus on instead.

Opening his refrigerator, she saw very little in it, settling on pouring him a bowl of cereal and toasting his last English muffin. If he had coffee, she failed to locate it.

He joined her, freshly-shaved, his hair damp from the shower. She caught the spice of his cologne and desire for him flooded her. Once more, she withdrew inside herself, worried that he was quickly becoming an addiction she could not quit.

Pouring the milk over his cereal, she handed him the bowl. "You are almost out of milk. Plus, there's no butter or jam for your muffin."

He looked sheepish. "I order out a lot from the

diner for dinner. And a lot of times, I'll just grab a donut and coffee at the station."

"I had bought groceries and restocked the pantry. I'll bring the perishables over when I return tonight. What time do you want me back?"

He placed the cereal bowl down and rested his hands at her waist. "Treat this as your place, Willow. You don't have to stay gone all day. I know you want to go home and paint some, but don't feel as if you have to drive around, waiting for me to come home."

Reaching into his pocket, Dylan took a key off his key ring. "Here's the key to the apartment. Come and go as you wish. I'll aim to be home by six, if that works for you. If an emergency comes up, I'll let you know if I might be late."

"Then let me cook dinner for you tonight. I'll feel better if I can provide that for you. I don't want to be a freeloader."

He kissed her. "*Yes* to a home-cooked meal. And no, I'd never think of you that way." He downed the rest of his cereal and rinsed the bowl. "I'll take the muffin with me." Then his voice changed, growing deep and formal. "Have a good day, dear. I'm off to the office."

She burst out laughing. "You sound like a sitcom dad."

He grinned shamelessly. "I am a man of many hidden talents." He snagged her around the waist and pulled her to him. "I'll even show you a few of those in bed later."

Kissing her once more, he released her. "Duty calls."

After he left, she decided to take Shadow for another run, unpacking and changing into jogging clothes. She kept the exercise to half an hour again, wanting to slowly increase her time and speed as Shadow adjusted to her. She didn't want to overtax the pup.

By the time she returned to Dylan's place, the square was coming to life, with more cars parked on the square and multiple people entering the diner. She nodded at a few people as she went around the corner of the building and up the outside staircase.

Willow fed Shadow and then showered and dressed for the day. Dylan had already made the bed with military precision. She washed and dried his cereal bowl and spoon and then took Shadow to her car, driving back to Boo's. She supposed she would always think of this house as her grandmother's.

On the way, her thoughts turned to Dylan and their night of intimacy. He had treated her with respect, making her an equal partner in their lovemaking. She had never participated as much in the act with any other lover, nor had she felt the deep connection with them as she had Dylan.

Could he be right? Could their paths have led them back to Maple Cove so that they would find one another once again?

Time would tell. And she was ready to soak up every minute of the week she would spend with him.

She arrived home and saw several pickup trucks in the drive. Three men were painting her house, and she recognized one of them.

Getting out of her SUV, she shouted, "Carter!" and waved.

He finished spraying a panel of wood and turned, grinning as he saw her. "Hey, Willow! Let me come to a stopping point."

He turned back to the side he painted, and she claimed Shadow from the car, snapping on his leash.

She let the Lab investigate a few new shrubs which had been planted. He sniffed and then left his calling card on two of them.

By now, Carter strode toward her. "I'd hug you, but I don't want to get any paint on you. This must be Shadow. Hi, boy. How are you? Is Shadow a good boy?"

The dog's tail began wagging frantically and Carter stepped closer, kneeling. He slipped off one of the gloves he wore and allowed the dog to smell him.

"That lick is the Shadow seal of approval," Willow told Carter, as the pup's tongue coated his fingers.

He petted the dog. "I heard you're living the good life now. That you've hooked up with a pretty artist who plans to spoil you rotten." He patted the dog's head and stood. "How are you holding up? We didn't get to talk much the other day. A lot of people turned out for Boo."

"I was pleased. Boo touched many lives in Maple Cove." She pointed to the other men painting the house. "Fellow firefighters?"

"Yes. We're all from Salty Point. I'll introduce you when we finish up the job. Pete's inside, knocking down your kitchen wall. I think it'll look good, opening up the space."

"I think so, too." She paused. "Carter, I'm sorry to hear about Emily. I didn't know she had passed away. I feel terrible that I didn't—"

"It's okay," he said brusquely. "It's been five years." He paused. "Five long years. I fell in love with Emily in kindergarten. I think we pretended to get married that first day of school. I was blessed to have her in my life as long as I did."

Willow knew not to mention the baby, but her

heart grew heavy. Carter would have made a wonderful father.

"She was special."

"She was—but I know it's time to move on. Em wouldn't want me to stay in a holding pattern the rest of my life. She would be the first to tell me to go out and live again." He shrugged. "Trouble is, Maple Cove is a small town. The single women here are few and far between. And the ones I do know and hang with— the Robinsons—they're like sisters to me. Not a romantic spark to be tended."

"What about Salty Point?" she asked.

"It's pretty much the same. A small dating pool."

"What about Portland? I know it's an hour away. But I've heard there are all kinds of dating apps now. Would you consider trying one of them?"

Carter laughed, shaking his head. "Not a chance, Willow. Now, if you knew someone and could set me up with her, I would trust your judgment."

For some reason, Tenley came to mind. Even though her friend was married to that asshole Theodore, Willow thought Tenley and Carter would be a good match.

"I have one good friend who's still single," she told him, thinking of Sloane. "The trouble is, she's an international journalist and rarely comes back to the US. When she does, her home base is New York."

He chuckled. "Oh, what's three thousand miles? Next time she's coming home, I'll just fly out and take her to dinner," he teased. "Listen, I should get back to work. I know Pete said you'd be working in Boo's studio during the day. I mean, your studio."

"I know. It's hard to think of Boo being gone. I may never get used to the idea."

"I get where you're coming from." A shadow crossed his face.

Willow took his hand and squeezed it. "You'll find someone again, Carter. She won't be Emily—but it will be a good thing. Just be open to whoever comes your way."

"Later."

He rubbed Shadow's head and loped away. She watched him, hurt tugging at her heart. Carter was one of the best men she knew. She did hope he could find someone to love.

"Let's go," she told Shadow.

They entered through the front door. She was reluctant to go through the kitchen because she didn't know how much dust was there and didn't want Shadow's coat to encounter it.

"Hello? It's Willow, Pete."

The contractor stepped into view. "Hi. Want to see a big lot of nothing?"

She followed him, surprised that the entire wall was gone, rubble and chunks of the wall lying everywhere. Her eyes roamed the space as she removed Shadow's leash.

"It looks twice as big now."

"It will flow well," Pete said. "I was thinking we could even put in an island here." He indicated a spot. "A large one, so that you could put stools on this side and use it to eat a quick meal. If you were entertaining, guests could sit and watch as you prepped and cooked.

"I like that idea. Walk me through it."

He described the layoff and stepped off the size of the island, both length and width.

"We could use the same quartz for the island that we're using for the countertops," he said.

"It makes perfect sense. Any idea of how much it might run?"

He gave her an estimate.

"Let's do it," she told him. I'm surprised I didn't think of that before. Then again, I'm coming off ten years of living in Europe. My Paris flat was just over 500 square feet. Kitchens are miniscule there. Everything can be pretty tiny."

"It must be hard adjusting to living here again."

"No, actually it's been nice to have that elbow room again. A larger shower. The nice, walk-in closet space. And I did grow up here. My parents died in an accident when I was three and Jackson six. Boo raised us. I barely remember them and have no recollection of our house, but I have extremely fond memories of living in this house and Maple Cove until I left for college."

"The town is a good one," Pete agreed. "I came here after a messy divorce. I was an accountant, if you can believe that, and wanted a new start. My dad had been a contractor, so I grew up working with him. Knew all about plumbing and electricity. Got licensed and came to the Cove."

"Did you have family here? I don't recall any Pulaskis during my time here."

"No, but my sister married a guy from here. They met in college. She knew how the divorce wiped me out financially and emotionally. She pushed me to make a new start—and here I am. I've been here seven years now, and my business has grown. I see my niece and nephew every weekend. I still have time to hike and fish, which I never did before. I'm pretty content."

She smiled. "The Cove is a nice place to live. Listen, I'll get out of your way and head up to the studio.

Shadow will stay with me, so don't worry about him being in your way."

Willow patted her thigh and the dog followed her up the stairs. She left the door to the studio open in case the smell of paint became too intense. Pulling out the sketches she'd made yesterday, she flipped through them, thinking of what she would be painting and how she wanted the final layout to occur.

She set an alarm on her phone, knowing how she often lost track of time when she worked. She left a time cushion in order to pack up some food from the kitchen and get back into town, where she would cook dinner for Dylan.

Work absorbed her for the next several hours. She blocked out everything else, focusing on her canvas. She did a light pencil sketch on the canvas itself, and then pick up her brush.

The alarm sounded, surprising her. It was easy to get lost in a painting once she began it. Willow cleaned her brushes and sealed the oil paints she had used.

Shadow came to his feet when she finished. She thought the dog smart and decided to leave off his leash, seeing if he would respond to her voice commands.

"Come," she told him, and he fell into step beside her.

Pete had cleaned up the demo remnants and was nowhere in sight. Willow took out a few canvas bags from a drawer and placed all the fruits and vegetables she had bought inside them, along with a carton of milk, some cheese, and a loaf of bread. She took a package of chicken from the refrigerator, intending it to be the star of tonight's dinner.

Then she took Shadow outside, telling him to go

pee. He ambled over to a bush and did so, returning to her side. She moved toward the car, the dog following.

"You leaving?" Carter called.

She turned and saw him on the upstairs balcony and moved back toward the house.

"Yes, I'm heading back into town. We need to get together soon."

"I'm having a few friends over Friday night. Pizza. Beer. A little game night fun."

"That sounds like fun. Will Rylie and Ainsley be there?"

"Yes. And I'll assume you'll bring Dylan."

"I can do that. He's letting me stay at his place while all the work is being done here."

"He is?" Carter grinned. "He didn't mention that when we watched Monday Night Football."

"He didn't know. I just asked him last night."

"Ah, so you made the first move. That's good."

"Oh, so I have the Carter Clark seal of approval?"

"Absolutely."

"Can we bring anything Saturday?" she asked.

"A couple of six-packs would be nice. Maybe a bottle of wine. The Robinson girls prefer that to beer."

Willow gave him a thumbs up. "Sounds like a plan. See you."

"Bye, Willow."

She walked back to the SUV and opened the door. Shadow leaped in and curled up. She was glad the dog was comfortable in the car. He traveled well, with no whining. Placing the canvas bags on the floorboard, she closed the rear door.

Getting behind the wheel, she turned the vehicle around and soon was headed back to Maple Cove proper when her phone rang. She rarely received calls, usually just texts.

The number was unfamiliar, but she chose to answer it.

"Hello?"

"Willow, it's Clancy. Do you have some free time tomorrow? I've drawn up some papers regarding the scholarship in Boo's name and wanted to run things by you."

"When would you like to meet? I'm open."

"Let's say ten o'clock."

"Ten will be fine. I'll see you then, Clancy."

She was eager to meet with the attorney and get the ball rolling regarding the scholarship. It was already December, and many students started hearing from colleges in February if they did not apply for early decision. She wanted the scholarship recipient to know exactly how much money was coming his or her way, because it could factor into the decision made regarding where to attend school.

The square was crowded when she arrived. No open spots were close to the diner, so Willow parked on a side street. She gathered her groceries and put Shadow back on his leash, not wanting to chance him running away in town. She would work more on his training once they returned home this weekend.

A part of her wished that Dylan could come with them.

"Too soon," she said aloud, leading the pup up the stairs and using the key Dylan had provided to let herself into the apartment.

She put away the groceries and washed her hands. She had decided to make chicken spaghetti, something Boo had taught her to make when Willow was twelve. It had become a Martin family favorite, and she had even made it for Dylan for Valentine's Day their senior year in high school. She wondered if he would recall that.

Going to her purse, she removed her cell and put on some music. She had always loved a movie Boo had introduced her to, *The Big Chill*, mainly because of the Motown music played in it. The kitchen scene was her favorite, where a group of friends cooked a meal together, laughing and dancing their way to completion. She called up the movie's soundtrack and began playing it as she put water on to boil and diced the chicken into bite-sized pieces.

Suddenly, someone grabbed her hand and lifted it over her head, twirling her around, Then Dylan pulled her close, dancing with her.

"So, you still like to listen to Motown?" he asked.

"I didn't hear you come in. You're early."

He smiled, causing her stomach to flutter. "No, Bear. I think I'm right on time."

CHAPTER 20

Willow entered Sid's Diner Friday afternoon. Only two tables were occupied, the lunch rush long past.

Nancy Mayfield greeted her with a hug. "Hello, Willow. It's so good to see you back in the Cove." She paused, grinning. "I hear you're keeping company with Dylan."

"I am," she said, not wanting to hide anything. Not that anyone could in a town the size of Maple Cove. "I've actually been staying with him this week while Pete Pulaski does some renovations on Boo's house."

"Are you selling—or staying?" the diner's owner asked, frank as always.

"I'm leaning toward staying, but I want the house in good shape regardless of what I decide." She paused. "Thanks again for agreeing to be on the scholarship committee and letting us meet at the diner. You being a former teacher had a lot to do with my asking you to help select the recipient."

"Go ahead and sit at that table in the back against the wall," Nancy told her. "I'll bring out coffee and iced tea. Pie, too."

"That would be terrific. Thank you, Nancy."

Willow moved to the table, removing from her purse the tablet that had her notes for the meeting. She set copies of the agenda she'd worked up at each place. By then, Dorothy Clark joined her.

"Hello, Mrs. Clark," she greeted, hugging Carter's mom. "Thanks for agreeing to serve on the committee."

"First, I'm happy to do so, simply because it's in honor of Boo. Plus, it's always fun to see how my former students have grown and matured. I can't wait to see the submissions we'll receive."

"Same here," Walt Willingham said, as he took a seat. "Dorothy. Willow."

"Thank you for coming, Sheriff Willingham."

"Nope. Not Sheriff Willingham. Just plain Walt, thank you very much. Your boyfriend gets to be called sheriff. Not me."

She felt her cheeks warm. "So, you heard Dylan and I are seeing each other?"

He chuckled. "I think everyone in the Cove knows that, after you telling Missy Newton off at the Hungry Bear the other night. Besides, at least half the Cove knows you're living in sin with our good sheriff."

Her face flamed now. "No, we aren't living together. I'm merely staying with Dylan while Pete Pulaski's doing some work at the house. I have a dog now and didn't think any of the local B&B's would allow Shadow to accompany me. He's a rescue and a little needy right now."

"I could say the same for Dylan," Walt noted. "Our boy could use some time, attention, and love."

"Walt, stop that," Mrs. Clark chided. "You're embarrassing Willow." She patted Willow's hand. "You're a grown woman and can see whomever you like, whenever you like. Actually, from what I hear, everyone in the Cove is rooting for you and Dylan."

"Thank you," she said, busying herself with her notes.

Nancy joined them, bringing a tray with four pieces of pie, an urn of coffee, and a pitcher of iced tea. She placed everything on the table.

"Serve yourself with whatever you'd like to drink. There are two peach and two apple slices of pie."

They took a minute to fill mugs and glasses, with Walt giving the women first choice at the pie. Mrs. Clark passed on a slice, so Walt took one of each.

"I always did like my sweets," he said, rubbing his belly.

He looked too thin and tired to Willow, but she didn't say anything. She didn't know if others knew Walt was terminally ill.

"Let's get started," she said.

Willow discussed the purpose of the scholarship, which would cover eight semesters. Hopefully, the winner could graduate in that amount of time or be well on their way to a degree. They talked about the application itself, Willow typing away as they made suggestions. She talked about each applicant having to submit a piece of art and the various types the committee might encounter when it came time to judge entries.

"Not everyone will enter with something conventional, such as a landscape painting. I'm expecting a variety of pieces, including mixed media. I suggest that we have applicants submit online pictures first with their application, then the finalists could provide the physical artwork for the final round of judging."

They discussed how long to give students to enter and what criteria to use. Some wanted financial need to be weighed equally with talent, while others thought the art should speak for itself. They came to a conclusion, and Willow put the finishing touches on the application.

"I'll e-mail a copy of this to you. Now that we have our timeline and a rubric on how to evaluate the entries, I'll contact the principal and the counselor at Maple Cove, and hopefully meet with them and discuss the best way to advertise and distribute applications."

She pulled up a calendar on her phone, and everyone did the same, noting dates so they would know when to be available to judge the entries.

"How and when should we announce the scholarship winner?" she asked.

"That might be something the principal could help you decide," Nancy suggested. "I know several scholarships awarded are announced at the end-of-year senior assembly, but you seem to want the winner to know well before that."

"I do," Willow said. "Having these funds might make a huge difference in the winner's plans for school. Next year, I want to start this process even earlier."

"Do you want us to serve again next year?" Mrs. Clark asked. "I don't mind."

"Let's see how the process goes, and we can talk about that after we've been through it one time. It might be good to involve others in the community, but I think it's important to always have an educator on the selection committee. I didn't want to ask anyone from the high school, though. I hoped to keep our judging impartial by eliminating any of the high school's faculty."

"Yes, the art teacher might have a favorite," Walt

agreed. "Or the principal. But I do think it's better to draw your judges from the Cove. More investment that way."

They finished up, with Willow promising to e-mail them not only the application they had settled upon, but her notes from when she met with the high school staff.

"I'll put my e-mail down as the one for them to submit to. Or I might create a new one that includes something about the scholarship or have Boo's name somewhere. Either way, I'll forward whatever we get, and you can look at things at your leisure. Then we can meet to decide the finalists—or possibly a winner if it's clear-cut. Regardless, this shouldn't take a huge chunk of your time."

"That's not a problem, Willow," Nancy said. "We're all happy to be a part of this for Boo."

"Thank you for coming," she told them. "And for the pie."

"Especially the pie," Walt seconded. "If anyone else needs me to serve on some committee and there's pie involved, just let me know." He rose and ambled off.

"Back to work for me," Nancy said, piling the empty plates on her tray.

"Thank you for leaving school early to meet with us, Mrs. Clark," Willow said.

The older woman smiled. "It's Friday. I didn't mind a bit." She consulted her watch. "In fact, I have time to head over now to the Bearded Barrel Brewery for happy hour," she revealed. "It's a Friday tradition for my teachers. We tend to get a little loud, but it's a nice way to blow off steam after a long week of teaching."

The principal rose. "Have fun at Game Night, dear."

Willow shook her head as Mrs. Clark left. Yes, everyone knew everyone's business in Maple Cove.

She left Sid's Diner and went outside, turning the corner and heading upstairs to Dylan's apartment. Shadow greeted her enthusiastically.

"Hello, boy," she said, ruffling his fur.

She went to the treat jar that Dylan had brought home and gave the dog one of the treats. He knew to sit, then shake, before she awarded it to him.

For the next hour, she worked on tweaking the format of the application and rubric, before e-mailing copies to her committee. She thought Walt wouldn't be here this time next year to participate. It might do to have one permanent member of the selection committee, such as Mrs. Clark, with two others who rolled off. Or have one member from the previous year help judge the next year, always switching that person out. She would talk it over with Dylan and get his opinion.

Going to the high school's website, she found the e-mail for the principal and sent him a request to meet with him regarding a scholarship to be funded by Boo Martin's estate, asking that the meeting take place sometime next week. The sooner she could publicize the scholarship and get the requirements into the hands of students, the better.

She heard the lock turn in the door, surprised to see Dylan enter.

"You're certainly home early."

Willow realized she used the word *home* and wondered if he had caught it as she placed her tablet on the coffee table. She had meant to check with Pete today about when she could move back to Boo's, but she hadn't even gone to paint today, having too much to do to get ready for this afternoon's meeting.

He took off his holster and locked the gun inside a

small safe and then came and sat next to her on the lumpy sofa, placing his arms along its back. "It was a quiet day. Thought I could sneak out early and spend a little time with you before we hit Game Night."

"You did?" Willow reached and unbuttoned the top three buttons on his uniform's shirt and slid a hand inside. "Are you thinking a little afternoon delight?"

He grinned, one hand cradling her cheek. "Actually, I was thinking a *lot* of afternoon delight."

Dylan kissed her thoroughly, causing ripples of desire to sweep through her.

Willow broke the kiss and stood, holding out her hand to him. He took it and rose, following her into the bedroom.

Afternoon turned into evening by the time they were done.

He kissed her temple. "We better hop into the shower, or we'll be late. I don't think you want to hear the ribbing we'll get if we are."

She stroked his chest. "You think they might know what we were up to?"

He chuckled. "Oh, they'd know. And never let us live it down." He kissed her. "You go first. But don't use all the hot water," he warned. "Else I'll have to go in and drag you out—and we'll have to do this all over again."

"Don't tempt me," she purred, feeling sexy and confident as she rose from the bed and headed to the bathroom.

They were both ready within thirty minutes and made it to Carter's house with three minutes to spare.

"Early," their host said as he opened the door. "I'm surprised. I heard the sheriff left the office before his usual time today."

Dylan shoved the two six-packs they'd brought at his friend. "Is nothing a secret in this town?"

"No," Ainsley answered, coming up the sidewalk, Rylie accompanying her. They held several pizza boxes in their hands.

Willow took a whiff. "That smells yummy. Where is it from? When I lived here, we usually got pizza at Eats 'n Treats Café. I know it's still on the square."

"This is from Crust 'n Stuff," Rylie told her. "Best pizza ever. An Italian family from New York runs it. The crust is divine."

They all stepped inside and she saw another guy already present. He smiled.

"Hi, I'm Gage. Gage Nelson. Got to the Cove this summer."

She took his offered hand. "Willow Martin. I came to Maple Cove when I was three and left after college, but I'm happy to be back." She looked to Carter. "Where do you want the wine?"

"I've got a corkscrew in the kitchen," he said.

"I'm so glad you brought wine," Rylie said. "I'm not that fond of beer."

"Same with me," she said. "I began drinking wine when I moved to Europe. I think I could live on water and wine to drink and nothing else."

"Two glasses of water to every one of wine," Gage said, and shrugged. "I'm a personal trainer. I can't help it."

"Oh, will you be eating vegetarian pizza?" Willow teased.

"Nah," Gage said. "Game Night is my cheat night. Pizza. Beer. Popcorn. Everyone needs a little food cheating. I think that's actually healthy for you."

"I made cookies," Carter volunteered, handing Willow the corkscrew.

"Cookies?" she asked.

"Yeah. Emily sucked at cooking. I learned how at the firehouse. Meatloaf and chocolate chip cookies are my specialties, but I can really cook just about anything."

"Willow made me chicken spaghetti this week," Dylan volunteered. "Same meal she made me on Valentine's Day senior year." He lightly touched her waist and kissed her cheek as she uncorked the pinot noir she'd brought.

"And he ate so much, we had no leftovers," she said, causing everyone to laugh.

They got drinks and took them to the big dining table. Carter opened the pizza boxes and everyone helped themselves to slices.

After she finished her first slice of pepperoni, Willow said, "You weren't kidding. This is terrific pizza. The crust *is* the best part. I could eat this once a week."

The conversation was lively as they ate. Willow told them about her meeting with the scholarship committee and the improvements being made to Boo's house. Ainsley talked about a new recipe she was testing, only revealing it contained chocolate. Rylie was heading out tomorrow for a Portland flea market, and Gage offered to accompany her. He was very quiet and a bit serious, and Willow thought his demeanor might have something to do with his military background. She knew he had been a Navy SEAL and wondered what he had seen. She wanted to ask him why he'd come to the Cove but didn't want him to feel as if she were prying.

Dylan mentioned a couple of cases from this past week, not naming any names, while Carter talked about a house fire in Salty Point, saying they'd barely gotten out a mother and her three-month-old baby. All in all, it was a relaxing, fun bit of socializing. She enjoyed getting to know the girls better and could see this group becoming very important to her.

"Let's put the leftover pizza in Ziploc bags," Carter suggested. "Leftovers usually go home with whoever brought them," he explained to her. "I'll grab the cookies and go set up."

"What's tonight's game?" Gage asked. "I hope not Trivial Pursuit. I suck at it. I only know the geography questions."

"The host picks the games," Dylan told Willow. "Carter always has some unusual picks."

The group took their plates and the pizza boxes into the kitchen and got refills on their drinks before heading to the den. Carter followed with a plate stacked high with huge chocolate chip cookies. Willow immediately snagged one and bit into it.

"Mmm. This is incredible. Why am I dating Dylan when I could be seeing Carter and his cookies?" she declared.

Everyone laughed as Carter retrieved a box and held it up. "Two games tonight. This is The Game of Things. It's a little bit of an icebreaker, especially when you don't know everyone well. You pick a card."

He chose one from the deck and read, "'Things... you shouldn't do in an elevator.' Then everyone writes down the first thing that comes to mind, and we collect the answers and try to guess who said what—and why."

"That's clever," Dylan said. "And possibly a little dirty." He grinned. "I think I like this game."

Carter passed out pens and small pads of paper so everyone could record their answer, tear off the sheet, fold it, and drop it into the pot.

After an hour, Willow stomach hurt from laughing so much. The game had gone from silly to risqué— and they were having a blast.

"Let's switch up," Carter suggested. "Pictionary. Guys versus girls."

"Oh, we are so winning," Rylie declared. She looked to Willow and Ainsley. "We need a team name."

They talked it over briefly as the guys huddled and did the same.

"Okay, we're ready," Ainsley said. "Meet the Women Warriors."

Dylan laughed. "We're the Macho Men."

Carter set up an easel with a large sketchpad and said, "I think you Warriors should spot us a few points to start."

"Why?" Willow asked.

"Because you, my dear, are an artist. Your team has an advantage in that they'll actually be able to figure out what you've drawn."

"Nope. Not a chance," Rylie said. "Willow is our secret weapon and we are going to mop the floor with you Macho Men."

It wasn't a whipping. It was an outright slaughter.

She laughed harder than she ever had, watching Dylan try to draw clues for his team. Carter and Gage were even worse. In the end, the Macho Men surrendered.

"I'm on Willow's team next time," Carter said. "She's smart and she can draw."

"I think we should stick to men versus women," Ainsley said. "I like women sticking together."

"If Carter bakes the cookies again, he should get to pick the teams," Dylan ruled. "These are damn fine cookies, my friend."

"Said as he eats the last one," Gage noted, making the others laugh.

They cleaned up and said their goodnights to one another by nine, respectful of Ainsley's need to get to bed, since she had told Willow that Saturday morning was her biggest day of the week. Willow got into Dylan's SUV. They were quiet on the way back. When they got to his apartment, he took Shadow outside while she slipped out of her clothes and into her robe, leaving her pajamas in the drawer.

Tonight was most likely her last night to stay here. She had enjoyed her week with Dylan. Cooking meals together. Making love. Watching the news. Even Game Night with his friends.

Could this be the life she wanted? She believed it was hers for the asking.

Yet fear paralyzed her as Dylan returned with Shadow.

He made love to her, slowly, tenderly, touching her everywhere, making her feel content and attractive. Afterward, Willow lay in his arms and sensed when he fell asleep, his breathing becoming slower and more even.

Was Dylan waiting for her to speak what was in her heart? And what exactly was that? Did she want to spend the rest of her life in Maple Cove?

Willow told herself she didn't have to come to a decision tonight.

But her heart knew that she already had.

CHAPTER 21

Willow awoke and lay still for a few minutes, knowing her mind was too restless to go back to sleep. She eased from the bed, thinking if she went for a run, it would clear her head. Shadow had taken to sleeping at the foot of the bed each night, and she saw him lift his head for a moment and then put it back down. She decided to leave the pup and run alone this morning.

Tiptoeing to a drawer, she lifted out running clothes, hearing Dylan's even breathing as she slipped from the room. She closed the door behind her and dressed in the dark outside the bedroom. She hydrated, downing two glasses of water, and then slipped her phone into her pocket, locking the door behind her.

It was a little after four. The square was deserted. She stretched for a few minutes and then set out at a brisk pace, pounding the pavement without thought to begin with, adjusting her breathing as she ran. She passed through the familiar streets, glad to have come home.

Home...

She might have been a citizen of the world for the last decade, but Maple Cove was in her blood and would always be home to her. Mostly because Dylan was here. Willow was fortunate enough to have an occupation in which she could work anywhere, where Dylan had made a commitment to this community and would serve as its sheriff for the next few years, until another general election occurred. Knowing how well thought of he was and how his history was tied to the Cove, she assumed voters would continue to re-elect him as often as he stood for office. If she wanted to be with Dylan, it meant putting down permanent roots in the Cove.

And Willow was fine with it. More than fine.

Having come to that decision, her entire body relaxed. She increased her speed dramatically. For the next hour, Willow kept to a brutal pace, pushing her body to its limits. She returned to the square on Orchid Lane, passing Pete Pulaski's house, but knowing it was still far too early to stop and touch base with the contractor.

She reached the square itself and jogged toward the gazebo, moving up its steps and stretching before sitting on a bench to cool down. The clock on the square said it was five-twenty. She thought she would give Jackson a call.

He answered on the second ring, and she could hear his footsteps as he jogged.

"Am I catching you at a bad time?" she asked. "It sounds like you're out running."

"I only left two minutes ago. I can jog a bit and talk before I begin my run. What's up? How is the work coming at Boo's?"

"They've been working all week. I'm going to

check in with Pete today to see what's done and what still needs to be finished. Most likely, I'll move back in this weekend." She hesitated. "I've been staying with Dylan."

"How is that going?"

"I love him, Jackson," she told her brother.

"Then go for it, Willow. Life is far too short not to seize that brass ring when it's there before you."

"My head tells me it's too soon, but my heart agrees with you. Dylan is the best man I will ever know."

"Have you told him that you love him?"

"Not yet—but I plan to do so today."

"I'll assume that means you'll be staying in the Cove."

"Yes. With Dylan being sheriff here, it ties us to the community."

"Then you should ask him to move in with you at Boo's. I know we share the house legally, but it doesn't matter to me."

"What if you take Clancy's offer and come back to the Cove?"

"We can cross that bridge at a later date. Right now, I'm focused on my murder trial."

"That's actually the reason I was calling you. How did this first week go?"

There was a long pause. "I would say it went extremely well," he finally said. "The DA's opening was strong. The jury responded to it. But my opening argument was the best I've ever presented."

"That's wonderful, Jackson. I wish I could have heard it. You know, I've never seen you in court. Maybe I should come down to L.A. when you put on your portion of the case so I could see you in action."

"Don't."

"You don't want me there?"

"That's exactly right. I don't want you tainted by this case. It's already made me feel as if I'm covered in slime. I'm affected in ways I don't want to talk about."

"Then I hope you'll give Clancy's offer serious consideration."

"I'm doing just that, Willow. Right now, I'm leaning toward a move to Maple Cove. Don't say anything to anyone yet, not even Dylan. And especially not Clancy. I need to get through this trial first, and then it will take some time to make arrangements to dissolve my partnership with Bill. But as of this moment, plan on me coming back to the Cove."

"That's the best news you could have given me, Big Brother. When you do, I expect you to stay at Boo's. Once you get here, we can figure out some kind of arrangement. Maybe I could buy you out of the house or what's left in Boo's accounts could go to you."

"We can think on it later. No rush. My focus now has to be on the McGreer case."

They ended the call, and Willow felt relief pour through her. She had worried about how this trial was messing with her brother's mind and confidence. It would be wonderful to have her brother back in Maple Cove.

She stood, ready to return to Dylan's apartment when her cell rang. It was Sloane calling and Willow sat again, eager to speak with her friend.

"Hey, Sloane. It's so good to hear from you."

"I didn't think that you would mind me calling so early, Willow. I know it has to be five or six your time."

"I don't care if it were the middle of the night, Sloane. I'm always happy to talk to you. I just finished a run and was taking a break. What's up with you?"

"I wanted to see how you were after Boo's memorial. I know Tenley wasn't able to get away to be there with you."

"Jackson was here. Also Gillian, our next-door neighbor. You know she's like family. But there's actually been an interesting development."

"You're back with Dylan again," Sloane guessed.

"How did you know?"

"Because the few times you mentioned him back in college, I heard something in your voice. Saw something in your eyes. I knew how special he was to you. You returning to Maple Cove would put you in his orbit again."

"You're right about that," Willow agreed.

Briefly, she ran through what had happened between Dylan and her since she had returned to the Cove.

"I've come to a decision, Sloane. I want to be with him."

"Like in forever be with him? Committed to him?"

"That's exactly what I mean. I'm going to tell him today. You know I've had some lousy relationships. Been hurt several times. But I do believe—as Dylan does—that fate brought us both back to the Cove and that we belong together."

"I'm so glad to hear that, Willow," her friend said. "You deserve some personal happiness to go with your professional success."

"So, tell me what's going on in your world?"

Sloane laughed. "Well, I'm leaving the Middle East. I'll be boarding a flight to Nairobi in the next few minutes."

"You're going to Africa? Why?"

"As my editor says, 'The Middle East is a dangerous place for Americans—and a lethal one if you're American *and* a woman.'"

"Did something happen to you, Sloane?" she asked quickly.

"I'll admit there have been a few incidents which have scared me. I won't go into any details because I don't want to think about them right now, but I'm frightened for myself, Willow. I need to get out."

"Why are you headed to Africa and not home?"

Sloane talked for a few minutes about her up-coming assignment, which Willow thought was plenty dangerous. She voiced that opinion.

"You know I can take care of myself," her friend said. "I've taken several self-defense courses over the years. I've earned my black belt. Even better, I've had one-on-one instruction with a former Israeli army guy, who's tutored me in Krav Maga, something the Israelis developed."

"Still, it sounds as if you're jumping from the frying pan into a flaming fire, Sloane. I worry about you."

"I'll know when the time is right to get out," her friend promised. "I'll admit I'm an adrenaline junkie, as well as a news junkie. Combining those together in hot spots around the world has been an incredible high. I do have a few feelers out with my agent, though, regarding a network job that would keep me stateside for the most part."

"I like hearing that," Willow said.

"Okay, they just called for me to board. I need to get going. I thought I would have time to also call Ten-ley, but we talked longer than I expected. Would you give her a shout today and tell her I'll be in touch soon?"

"I will," she promised, knowing she didn't have

time to go into the problems Tenley was experiencing. Besides, that would be Tenley's to share with Sloane.

She stood and stretched her muscles a little, seeing a couple of people walk into the diner. She decided to walk over to Buttercup Bakery even though she didn't have her wallet on her, intending to get breakfast for her and Dylan. Only one person was in line ahead of her, and Willow waved to Ainsley.

Her friend came out to the counter. "My, you're up early for a Saturday morning. It looks as if you've been for a run."

She laughed. "I suppose I do look pretty sweaty. I thought I would stop in and get something for Dylan and me to eat, but my wallet is upstairs."

"I know you're good for it," Ainsley said. "Game Night was fun. Dylan has never looked happier or more relaxed to me. You two just look like you belong together."

"I think so, too. Can I have two coffees? And whatever you think is tasty this morning."

Willow left the bakery with the coffees, two Cheese Danishes, and two sausage rolls, as well as a promise to call Ainsley for lunch one day this upcoming week.

She went up the stairs and let herself into Dylan's apartment, going to the kitchenette. She plated the Danish and sausage rolls as her phone chirped. Checking it, she saw it was a text from Pete.

Work almost complete. Should be done today by mid-afternoon. Come by if you can to check out things before the crew leaves in case you spot something which needs to get done.

Willow texted back, telling Pete she would stop by around noon in order to walk through the house and look at what had been completed. He sent her a thumbs-up.

"You're up early."

She turned, seeing Dylan standing in the bedroom's doorway. He came toward her, wrapping his arms around her and nuzzling her neck.

"I'm too sweaty for this," she protested.

"Or you're not sweaty enough," he countered. "I can think of a fun way to work up a sweat." He sniffed. "Unless those are sausage rolls in that bag."

"They are," she confirmed. "Ainsley sent that and some Cheese Danish."

He gave her a quick kiss. "Food wins out—for now."

Dylan carried their coffees as Willow picked up the plates and set them on the coffee table.

"I'm going to get a towel to sit on," she said.

He snagged her around the waist and pulled her into his lap. "This couch is ancient. Nancy couldn't remember how old it really was. I don't think you could hurt it." He grinned. "Just in case, you can sit on me, Miss Martin. Now, where did you run?"

They ate and sipped their coffee as she told him about her run and conversations with both Jackson and Sloane.

"I hope Jackson's trial ends soon," Dylan said.

"I had hoped he could come to the Cove for Christmas. If the trial is still going on, though, I doubt that will happen. With Christmas on a Monday, the judge would probably have things pick up on Tuesday."

"Do you think he'll take over Clancy's law practice?"

Holding to her promise not to say anything, Willow merely said, "I really hope he will."

"I'd like to meet Sloane. And Tenley," Dylan continued. I know how close you are to both of them. It sounds as if Sloane may be approaching burnout. I saw that in the military."

"She's covered war zones. Famines. Hurricanes. Sloane is terrific at what she does, but I hope her agent can out work something that will allow her to come home and stay. The situation she's going into in Africa has me worried for her. I'm also worried about Tenley."

Willow shared what Tenley had told her in their last phone call.

"I never liked Theodore," she admitted. "I couldn't understand what Tenley saw in him. I haven't spent much time around them since she met him after college, but the few times I've been in his company, he just didn't seem to be her match." She paused. "You know who I think would be? Carter."

"*Our* Carter?"

"Yes. We talked at the house the other day. He's ready to start dating again. He said Emily wouldn't want him to give up on living. He indicated, though, that the pickings were slim around here, as far as the dating pool went. I suggested a dating app and trying Portland."

Dylan laughed. "Carter swiping left or right is the last thing I can see happening."

"Do you think Ainsley or Rylie might ever interest him? He said he looked upon them as sisters, but sometimes things can shift between people."

He set down his coffee and hers. "And sometimes things don't change—unless you count them getting better."

His kiss lingered. She tasted the coffee and the

man and knew it was the right thing to tell him how she felt.

Then he stood, carrying her into the bedroom, and all thought of talk fled as Willow immersed herself in this incredible man.

CHAPTER 22

Dylan dressed after showering, listening as Willow sang in the shower. Slightly off-key. He grinned, thinking he would gladly wake up every day to this if she would agree to it.

Was it too soon to bring up living together?

He wasn't sure. Willow's mercurial moods had sometimes baffled him when they were teenagers. Now they were adults, he thought he read her pretty well, despite all the time they had spent away from one another. He wanted to be with her whenever he could. Living together would make that a whole lot easier.

More than anything, he wanted to tell her he loved her. Again, fear of her being spooked had kept him from doing so. He knew what she would say. That it was too soon to make that kind of statement. That she needed more time. That they still didn't know who they were together.

He did, though. He knew he was the best version of himself when he was with Willow. She was his person. The only one he wanted to come home to each night.

Then why the hell was he tiptoeing around on eggshells?

He would tell her today. If she wasn't ready to hear it, then too bad. It was time she put on her big girl panties and listened to what he had to say.

Dylan only hoped it wouldn't send Willow running.

He checked in at the station. Oswald Jones told him things were quiet and that Dylan should enjoy his weekend with Willow and Shadow. He hung up, shaking his head. Not only did everyone in Maple Cove know about him seeing Willow, they also knew the name of her dog. He used to get irritated when he was growing up at how everyone seemed to know his business. Now, however, Dylan realized the Cove was like a village, taking care of its own, watching out for everyone.

He called down to the diner and placed an order with Nancy.

"Picnic food," he told her. "Maybe fried chicken. Something easy to eat. Willow and I are going to the beach."

"Give me ten minutes, Dylan."

Willow came into the room, wearing black leggings and a turquoise sweater, her hair swept back into a ponytail. She carried her suitcase and placed it beside the door.

Pulling her into his arms, he said, "You look scrumptious." He kissed her at length. "You taste scrumptious."

"Later, Romeo. We need to get back to my place. I promised Pete I'd come by at noon and walk through with him. You can be my second opinion and see if there's anything he missed."

"Are you sure you want to take your suitcase? The work might not be completed."

"Pete said it would be by mid-afternoon. Oh, I need to get Shadow's food."

She pulled away from him and went to the kitchenette. "Both bowls are empty. I guess he finished his morning meal." She picked up the sack of food from the vet and brought it over.

"Here, I'll take that for you. And the suitcase. You get Shadow."

They slipped into their jackets, and she clipped the leash to the dog's collar before they went downstairs. Dylan opened the back of his SUV and placed the luggage and food inside as Willow settled the dog in the back seat. He opened her door.

"I ordered something quick from the diner. I know we had talked about going to a winery for a picnic, but I thought since we would be back at Boo's, we could just go down and eat at the beach right there."

"That's a great idea."

"Be right back."

Dylan went inside the diner. Nancy met him with a basket.

"I'll want the basket back. Have a romantic time. Sid and I always used to picnic, though we waited for warmer weather." She smiled. "I suppose you'll keep Willow warm."

"Or she might need to keep me warm," he countered.

Taking the basket to the SUV, he opened Willow's door and said, "Might want to put that at your feet. I was afraid it would tempt Shadow too much if I set it in the back seat."

She inhaled deeply. "Oh, fried chicken. Hey, it may tempt *me* to open it and eat a leg on the way home."

He laughed and returned to the driver's side, pulling away from the square and heading out of town toward Boxboro Highway, which connected Maple Cove to Salty Point. Boo's house was just off the highway.

Dylan reached for Willow's hand, simply wanting to touch her. He laced his fingers through hers and they rode in amiable silence to Boo's.

When they arrived, she said, "Leave everything in the car for now in case Pete's not ready for us. I'll bring Shadow in, but we can get the rest later."

As they got out, he said, "I really like the colors you went with for the exterior. The new landscaping really spruces things up."

She was busy snapping photos with her cell. "I'll send these to Jackson later."

This time, Willow left Shadow off his leash. They had worked on some simple commands during her stay, and she said she might want to see if she could find a trainer for Shadow. The dog seemed intelligent and already followed the few commands with ease. As usual, he stuck close to Willow as they entered the house.

"Pete!" called Willow. "We're here." She glanced down at the ground. "Look how these floors turned out. They're gorgeous."

"Thank you," Pete said, coming down the stairs. "It took just a little sanding to bring out their natural beauty. Hey, Dylan."

"Dylan is going to walk through with me if that's okay," Willow said.

"Not a problem. I'll tell you what we've done in each room. Look closely. See if there's anything we missed."

The contractor led them on a tour of the house.

Dylan admired the work that had been done and said so, as Willow took pictures of each room.

"You've accomplished quite a bit this week, Pete," he praised. "Everything looks terrific."

"Thank you. Of course, it couldn't have been accomplished so fast without my crew. Carter worked four of the days," Pete told them. "Even took two days off from the firehouse to see a few of the projects through."

Willow's eyes teared up, and Dylan squeezed her fingers. "That's what friends are for," he said softly.

They ended up in the kitchen, and Willow said, "This is a showstopper. Painting the cabinets instead of replacing them was a brilliant idea. I love the new backsplash and the quartz countertops. Best of all, this island is to die for."

"It will be nice for Game Night," Dylan said. "You can spread out the food here. Lots of room to prep on it and even eat."

"I'll need to get some barstools." She frowned. "I didn't see anything like that at Rylie's shop. It may take a trip into Portland to find what I like."

"If you don't see anything that catches your eye, let me know," Pete said. "I know a guy who knows a guy who provides furniture for game rooms. Pool tables. Bar stools. That kind of thing. He might have something you like."

"I'll keep that in mind," she said. "I think we're all finished here. How do you want to settle up?"

Pete gave her a few payment options, and Willow wrote him a check for the full amount from Boo's account, using one of her checks.

"Take this to the bank Monday. I'll call ahead and they should honor it. They're printing new checks for Jackson and me to use. I can't thank you enough, Pete.

If you need any kind of reviews posted, just text me the links. I'd be happy to spread the word."

"I can always use the business," he said, giving her back her key. "A satisfied customer always helps bring more in. Thank you, Dylan, for recommending me to Willow."

"Anytime, Pete."

Willow saw the contractor out while Dylan collected her suitcase and Shadow's food from the SUV. She had bowls placed on a mat by the time he returned. Shadow immediately dug into his food.

"I want to get bowls with his name on them," she said. "That's on my To Do list."

He settled his hands on her waist. "What's on my To Do list now is to eat. I'm starving."

"Then let's grab the picnic basket and head down to the cove." She glanced at Shadow. "I think we can leave him here for now. He'll probably be ready for a nap now."

They stopped at the car and claimed their lunch, along with the blanket to sit on. Willow checked to see if there were any drinks inside the basket and found two cans of Coke, along with a couple of bottled waters, napkins, thick paper plates, and plastic ware.

"Nancy thought of everything," she said.

"She usually does. She's a great landlord. Lets me charge meals, and then I pay for them with my rent at the end of each month."

"I remember when she was a teacher when I was in grade school. Just before I hit fifth grade, Sid died. That's when she left teaching and took over the diner."

"She told me Sid lived above the diner before they got married. Once they did, they bought a house a few blocks away. She still lives there. No one had rented the apartment upstairs for many years."

"I'm sure she was glad to get such a law-abiding tenant," Willow teased.

Dylan tossed the blanket over his shoulder and took her hand. They went across the lawn and through a grove of trees, making their way to the path that led down a steep hill to the beach. He couldn't remember how many times they had come this way, spending hours on the sand or in the water or exploring the cove to the north.

As they reached the bottom and the water appeared, he was glad he returned with Willow. This would make a perfect spot to propose. Forget about living together. He wanted the real deal. He intended to tell her that he loved her and then ask her to marry him. Not tomorrow or next month or even next year. Just whenever she was comfortable doing so.

She took the blanket from him and spread it out. He found a few rocks to anchor the four corners and they sat, opening the basket and pulling out various items and placing them on the paper plates.

Sinking her teeth into a chicken leg, Willow sighed. "Oh, fried chicken might just give me an orgasm. I haven't had this in years. Years!" she declared.

"You mean it's not a delicacy on French menus?" he teased.

"Nope. I did develop a taste for French food, though. German food was pretty good. English food was a little bland, although they have a ton of Indian restaurants in London. Curry was probably my favorite dish to eat in England. But France?" She waved the leg around. "*En France on mange bien!*"

"Meaning?" he asked.

"In France we eat well."

"What were your favorite dishes?"

"Cassoulet. That's white beans with a variety of

meat in it. Goose. Duck. Pork sausage. And *bouef bour-guignon*, a beef stewed simmered in red wine with gar-lic, mushrooms, and onions."

"That sounds heavenly."

"You'd love it and ratatouille, too." She paused. "Maybe you'd like to go to Paris someday."

He cupped her cheek. "Only if I went with you, Bear." Dylan almost added something about a honey-moon but stopped himself at the last minute.

They finished eating and packed everything back into the picnic basket, setting it aside. Willow climbed between Dylan's legs and rested her back against his chest, his arms around her, as they watched the waves roll in and out.

He could have stayed this way forever.

Drawing up his courage, he cleared his throat, ready to let Willow know what was on his mind.

Instead, she turned and faced him, her hands taking his. Her violet eyes were luminous, luring him in.

"Dylan? Will you marry me?"

CHAPTER 23

Willow saw the shock on Dylan's face even as it reverberated through her. She had had no idea those words would come out of her mouth—until they did.

But she was glad she had spoken to them.

"What?" he asked. "I... don't think I heard you right. I thought you said—"

"I asked *you* to marry *me*, Dylan Taylor. And I'm waiting for your answer."

He shook his head in disbelief. "Bear, I don't know if I have one for you."

Disappointment flooded her. She tried to release his hands, but he tightened his grip on her.

"You know my answer without me having to say a word," he said. "It's *yes*. A thousand times *yes*. But I'm struggling with the why."

"Why I asked you? Or why I wanted to get married?"

He nodded. "You've mentioned numerous times how long we've been apart from one another," he began. "You've also pointed out that we are different people than when we dated as teenagers. You've only been back in the Cove a week."

He paused, his gaze boring into her very soul. "But I haven't seen those as obstacles. I think at our core, we are the same people we always have been. We have a little life experience apart under our belts now, but I know what I want. What I have always wanted. And that is a life with you."

His gaze continued to search her face. "I'm committed for three years to serve as sheriff of Maple Cove. I can't walk away from that, so if you want to do something long distance, we can. But I want you to know that I love you, Willow Martin. I would do anything for you. I would go to the ends of this earth to be with you. That means if you want to move back to Europe, I'm in. if you want to stay stateside, I'll live anywhere you wish. I just need to finish out my term for the people of the Cove. I owe it to them."

Her throat thickened with tears, and she smiled at him through watery eyes. "I love you, Dylan. More than I ever thought possible all those years ago. I think it took me going through bad times—terrible times—with other men who couldn't hold a candle to you. You are my rock. My heart and my soul. I want to spend the rest of my life with you. I was afraid if you asked me to marry you, you would never quite be sure of how deeply committed I am to you. That's why I've asked you. Yes, our physical intimacy did factor into my decision, but it goes well beyond that. I feel you are my soulmate in every aspect. I can't imagine my life without you. I don't want to live my life without you in it. I also want that life to be in the Cove. My wanderlust days are over. I want to sink roots deeply in this place. With you.

"I love you so much, Dylan. I plan to show you just how much every day for the rest of our lives."

She saw love for her shining in his gray eyes as he said, "I love you. I have always loved you. Even when we were apart and I didn't even know I still did. I think that's what kept me from committing to any other relationship with a woman. You were my gold standard, Willow. We go together." He grinned. "Like peanut butter and jelly."

"Am I the peanut butter or the jelly?" she teased.

"You are my golden girl. Don't expect it to be smooth sailing for us, though."

"Because I can be a bear sometimes?"

"Maybe a little," he admitted. "But I'm no saint either. I'm just a man who loves one woman—and I'm thrilled that she loves me back."

They leaned toward one another for a sweet, tender kiss. If Willow had any doubts, they had all fled since she'd opened her heart to this incredible man and told him just how she felt.

He broke the kiss. "You're certain you want to settle here in the Cove? I meant what I said. I would follow you to the ends of the earth."

"The ends of the earth aren't all they're cracked up to be," she told him. "Yes, I want to take you to the places I've lived and share them with you. But our life together should be lived out in Maple Cove. Hopefully, with a family."

"You want kids?" he asked.

"I do. Unless you don't."

"I've always wanted them. I know two people can be a family, but I believe children would add a wonderful, rich layer to our lives." He hesitated. "I worried that you thought it would be too soon, and that's why I kept quiet. Why I didn't tell you I loved you."

She touched her palm to his face, caressing his cheek with her thumb. "You told me every day that you loved me, Dylan. In every glance. Every smile. Every touch. I knew. No words were necessary."

"They are to me. You will hear them each day. Probably more than you want to. You might even get tired of me saying them—but I love you, Willow Martin."

They kissed for a long time, each kiss sweeter that the one before because of the new commitment that now lay between them.

Dylan broke the kiss and asked, "When can we get married? A day? A week? A year? You know I would wait forever. As long as you wish. But I hope we can still live together in the meantime. This is our second chance, Willow. We've spent too much time apart. Wasted time which I plan to make up for."

"Where would you be interested in living?" she asked. "You were going to talk to Shayla Newton about a house."

She saw his sheepish grin as he said, "I did mention it to Shayla. I also told her it was a mere fishing expedition."

"Why?"

"Because when I asked your opinion, you told me it was my house, and you had nothing to do with it. I'll admit that hurt me, Bear. I almost lost hope."

"I'm sorry, Dylan. I think I was still trying to protect myself and not become too involved with you. You had a way into my heart, though. I'm grateful you didn't let me pushing you away stop you."

"Stop me? Hey, you're the one that asked me to get married, not the other way around." He laughed.

"You're never going to let me live that down, are you?"

"Probably not. But it can stay between us." He framed her face in his hands. "But I love that you did ask me, Willow. You're right. It does let me know that you are committed to us. What do you think if we moved to Boo's house? I know half of it has to belong to Jackson, and we'd need to take that into consideration."

"Jackson would be fine with it," she told him, still holding back that her brother would most likely move to the Cove. Though she didn't want to keep anything from Dylan, she had promised Jackson to wait before revealing his plans.

"I told him that I was staying in the Cove, and he said we could work things out. Boo left us some money in her banking accounts, and I offered for him to take what was left in them after I pay Pete for the renovations. Or we even talked about splitting those funds and me buying out his part of the house."

She kissed him softly. "It would mean a great deal to me if we did live at Boo's. The art studio is a perfect space for me to work in." She smiled. "And it is plenty large. You know, for a few kids."

Willow paused. "I don't want a big, fancy wedding, Dylan. I was never one of those little girls who planned out all the details of her wedding, from the kind of flowers to the dress to who would serve as my attendants. If it's all right with you, I'd rather slip away and get married. Maybe have Jackson there to witness it. I would love if Tenley and Sloane could also come, but that wouldn't be possible. Tenley told me she was going to try and get away and come to Oregon sometime in January, and Sloane has just accepted a new assignment in Africa. So I would be happy simply to have Jackson there for me. What about you? What are your feelings regarding the ceremony?"

"You read my mind, Bear. A no-muss, no-fuss wedding is fine with me. I've seen people sink thousands of dollars into a wedding and reception when that money could have been put to better use. While I don't mind getting married at a courthouse, I could definitely see having a big party to celebrate our marriage. After the fact."

"I'm all in for a party. Lots of music and dancing. Some food and drink."

"So, we're back to the timing. When do you want to get married?"

She laughed. "I guess I can Google how to get a wedding license in Oregon and see the wait period, at the same time I'm researching how to get my driver's license. Could we give it at least a week? I'll need to check with Jackson and see about his trial. I was hoping to get him up to the Cove for Christmas, but he didn't think that was going to be possible."

"What if we got married down in L.A.?" Dylan asked.

"It's a thought. I guess I can look into that, as well. Or maybe we should elope to Vegas and have 'Elvis' marry us." She grew solemn. "It really doesn't matter where the ceremony takes place. I am already committed to you in my heart. It will just be a formality."

"I feel the same, sweetheart."

Willow smiled. "You've never called me sweetheart before."

"Do you like that? Or should I stick with Bear?"

She threw her arms around him. "You can call me either or both. Just don't ever stop loving me, Dylan."

He kissed her deeply and Willow had never felt as close to another person as she did Dylan in this moment. Now that she had finally committed to him heart and soul, it seemed all the tension fled her body, replaced by love for this wonderful man she would soon call husband. As he pointed out, she knew there would be some bumps along the way. She was hard-headed and had a bit of a temper, but Dylan's easy-going nature would always be a good balance to her mercurial moods.

She was glad he wanted children. She had only mentioned doing so in passing to Jean-Luc, and he had brushed aside the idea without giving it any consideration. She realized now how selfish the Frenchman had been and how little he had given of himself to her in their one-sided relationship. With Dylan, things would be much different. They already had a history together and a deep, abiding love, which would only grow through the years to come. She felt she could tell him anything. Her deepest secrets. Her greatest fears. And he would also celebrate every victory with her and comfort her in every defeat.

Life would be good with this man, and Willow would do everything in her power to be the best wife, lover, friend—and eventually, mother—that she could be.

"Ready to go back?" he asked.

"Yes. Shadow will be wondering where we went."

She removed the rocks anchoring the blanket, and he folded it and grabbed the picnic basket. They returned up the steep incline to Boo's house. Now, with the new coats of paint outside and the changes within, it was becoming their house.

Inside, Shadow eagerly greeted them. Dylan said he would take the dog for a walk if Willow would look up how to obtain a marriage license in Oregon and California.

"Are you that eager to marry me?" she asked, running her fingers up his sleeve.

He caught her hand and brought it to his lips for a kiss. "More than ready."

She retrieved her tablet and opened a document for taking notes. In quick time, she learned that they could get the application in Oregon online, or request it in person. She favored completing what they could online and then showing up in person to complete the rest of the process and pay the licensing fees. They would also have to return to pick up their certified marriage certificate after the ceremony was held, since the state required the officiant to sign and mail in the certificate so the marriage could be legally recorded in state records.

The state required a three-day waiting period, which could be waived for a small fee. The license would be good for sixty days. A note of interest said not only could an Oregon judge marry them, but a military judge, as well. She wondered if Dylan might have someone from his army days that he might want to officiate.

She switched up her search, moving to California's requirements, and found good news. The state didn't require the bride and groom to be residents of California. They would merely go to a county clerk's office with their picture IDs and obtain a license good for ninety days. Many of the county clerks would perform civil marriage ceremonies in their offices. In fact, California was more liberal in the number and kinds of people who could serve as the officiant. As in Oregon, they would need to pay for a certified copy of their license after the marriage certificate had been filed with the state.

Dylan returned with Shadow and she shared with him the information she'd learned.

"I suppose it will all hinge upon Jackson and his

schedule," he said. "The cost is reasonable in both places. It might be smart to obtain a license for both states and use the one most convenient for us. As far as a judge goes, I don't have anyone in mind that's stateside now. I did know a few from my MP days, but we'll have to find someone to do the ceremony."

"That's a thought. Let me call Jackson. If we get married in L.A., he might have a suggestion, since he's tried cases in front of so many judges."

She was disappointed when her brother didn't pick up. Even though it was a weekend, she figured he was at the office, hard at work on the McGreer case, his ringer off.

"Call me when you get this," she said after the beep, not wanting to leave her good news in a voicemail.

"He wasn't answering," she told Dylan when she hung up. "I'd rather him hear about our wedding directly from me than on a recording."

"Agree. We'll need another witness in any case. Would you mind if I asked Carter?"

Willow slipped her arms about his waist. "I think that would be perfect. He was there at the beginning. I just hope it won't make him too sad, with Emily being gone."

"He and I had a talk the other day at lunch. He showed up at my office with sandwiches. Like he shared with you, he's ready to start dating again." Dylan kissed her. "I think Carter seeing us as a loving couple might give him hope that he'll find love again someday."

"Speaking of love," she said. "How about you and I go upstairs and try out the bed?"

Her fiancé grinned. "Are you still sleeping in your old room? I always wanted to see it."

"But Boo was old-fashioned and made us always stay downstairs."

"Hey, it didn't keep us from making out." He gave her a slow, bone-melting kiss.

"I've actually moved to the primary bedroom now. It's bigger."

Mischief lit his eyes. "Well, we could christen that bed—and then move to your old room. Just for the fun of it."

Willow snuggled close. "I like your idea of fun, Sheriff Taylor. Lead the way."

CHAPTER 24

Willow suggested they go hiking again the next morning. She couldn't believe it had been only a week since they had gone out, finding Shadow. Finding each other.

Finding love again...

Shadow eagerly jumped into the car, and Willow thought of the shy, hesitant dog who had approached them in the clearing and how far he had come in such a short time. She could say the same for herself. She had thought to guard her heart against Dylan but discovered she needed him in her life. That he made her whole. That they were better together than they were apart.

After hiking several hours, they returned to Boo's, and Dylan made sandwiches for them while Willow took a quick shower.

As they ate, he said, "I think I'm going to go to the station for a couple of hours this afternoon and catch up on some paperwork. My mind wandered quite a bit this week, and it stacked up."

He reached for her hand. "I love you, Willow. Your love will ground me and everything I do."

"I feel the same," she told him, squeezing his fingers. "Would you come back here for dinner?"

"I can do that. Probably about five or five-thirty, if that's all right with you. Right now, I'm going to run home and shower off the hike and then head to my office."

He kissed her goodbye, and she and Shadow watched his SUV pull away from the house. They had talked about whether he should move in with her this week or not but hadn't come to any decision just yet. She decided she would call her friends and share her good news with them. She realized Sloane would be asleep now, so she dialed Tenley's number first.

"Hi, Willow," Tenley greeted. "What's up?" her friend asked.

"Can you talk a few minutes?" she asked, aware of how things weren't quite right in Tenley's household.

"Sure. Theodore is at the office. I'm working on a new PR campaign, but I've got all the time you want to talk."

"I have some news for you. It's pretty wild." She paused. "Dylan and I are getting married."

Tenley's squeals were so loud that Willow had to pull the phone away from her ear. She smiled, knowing that even though her friend wasn't happy, Tenley was joyful regarding Willow's situation.

"That's fantastic news, Willow. Give me the details. Don't you dare leave anything out."

She walked through the last week and the proposal.

"I think it speaks volumes that you proposed to him," Tenley commented. "I know ninety-nine of out one hundred people would think you were crazy to do so, especially after so short a time, but I've known you too long and trust your judgment."

"My heart spoke to me, Tenley. It told me not to blow this second chance. Why waste time when I could be with the man I love?"

"When is the wedding? I doubt you'll wait long. I know I said I was coming next month, but I'm sure you'll already be married by then."

"You're right. We've decided to do a small courthouse wedding. Either here in Oregon or possible down in L.A., so Jackson could be one of our witnesses."

"I may have to re-think coming to see you," her friend said. "You'll still be in the honeymoon phase."

"No, you have to come. You promised. Dylan is dying to meet you. Sloane, too. Tell me you'll come, Tenley. Please."

After a long pause, Tenley said, "I'll come."

"Thank you. I need my Tenley time."

They talked about a few things going on with Tenley's job, especially the new campaign she was embarking upon. At least her friend sounded upbeat and happy in her professional life if not her personal one. Once more, Tenley refrained from mentioning anything about her marriage, and Willow knew they would have many long talks once Tenley came to the Cove.

Since she couldn't call Sloane just yet, Willow puttered into the kitchen, wondering what to make for dinner. She spied Boo's recipe box and went to it, flipping through the cards. Seeing Boo's familiar handwriting caused a lump to grow in her throat. At least she had this small part of her grandmother and decided she would make lasagna. It had been Boo's favorite meal to cook for her grandchildren. Willow pulled out the card and skimmed the recipe, deciding she had everything she needed except the bell pepper.

She hated to drive in to the Cove just for that and thought she would text Gillian to see if she had an extra one.

I'm back home & the renovation is complete! Want to come see the house? If you have a bell pepper, I need one for lasagna.

Willow immediately saw the flashing dots, and Gillian replied, saying she was on her way with the bell pepper.

Going to sit out on the porch with Shadow to await her neighbor, Willow breathed in the clean Oregon air. While she had loved each of the cities she had lived in, nothing beat Maple Cove. A few minutes later Gillian appeared from the woods that separated their two houses, carrying a plate wrapped in foil and the requested bell pepper.

She climbed the stairs and embraced Willow. "I love this color. Funny how a fresh, different coat of paint can make such a difference in a house's appearance." She gave an admiring glace to the flowerbeds "The landscaping also looks wonderful. Boo would be pleased with what you've done."

"Come inside and see the rest. Pete Pulaski and his crew did a terrific job."

They went to the kitchen first, which Willow knew Gillian would enjoy seeing most. Her friend oohed and ahhed over the updates, her careful eye inspecting all the work.

"This island is a dream," she told Willow. "Making lasagna will be easy, spreading out on it." Gillian set down the plate and bell paper. "I made a cake this morning. German chocolate. I was about to see if I could bring a few pieces over when you texted me. I assume you're making dinner for Dylan."

"Yes."

She had let her neighbor know she was staying at Dylan's this week while the house updates occurred and decided now to tell her about the upcoming marriage.

"I'm swearing you to secrecy on this."

Gillian laughed. "Are you going to tell me you're getting married?"

"How did you know?"

"How could I *not* know?" Gillian asked. "You're positively glowing, Willow. I remember how close the two of you were before you both left the Cove. And don't forget—I watched the two of you last weekend when all those people were here. Dylan never left your side."

"You don't think it's too soon?"

"Not at all," Gillian assured her. "Very few people are awarded a second chance—and that is exactly what you and Dylan have gotten. Don't worry about conventional wisdom or any gossip that might occur. Follow your heart. Dylan is a good man. You couldn't do better." She wiped a tear away. "Boo would've been so pleased."

Gillian hugged Willow.

"Thank you for being such a good friend to Boo and me," she said. "You've been family to us all these years. You'll have to be the substitute granny when we have kids."

Gillian's face lit up. "Oh, I would like that so much, Willow. Now, let's go see the rest of the house."

Willow gave Gillian the grand tour. They returned downstairs, and Gillian asked, "Will you and Dylan live here?"

"That's the plan. I don't think Jackson will have a problem with it. As far as our marriage goes, we're not going to be telling anyone until after the fact. We will have a party, though, to celebrate. Hopefully, we'll be married by Christmas, which is two weeks away."

"My lips are sealed," Gillian promised. "If you need any help planning the party, though, you know where to come. If I were you, I would have Ainsley bake you a wedding cake. Every girl needs one."

After Gillian left, Willow gathered everything she needed to make the lasagna, putting on water to boil the noodles and browning the ground meat. She chopped the bell pepper and onion and got out one of Boo's nine by thirteen glass dishes. After the sauce had simmered half an hour, she ladled some of it into the dish, layering cooked noodles, meat, and cheese, then repeating the pattern until she'd used all her ingredients

It would take over an hour to bake, so she preheated the oven and then slid the casserole dish inside, setting the timer. They would have to make do without a salad, but she did find a loaf of frozen sourdough bread in the freezer and took it out to thaw, helping it along some by sticking it in the microwave. By now, it was a little after four, and although still early halfway around the world, she decided she couldn't wait any longer and dialed Sloane's number.

Sloane answered on the first ring, and Willow said, "I hope I'm not waking you up, but if I am? It's for a good reason."

"I was awake. I'm working. As usual. I have to keep crazy hours because of when the network wants to air a segment. I'll be on-air on the nightly news in less than an hour. At least Eastern time."

"I'll be sure to tune in and catch your report," Willow promised "In the meantime, I wanted to let you know that Dylan and I have decided to get married."

Sloane reacted in a similar manner to Tenley, a loud squeal coming across the line from half a world away.

"You've got about five minutes before I need to go, so squeeze as much as you can into that time," her friend told her.

Willow quickly recounted how she had come to trust Dylan and how she had been the one to propose to him.

"That totally shows how committed you are to your relationship, Willow. He'll never doubt how much you love him, because you were the one to make this first move."

"He said as much. I knew I would have to do something bold to let him know just how much I cared. He is the love of my life, Sloane. I almost don't mind that I suffered through my twenties with men who weren't good to me. I would do it all again as long as I knew Dylan would be at the end, waiting for me."

"I think this is one of the most romantic things I've ever heard, but I've got to go, Willow. I want to hear more about this, and I want to meet Dylan. I know that's impossible right now, but let's figure out a time we can all talk. You can put me on speakerphone or FaceTime. Gotta go. Love you."

"Love you, too," Willow echoed.

She left the kitchen and moved to the sofa, where Shadow sat. Settling next to the pup, she petted him, the motion soothing her. Then her phone rang, and she saw it was Jackson.

"Finally," she said.

"Sorry. I've been swamped with this murder case, Willow."

Sympathy filled her, knowing how affected her brother was by defending a man who had committed such a heinous crime, one Jackson suspected had done it more than once.

"That's okay. I understand. I needed to talk to you about something very important. That's why I left a terse voicemail."

"Does this have anything to do with a dark-haired sheriff?" Jackson teased.

"As a matter of fact, it does."

For the third time that afternoon, Willow launched into an explanation of the circumstances surrounding her engagement and how they wanted to get married as soon as possible.

"I envy you and am thrilled for you," Jackson told her. "When is the wedding?"

"That's why I'm calling you. We want it as soon as possible. Perhaps even this weekend. You know I want you there, Jackson."

"I don't see how that can happen, Willow. I don't want to disappoint you, but I'm in the middle of this trial. Lawyers trying murder cases don't have the luxury of a personal life."

"Dylan suggested that we get both an Oregon and California license."

"California?"

"Yes, we thought about flying down to L.A. so that you could be at the ceremony."

"Wait a minute. Let me think." Jackson was silent, and Willow waited patiently.

"If you really mean it and are willing to come down here, I can help arrange things for you. I can e-mail you a copy of the application. Fill it out and send it back to me. I can make the arrangements for Friday. The judge usually ends things by four or four-thirty on Fridays. That's been his pattern the past two weeks. I could arrange for the county clerk to have everything ready to go, and I have a judge I play basketball with that would be happy to perform the ceremony. You could get married in his chambers by about five this coming Friday, if you're willing to move that quickly."

"Oh, Jackson, that would be incredible. Dylan talked about Carter possibly being our other witness."

"Yes, you'll need two. If Carter can't make it down here, I can always have my paralegal or Bill Watterscheim serve as your other witness." He paused. "I'm happy for you, Willow. I know you've been through the ringer as far as relationships go. I think it's pretty cool you've actually come full circle and are winding up with your first love. Second chances are rare. You're one of the lucky ones."

"I think so, too."

"You definitely need to make Boo's house yours, Willow."

"But what if you come back to the Cove?"

"If I do, you can put me up in a room until I find something I like. I know a lot of the places on the square have upstairs storage, and some of the tenants have lived in it at one time or another."

"Dylan's been renting out the space above Sid's Diner. Nancy said Sid lived there before they got married. If no one rents it after he leaves, you might consider it. The apartment is small, but it would do until you found somewhere you wanted to live."

"That's a thought. But if I come—and it's still an *if*, Willow—I'll also need to rent office space."

"Wouldn't you take over Clancy's?"

"I haven't thought that far ahead," her brother admitted. "His offer is tempting. I just need to get this trial over and done with, and then really sit and think things through. In the meantime, I'll pull the marriage application and send it your way."

Five minutes later, the notification popped up on her phone. She opened the e-mail and saw Jackson had forwarded a California marriage license application. She went to her tablet and opened up the e-mail again on it, filling out as much as she possibly could. When she finished it, she returned to the kitchen. It was a few minutes after five and the lasagna was ready to come out. Boo had always let it rest five to ten minutes. The sourdough had thawed, and Willow placed it inside the oven, hoping Dylan would be here soon.

As she set the table, she heard the doorbell ring and realized he didn't have a key to the house. She went and met him at the door, and he kissed her, following her back to the kitchen.

She opened a drawer and handed him the key Pete had returned to her yesterday.

"This is for you. I finally spoke with Jackson and got his okay. The house is ours. We'll iron out the details later."

He pulled her close for a lingering kiss. "That's terrific news. I've always loved this house." He inhaled. "And if I'm not mistaken, I smell Italian."

"It's Boo's lasagna recipe," Willow confirmed. "Hopefully, it came out okay."

They sat at the kitchen table and over dinner, she told him about how they would need to book flights to California for the Friday ceremony Jackson would be arranging.

"He sent me the application. I have most of it filled out, but I need a few details from you, such as your Social Security number."

"When on Friday?" he asked.

"After his trial finishes for the day. We'll meet him and then walk down to the county clerk's office. Get the paperwork taken care of and then head to the chambers of a judge he knows, one of his basketball playing buddies. Will that work for you?"

"For me, yes. I know Carter is pulling a Thursday through Sunday shift, though."

"We can wait if you want," she told him.

"No. I want to do this. Carter can be there to help us celebrate."

"Jackson said his law partner or paralegal could be our other witness."

"Then let's go with that."

They cleared the dishes and then Dylan fed Willow the information she needed to complete the application. She e-mailed it back to Jackson and told him Carter was out and they would need another witness.

They curled up and decided to watch a movie together. The opening credits had just finished rolling when Dylan's phone rang, and he answered it. After listening a moment, he said, "I'll come in now."

"Trouble?" she asked.

"A little." A shadow crossed his face. "A car wreck on the Boxboro Highway. Near the same stretch where my family died."

Willow wrapped her arms about him. "I'm sorry, Dylan."

"Two fatalities. One injured."

"You need to go," she urged.

"I know we haven't worked out any details yet as far as me staying with you or not this week. Tonight will be a late one, though. I'll just head home once I wrap things up."

"Call me if you want to talk," she said. "No matter how late."

"Okay."

He hugged her tightly and then released her. "I'll call you tomorrow morning."

Willow watched him leave, saying a quick prayer that Dylan would manage to see things through without too much grief surfacing.

CHAPTER 25

Dylan rubbed his eyes, weariness filling him. The hardest part of his job was making the notification to someone that their loved one had died. He'd done it several times while serving as an MP, but this was the first time he'd done so as sheriff in Maple Cove.

He had taken Linda Goodnight with him. The deputy was forty, and had two boys, eight and ten, of her own. Though off-duty, Linda had agreed to come with him.

The two killed had been a father and daughter, the girl only five years old. They had gone to Portland for the weekend to visit the father's parents who lived there. The mother had been out of town on business and had returned earlier in the evening. When Dylan and Linda arrived and gave her the bad news, she had let out a guttural scream and then collapsed to the ground.

He knew some of what she would go through in the next hours, days, and weeks to come. Survivor's guilt would plague her—as it had him. There would be a thousand details to handle. For him, it had been the little things that almost did him in. The laundry that had been left in the dryer. Seeing Grace's painting drying on the kitchen table. His father's briefcase sitting atop his desk. When Dylan ate the last frozen casserole his mom had placed in the freezer, he had wept.

He turned off the light in his office and was glad he wasn't bringing his foul mood home to Willow. He preferred being alone now, walking the short distance to his apartment and heading up the stairs. He appreciated that Raymond Garcia had volunteered to go to the hospital and interview the driver who had caused the accident. Deputy Garcia had already told Dylan that the breathalyzer told them the driver had been drunk when he crashed into the pair. Dylan didn't know if he had it in him to talk to the man without tearing him limb from limb. He wondered if Walt had felt the same way when faced with dealing with the driver who killed Dylan's family.

It took a huge effort to climb the stairs to his apartment. He fished for his keys and let himself in. Already, this place didn't seem like home anymore.

Because home was where Willow was.

He removed his jacket and hung it up and then slipped out of his shoes. He stood without moving, too tired to even think what to do next.

A knock sounded at his door. For a moment, he wished it were Willow coming to be with him, but as he answered it, anger surged through him.

Missy Newton stood there, her hair mussed, smeared mascara under her eyes. The last thing he needed to do was deal with was a drunk Missy.

"You can't show up like this, Missy," he told her.

She met his gaze. "I didn't have anywhere else to go, Dylan. I need to file a complaint."

"Then do that tomorrow morning at the station," he said gruffly. "It's late."

She burst into tears. "I need to talk to you before I do that. Please. Can I come in? I need to show you something."

Reluctantly, he stepped aside and Missy entered. Dylan shut the door, wondering what she needed him to see and what kind of complaint she had.

Missy let her purse drop to the floor and slipped off her jacket, wincing as she did so. He perked up, realizing something was wrong with her beyond having too much to drink. Before Dylan could ask her anything, she reached for the hem of the turtleneck sweater she wore and pulled up, bringing it over her head and allowing it to fall to the ground.

She had dark bruises on her throat, along with some on her torso.

"Who did this?" he asked gently, not wanting to frighten her more than she already was.

"I... don't know if I should tell you," she said. "I'm scared of him. I'm afraid if I press charges, he'll come after me."

Dylan took her elbow and guided her to the sofa. She sat and he joined her.

"I think you should tell me, Missy," he said, his voice calm, hiding the fact he wanted to pummel whoever had hurt this woman.

"He's threatened me," she said.

"Has he done this kind of thing before?"

She hesitated. "He's slapped me around a little. This is the most he's ever done."

"Tell me his name, Missy," Dylan said firmly, thinking it might be Rick Mercer, since he had seen them together at the Hungry Bear only last Monday night.

She hiccupped. "Can I think about it?"

"Yes. But you don't want him to do this again to you. He might if you don't press charges. He might hurt someone else, too."

"I know," she said, her voice small. "I just need to think about it. He has a key to my place." She hesitated. "Could I stay here tonight, Dylan?"

He shook his head. "I don't think that's a good idea."

She bit her lip. "Then I guess I'll sleep in my car. I just hope he doesn't drive around looking for me."

Guilt flooded him. "Okay. You can stay."

"Thank you, Dylan. I'll just sleep on your couch."

"No, you can take the bed. I'll sleep here."

She stood. "Can I use your restroom?"

"Sure. It's right through the bedroom door."

Missy went inside the bedroom. Dylan followed her. The bed was made and he pulled back the comforter and sheets, doubting she had the energy to do so. He fluffed the pillows and then waited for her back in the den.

When she appeared, she said, "Hot tea always helps me sleep."

He smiled ruefully. "I'm afraid I don't have any. You're talking to a bachelor."

She claimed her purse. "I always carry teabags. If I can use your microwave, I can heat the water. Would you share a cup with me?"

"Sure," he said, afraid she would fall apart if he said no.

Dylan pulled two mugs from the cabinet and filled them with water. He placed them inside the microwave and started it.

"I... I might want to take a shower. You know. Wash off everything."

"Were you raped, Missy?" he asked, on high alert now.

"No. Nothing like that. I'm not trying to hide evidence. I just..." Her voice trailed off.

"I'll go set out a towel and washcloth for you. Be right back."

He left and was glad he still had a clean towel for her, leaving it on the toilet seat. When he returned to the kitchenette, she was dunking the teabags in the mugs.

"Thanks for letting me stay, Dylan," she said softly.

"Not a problem," he assured her.

She carried the mugs into the bedroom, and he followed her there. Missy handed him one and then she climbed onto the bed, propping up a pillow and settling against it. She took a sip.

"Ah, the perfect temperature. There's nothing like a good cup of tea."

He felt awkward standing there, so he went to the opposite side of the bed and perched at its foot, taking a sip of tea. The warmth felt good going down, and he realized he probably needed this cup of tea as much as she did after the night he'd had.

"Do you want to talk about it?" he asked. "Sometimes, saying things aloud, especially to someone else, helps me think."

"I don't want to talk about it," she said abruptly, sipping her tea again. "Let's talk about something else. I'll think about it later."

He knew some victims could compartmentalize what had happened to them. It seemed Missy Newton was one of them. She had reached out for help but now shut the door on the incident. He would need to give her the time to process it.

Dylan began talking about the Seahawks, knowing

Missy was a football fan. They spent about fifteen minutes together. He finished his tea, his eyes growing heavy.

"I'm really tired, Missy," he told her, his words slurring slightly. "It's been... a long... day."

"I know it has been, Dylan. But I'm here now."

Something in her eyes didn't set well with him. But he was having trouble keeping his own eyes open. He tried blinking rapidly, but it was as if he was no longer in control of his body. A numbness set in. A sudden suspicion dawned on him, but he was becoming too weak to even think it through.

"That's all right, Dylan," Missy cooed. "I know you're tired. You should stretch out and get a little sleep."

She set down her mug and stood, coming around to his side of the bed. He felt himself tip over onto the mattress, not able to control his body anymore, as if he'd become suddenly paralyzed. She pulled him up so that his head rested on the pillow and lifted his legs, placing them on the bed.

"You just go to sleep. Everything will be fine."

A wave of dizziness hit, coupled with the drowsiness. Dylan fought against both a few more seconds and then succumbed to the darkness that swallowed him.

WILLOW AWOKE for the first time in a week without Dylan beside her. Even with Shadow firmly pressed against her legs, the bed felt empty without her fiancé in it.

She picked up her phone to see if she had missed a text or call from Dylan. Nothing. It was almost six and though she wanted to text him, she didn't know how late he had been up last night. She hoped he would call soon.

Rising, she dressed in her running clothes and was slipping on her socks and shoes when her cell pinged. She pulled it from her pocket and saw a text from Dylan.

Come over for a morning surprise!

A wide smile crossed her face. Eagerly, she texted him back.

Up for a little morning delight?

Willow waited a moment. When Dylan didn't respond, she didn't think anything of it. Instead, she hit the restroom and brushed her teeth.

"Come on, Shadow," she told the dog, who jumped from the bed and followed her downstairs.

She let him out to pee, watching him from the porch. He was good about not straying, and she wondered if she could train him on her own instead of taking him to a trainer.

He returned to her and she let him inside, scooping kibble into his bowl and giving him fresh water.

"I'll be back later," she told him, before grabbing her keys and purse and heading out the door.

She made it into Maple Cove and parked on the square, which had several cars in front of the diner. She didn't see Dylan's SUV anywhere and took out her cell again, making sure she hadn't gotten her wires crossed and thinking she was supposed to meet him somewhere else. No, he just said to come over. Surely, he meant his apartment and not the station.

Willow locked her car and headed to the side of the building, hurrying up the stairs. She felt giddy as a schoolgirl, anxious to see him. She hoped last night had gone better than he expected, but she would refrain from asking him about it. If he brought up the wreck and wanted to discuss it, she would be happy to let him talk. When his parents and sister had died in the car crash, she had hoped he would seek counseling. She doubted that had occurred since he'd left for the army and basic training so soon afterward.

She knocked lightly, having given him back his key. When he didn't answer, she knocked again, a bit louder this time. Still no response. Turning the handle, she found the door unlocked and grinned. She assumed he was waiting for her in bed.

Moving across the den, she opened the bedroom door. A light from the bathroom was on, helping her to see into the darkened room. But what she saw didn't make any sense. Dylan was in bed, the sheet pulled low on his hips, his body bare.

And Missy Newton lay sprawled across him.

A naked Missy Newton.

Bile rose in Willow's throat as she stood staring at the scene, frozen to the spot.

Then Missy yawned and stretched. "Oh!" she said, so fake that Willow knew immediately that Missy had been the one to send the text.

It didn't matter who sent it—because the text had helped her discover the truth.

That Dylan was cheating on her. With Missy, a woman he claimed he wanted nothing to do with. Nausea filled her as she thought back to Missy confronting her last week at the Hungry Bear. Had she and Dylan been seeing one another all along? Had Missy been here first—or had Dylan already tired of Willow as she had feared? He hadn't wanted to spend the night at her place last night. Was it because he'd already arranged to be with Missy? Had there even been a car fatality?

Willow thought she might be ill and turned quickly to flee the room. She changed her mind and ran to the bathroom since it was closer, falling to her knees and vomiting into the toilet.

When she rose and turned, Missy stood in the doorway, a triumphant smile on her face.

"Dylan didn't want to tell you about us," she revealed. "He felt sorry for you because your grandmother died. And he got sucked in by you, just like before. I tried to warn you, Willow, but you weren't ready to hear it. Dylan doesn't love you. He loves me."

Her thoughts whirled until she was dizzy. "I don't believe you," she said shakily.

Missy shrugged. "Believe whatever you want. But he didn't come to you last night, did he? Because he'd already planned to be with me. We laughed about you, Willow."

"No, that's not true," she said, denying Missy's words.

"Whatever. But I was trying to give it to you straight. I've been in your shoes, and it isn't fun when your man is running around on you. I just thought you should know."

Missy turned and padded back to the bed, slipping beneath the sheets and snuggling close to the still-sleeping Dylan.

Giggling, she said to Willow, who'd stepped from the bathroom, "He's already hard. If you'll excuse us, we have some catching up to do."

Missy turned away, tossing the sheets back and straddling Dylan.

"Hey, baby," he said sleepily.

Willow ran from the room, tears blinding her.

CHAPTER 26

Dylan woke to Willow nuzzling his neck, her weight atop him. He tried to smile, but a headache blinded him. His hands went to his head, pushing on it. He moaned. Willow moved from him, her weight suddenly gone.

"My head's killing me, Bear. Can you get me some aspirin?"

She left and he tried to open his eyes. A wave of dizziness swarmed through him, and he gripped the sheet in his hands. His body trembled uncontrollably. He reached for the other pillow and clasped it to him, trying to hold on and anchor himself.

It was odd. He could smell Willow's floral perfume, but another feminine scent coupled with it. Confusion filled him. His mouth was so dry. He swallowed, hoping Willow would return soon with the aspirin.

The next thing he knew, light flooded the room. Dylan opened his eyes, his mouth feeling as if it was stuffed full of cotton. He heard something in the distance and couldn't understand what it was. He pushed himself up with one hand and sat on the edge of the bed, his limbs weak as if he'd just fought a bout with the flu—and lost.

Where was Willow?

The noise started again, and he realized it was his cell ringing. Dylan pushed himself to his feet and stood a moment, unsteady. He ventured a few steps and reached out, leaning against the wall, his heart racing. Something was wrong with him. It was as if he'd gone on some huge bender. But he hadn't had a sip of alcohol. At least, he didn't think so. No, he didn't recall drinking. Hell, he didn't recall much of anything. Hiking with Willow. Yes, they'd done that. No, wait. That had been last weekend. When they found Shadow. Or had they gone again? Confusion filled him.

The ringing ceased. Dylan slowly made his way into the bathroom and caught the faint scent of vomit in the air. Had he been sick? Was it the flu? He hadn't been sick in years. He gripped the bathroom sink and looked into the mirror. Bloodshot eyes. Disheveled hair. Stubble.

He raised a hand and felt his forehead. It was cool to the touch. Then why did he feel so awful?

And why couldn't he remember anything?

He turned on the faucet and cupped his hands, drinking the cold water. It hit his belly and almost came back up. He waited a moment and then leaned down again, splashing water on his face. Grabbing for the towel, he dried it and stared at himself in the mirror again.

Something was very wrong. He needed to talk to Willow. She would know what had happened.

Dylan stumbled from the bathroom, slowly making his way outside the bedroom. His cell started ringing again and he fell to the couch, picking it up from where it lay on the coffee table.

"What?"

"Dylan? It's Pam. Are you all right?"

"Why?"

The dispatcher paused. "Well, I know about the wreck last night and that you worked late. You didn't come in this morning. We... we were worried about you."

Wreck?

Flashing lights appeared in his head. Then nothing.

"Wreck?" he echoed.

"Yes," Pam said. "The father and little girl who were killed."

Dylan had no memory of that. "I worked it. Yes," he told her. "I'll be in later."

"Raymond wants to meet with you about the statement he took."

"Okay. Later," he repeated.

He hung up without saying goodbye. Fog still clouded his brain. He closed his eyes, willing the dizziness to pass.

Then he opened them again and called Carter.

"What's up?" his friend said cheerily.

"Come over," he managed to say. "Bring your... bag."

"Where are you?" Carter's voice turned serious.

"Home."

"Is Willow with you?"

"No. I don't think so."

"Hang tight, buddy. I'll be right there."

Dylan's head fell back.

The next thing he knew, he heard Carter's voice. "Dylan. Talk to me, buddy."

He opened his eyes and saw a blood pressure cuff around his arm. Carter placed the rounded disk of a stethoscope against Dylan's heart.

"Can you tell me your symptoms?" Carter asked.

"Headache. Dry mouth. Dizziness." He trembled again. "The shakes."

"Have been drinking, Dylan?"

"No. I don't think so."

Carter frowned. "I'm going to take a blood sample."

He felt the cold wipe against his arm and then the sting of the needle.

"What's the last thing you do remember?"

He thought hard. "I'm not sure. Wait. The beach. Willow."

"Good," Carter encouraged. "What else?"

"We're... engaged." He frowned. "But nobody knows. Maybe Jackson. And you."

"I didn't know, Dylan. You hadn't told me, so that means it was a recent event. Do you remember what day that happened? I saw you Friday at Game Night."

"Maybe Saturday? What's today?"

"Monday."

Monday. He had no recollection of Sunday.

"Do you remember the wreck last night?" Carter asked.

He rubbed his temples, trying to ease the pounding. "Pam just told me on the phone. A father and daughter killed."

"Yes. They were hit by a drunk driver. I heard about it. I assume you worked the scene. They would have called you."

Frustration filled him. "I don't remember, Carter."

His friend held up the vial of blood. "If this is what

I think it is, the lab won't find it. I think you were roofied, Dylan."

"Huh?"

"Rohypnol. Your heartbeat is erratic and faster than it should be, especially since you're so lethargic. Your BP is much higher than usual. Do you understand what I'm saying?"

"I think. I remember investigating a few cases in the military. I'm sorry, Carter. My brain is so fuzzy."

Carter walked away and returned with two bottles of water. "Drink one now. The whole thing."

Dylan did as instructed and wiped his mouth with the back of his hand.

"I'm taking you to the hospital. We need to get an IV in you and get this blood work run. I suspect it'll already be too late to find a trace of the drug in your system. Be right back."

Carter returned and helped Dylan to dress, easing him to his feet. "My car is right downstairs. I've already called this in, so the emergency room is expecting us."

"Willow?"

"I'll call her on the way." Carter slipped Dylan's phone in his pocket. "Let's go, buddy."

He didn't know how long it took to get to Carter's car. His friend had to buckle him in as if he were a child.

"Close your eyes. We'll be there soon."

Dylan shut them but could hear the calls Carter made. The first was to the station. It was cryptic but asked for a deputy to meet him and Dylan at the hospital. The second was to Willow.

"Hey, Willow, it's Carter. I'm using Dylan's phone to call you. Didn't have your number. Listen, I think you should come over to the hospital as soon as you can.

Text me when you get there, and I'll come get you. I'm taking Dylan in now. Nothing to worry about. He's fine. Just a little confused. I'll explain when you get here."

Dylan felt strong arms lifting him from the passenger seat, placing him in a wheelchair.

"Dr. Peterson's ready for him," the voice pushing the chair said.

"Thank you," Carter said.

He found himself hoisted from the chair and up onto a table.

"I'm Dr. Peterson, Sheriff Taylor. I'm going to poke and prod a bit if that's okay."

He nodded and winced.

"Headache?"

"Yeah. It's raging."

"He needs an IV, Doc," Carter said.

"All in good time," the physician said.

"I gave the blood sample to the nurse who met us," Carter added.

"He'll put a rush on it. Good thing the sheriff called you and you took one."

"I think it's too late. It'll probably be out of his system. He doesn't remember any of yesterday. Possibly a little of Saturday."

"That's to be expected if it's Rohypnol. Some victims lose days. Even a week."

"Victim?" he repeated.

"Yes, Sheriff," the doctor said, shining a pen light into Dylan's eyes. "Our best guess is someone slipped you Rohypnol. That's why you're feeling sick and woozy and don't remember much of anything. You may not regain your memory. We may never know who did this to you."

"I aim to find out," a voice said.

Dylan recognized Deputy Oswald Jones, his second-in-command. Relief filled him. Then he asked, "Willow?"

"I left a message for her, Dylan," Carter assured him. "You know Willow. She could be out running. Most likely, she's in her studio painting. I'll bet she turns her phone off when she does that."

"Get her," he said. "Please."

"Okay. I'll go to Boo's and do that."

Carter left the examination room, gesturing for Oswald to follow him. Dylan supposed Carter would fill the deputy in.

The doctor asked him a few more questions and then told him, "We're going to place you in a room and get an IV going. You need to get rest."

"Carter? Willow?"

"Carter left to go bring Willow here. I'd say get your beauty sleep while you can so you can look good for your girl."

The next thing he knew, Dylan was back in a wheelchair. He didn't recall how he got there. A burly nurse helped him into a bed and inserted a needle in his arm, taping it into place.

"The IV will help restore your fluids, Sheriff. Once you're more balanced, the headache should cease. Try to get some sleep."

"Okay." He closed his eyes, wishing Willow were here with him.

~

WILLOW LED Shadow into Dr. Shorter's clinic, where the receptionist greeted them.

"You must be Shadow," the woman said. "Dr. Shorter told me what a beauty you are." She looked up. "And you're Boo's granddaughter. Boo was in my book club. I'm Sandy. Let me take you back to a room. Dr. Shorter will be with you shortly. How's Shadow liking the food Dr. Shorter gave you?"

"He eats every scoop," she said, trying to smile at the woman.

Even while her insides were ripped apart.

She felt as if she were on autopilot standing there, realizing this was how she always dealt with problems. She compartmentalized—and kept going—putting the pain of Dylan away where she wouldn't have to examine it, question it, or think about it.

Because if she dared to think about it, it would destroy her.

"Do you have the stool sample for me?" Sandy asked brightly.

Fortunately, Willow had remembered at the last moment and claimed the freshest one from this morning, placing it in a Ziploc bag.

The receptionist left them in the room, which had a table for Shadow and a seat for her. She let the dog stay on the floor for now, unclipping his leash. The pup sensed something was wrong and moved between her legs, resting his head on her thigh.

"I'm okay," she lied to the dog, knowing she would never be okay again.

Dylan's betrayal cut her to the quick. Yes, her previous lovers had all cheated on her, but she would never have thought Dylan capable of doing so. Not after they had shared so much with one another this past week. She supposed the sex had just been sex to him, where for her, their physical relationship had held a much deeper meaning than ever before. Combining the emotions she felt for him and adding love to the mix was now poisoning her. The connection she thought they had forged, the oneness that she had felt with him, wasn't unique at all. She had bared her soul to him—and she had been merely another lay to him. Willow felt used. Hurt. Emotionally raw.

She had to leave the Cove. She didn't want to live in the house where they had planned to start their lives as a married couple. The one where they would raise their children. That was to be their beginning—and she couldn't face living there alone. Actually, she couldn't even think of staying in town now, where she might run into him at any time. Willow didn't want to see Dylan Taylor. Didn't want to think about him. She wanted to go far away and nurse her wounds in a dark cave.

Stroking Shadow, she was eternally grateful she had him to comfort her. Willow didn't think she would be able to get through the next few hours—much less days—without the dog's company. Once she got home, she needed to pack up and leave Maple Cove.

For good.

She had no idea where to go. South to L.A. held no appeal for her. True, she liked the beach but couldn't stand the city's traffic and smog, having spent her college years there. Maybe she could find another town along the Oregon coast. No, too close. Maybe Northern California. She'd been to San Francisco a few times. The cosmopolitan city held some appeal to her. It had a thriving art community. She wouldn't necessarily have to live in the city. She could try for one of the small, seaside towns nearby.

Tears began to roll down her face. She opened her purse and found her tissues, blowing her nose and blotting her eyes, trying to pull herself together. She didn't need the vet to see her weeping on the cusp of her abandoning the Cove. The gossip would already be vicious.

Why should she care? She would never come here again.

Dr. Shorter entered and smiled. He paused a moment. "Are you okay, Willow?"

"Fine," she told him, dabbing one eye. "I had something in my eye. I got it out, but I know I look a mess after it watered so much. Let's talk about Shadow," she suggested, trying to turn the conversation.

The vet knelt. "How about we get up on the table, young man?"

He lifted Shadow and Willow stood nearby, hovering like an anxious mother.

She answered the vet's questions and after several minutes, he pronounced Shadow in excellent health.

"The running is good for him. I think you can increase his morning scoop to one-and-a-half. Sandy's analyzing the stool sample now. If you'll excuse me, I'll go see if that turned up anything."

When he returned a few minutes later, it was good news. "Nothing out of the ordinary. We do need to give Shadow his shots now, and I'll also give you some heartworm medicine. I would like to see him back here in about three months. He should be a year old by then. I want to check his weight and make sure he's thriving. Adjust his feeding schedule if necessary."

"I may not be here then," she revealed, playing her cards close to the vest.

"Oh, I thought you would be staying in the Cove. Heard you've fixed up Boo's place."

"Yes. To sell," she said.

"I see. Well, give me a call when you get settled wherever you're going. I'll recommend a vet in the area if I know any. If I don't, I'll find a good one for Shadow."

He offered her his hand. "It was a pleasure meeting you, Willow." He patted the dog's head. "And you, too, Shadow."

They left the exam room, and she paid the bill at the desk. It included another bag of food, which Sandy carried to the car for her. She thanked the receptionist and drove home, this time letting her tears flow freely. If she cried enough, maybe her well would finally run dry.

Leaving the bag of food in the car since she knew she would be gone by the end of the day, she led Shadow inside. She looked around what she had thought would be the home she would live in forever. With Dylan. With their kids. Frustration filled her and she let out a primal scream, startling the dog.

"I'm sorry, Shadow," she called out as he ran up the stairs.

Her cell buzzed in her pocket. She removed it, dread filling her. If it were Dylan, she simply wouldn't answer it. He had already called once this morning. She had deleted the voicemail he left without listening to it.

It was him again. She shoved the phone back into her pocket and went upstairs to pack. Moments later, a text came in.

Willow—it's Carter on Dylan's phone. Where are you? I've been calling you.

Why would Carter have Dylan's phone? And what would he want? Did Dylan think he could have his friend try to mend the ginormous rift between them?

No, she would nip this in the bud now.

Don't text me again. I'm deleting your number.

She sent the text and then went to her contacts,

eliminating Dylan's number. It was as if someone had stabbed her in the gut as she hit the button, erasing him from her life for good.

Her phone rang again. This time it was an unknown caller. She supposed it was Carter, using his phone to get in touch with her. She let it go to voicemail and then deleted the message.

She went to her studio and boxed up her favorite brushes. The oil paints and canvases could remain behind. Maybe Gillian could collect them for her at a later date. She realized that with the likelihood of Jackson moving to Maple Cove, he would become a part of the community. It would hurt her, but Willow couldn't see him here. They could meet elsewhere. Maybe she should move back to Europe and put as much distance as possible between her and the Cove. She decided she would just get in the car and drive and see where she wound up at the end of today.

Willow took the box of brushes to her car and returned to her bedroom to pack. She hadn't brought much with her, so it wouldn't take too long.

Then the doorbell rang. She glanced outside and saw a truck next to her SUV. She recognized it from being here last week and figured it had to be Carter's.

She unlocked the window and raised it. "I'm not answering my door, Carter. Not for you or anyone."

He stepped from the porch into view. "Wait, Willow."

In response, she slammed the window and locked it again.

Seconds later, the doorbell started ringing again. Carter continued to press it, causing Shadow to bark excitedly, running in circles.

"This is ridiculous," she said aloud, storming down the stairs and throwing the door open.

"You didn't listen to my voicemails," Carter accused.

"I didn't. I don't want to hear from Dylan—or his trusted friend. It's over between us, Carter. I'm leaving the Cove."

She slammed the door, but Carter jammed his foot in, forcing it open. Stunned, she stepped back.

"Dylan needs you, Willow. Someone slipped him a roofie. He doesn't remember the last twenty-four hours. Maybe more. He's sick as a dog. I took him to the hospital."

Willow gasped, a sudden clarity enveloping her. "Oh, Carter. I think I know who did it."

CHAPTER 27

Willow sat next to Carter, guilt and shame filling her. She listened as he called the Maple Cove Sheriff's Department and was passed on to a Deputy Jones. Carter outlined what Willow had shared with him, and Jones said he would locate Missy Newton and take her into custody. He would then come to the hospital and speak directly with Willow.

As they drove along the Boxboro Highway to the hospital, Carter filled her in on Dylan's condition. As she listened, Willow felt awful at how she had reacted.

"I jumped to some pretty terrible conclusions, Carter," she admitted. "I wasn't thinking clearly."

She mentally kicked herself. How could she have thought Dylan, who had loved her so completely, unlike any other man had, would be capable of such a thing? That he was lying there drugged and she suspected him of something so terrible? How could she have believed Missy?

"It had to be shocking to you to come in and find Dylan with Missy like that," he said, taking her hand and squeezing it reassuringly. "But Dylan has all the signs of someone who has ingested Rohypnol. The elevated heart rate and BP. The massive headache and brain fogginess. And the memory loss, in particular. That's why the drug is known as a date rape drug. Victims know something has happened to them, but they are so fuzzy on the details once they awake that it oftentimes doesn't result in a conviction. Many times, a victim can't even remember several days leading up to the incident.

"At least Dylan still remembers we are engaged. If he had forgotten that, I don't know what I would've done."

"He would've asked you again, Willow. He loves you. He has for a long time."

She kept to herself that she was the one who had done the proposing and that she wondered if Dylan would even want to marry her, since she had showed such little faith in him. Willow mentally berated herself. If she had only thought rationally, she would have known something was very wrong. Dylan had never been involved with Missy Newton. Why would he tell Willow he loved her and agree to marry her, filling out their marriage application and sending it back to Jackson, much less plan to go with her to L.A. in a few days get married at the courthouse?

Instead, she had let her past experiences color the present, making her deeply ashamed of her behavior. She would do whatever it took to make it up to the man she loved and never doubt him again.

They arrived at the hospital, and Carter explained that Dylan had been admitted to a room after they had tended to him in ER. They went directly to his room, and she saw the IV hooked up to him. Dylan was sleeping, and Carter told Willow that getting fluids into him was very important in his recovery process.

"He will definitely have gaps in his memory, so you'll need to be patient with him."

"I can't thank you enough, Carter. For recognizing his symptoms and getting him to the hospital. You've always taken such good care of him. Dylan is lucky to have a friend like you."

Dylan began to stir, and Willow stepped to the bed, taking his hand. Carter went to stand on the other side.

Slowly, Dylan's eyes opened, blinking several times. Then he caught sight of her and gave her a crooked smile.

"Hey, Bear."

"Hey, you. How do you feel?"

"Better than before." He turned and saw Carter. "You helped me."

"I did. You were in a pretty bad way, Dylan, but you had the sense to call me." He glanced across the bed to Willow. "Besides being a fireman, I'm also a certified EMT. Dylan remembered that on some level." He glanced back to Dylan. "Do you remember anything from this morning?"

"I remember you talking to me. You made me drink a lot of water. Other than that, it's a blank."

Carter said, "I'll leave you two alone and go wait for Oswald. You might want to walk Dylan through the last few days, Willow, and see what he remembers. Help him fill in any gaps."

She perched on the edge of the bed as Dylan's fingers tightened around hers.

"I gave you a scare, I guess."

"You did. Think over the last few days. What do you recall?"

He thought a moment. "Game Night at Carter's." He grinned. "You kicked some serious ass, Bear. I think I want to be on the girls' team next time."

"No can do," she said lightly. "Anything after Game Night?"

He was silent a good two minutes before he said, "The beach."

"Do you remember which beach?"

He nodded and winced. "Sorry, my head still feels like it wants to explode. It was the beach by Boo's. Wait. We went to Boo's. The house. It was finished, wasn't it?"

"Yes, that's right," she encouraged. "We went all through it with Pete."

"Okay. I recall parts of that. The kitchen looked really nice. And then we went to the beach. I know we came back happy. Engaged." He smiled. "You asked me to marry you."

She smiled gently. "I most certainly did. I wanted you to know just how much I loved you and how committed I was to you and a life together. Anything else?"

Dylan sat again, staring into space. Finally, he said, "No, nothing after that. I'm sorry if I'm forgetting the mind-blowing sex we had to celebrate being engaged. Fill me in on what I'm not remembering."

"I talked to Jackson. We decided to get married quickly and quietly and then have a party afterward. I did want Jackson at the ceremony, though. You suggested we fly down to L.A. Jackson sent us a marriage application. We filled it out and sent it back to him. He's arranging everything for this coming Friday afternoon after the jury is excused for the weekend. We're going to be married in the chambers of a judge he's friends with."

He thought a moment. "Basketball? Something about basketball?"

"Yes," she said, excited. "Jackson plays basketball with the judge. That's good, Dylan. Anything else?"

"No. Did we book flights yet?"

"No, you got called away."

"I can't remember why," he said, frustrated. "I hate that someone robbed me of my memory."

"We have a pretty good idea who did so," she revealed.

"What? Who?"

"I think we should wait for Deputy Jones to get here."

"Tell me, Bear. Please."

"I don't know everything, Dylan. We were going to watch a movie after dinner. I had made Boo's lasagna for you."

"I don't remember that at all."

She smiled. "There were plenty of leftovers, so I'll feed you some. Maybe that will jog your memory a little. Anyway, we were just sitting down to watch a movie when you were called to come to a traffic fatality. You left to go deal with it, and you told me you would be pretty late and you'd just stay at your place in town. We hadn't yet decided how this week would play out, and you didn't have any clothes at Boo's."

He frowned. "So, I went to this scene. It must have taken a few hours, being there and then going to the station to file the reports. And then I must've gone back to my apartment," he said.

The door opened, Carter returning and with him, Willow assumed, was Deputy Jones. Introductions were made, and then the deputy said, "How are you feeling, Sheriff?"

"Like a sixteen-wheeler ran over me, Oswald. Other than that, I'm just fine."

A physician entered, wearing his white coat with *Dr. Peterson* embroidered above the pocket. He introduced himself and then told Dylan, "The blood work came back, and as we thought, no indication of the Rohypnol was in it. It doesn't surprise me because it dissipates from your system pretty quickly. But you had all the classic signs. I did my residency at a hospital close to a university and saw quite a few cases of it in the ER."

"Someone gave me this deliberately," Dylan said, pondering the situation. "But we don't know who. Only when. Sometime after I got home from working the traffic fatality last night."

Willow thought how she had told Dylan only a few minutes ago that they had an idea of who had dosed him—and he'd already forgotten. It let her know just how serious the situation was and how affected his memory was.

"Actually, Dylan, we have taken a suspect into custody, based upon what Miss Martin has told us," the deputy said.

Dylan's gaze flew to her. "Who? Tell me."

She swallowed. "I received a text from you early this morning, asking me to come over. When I got there, I found you...with someone."

Dylan frowned. "When you say found me, what do you mean?"

"You were in bed. With Missy Newton."

He jerked his hand from hers. "What? Absolutely not. There's no way, Willow, that I would ever betray you, much less with someone like Missy Newton."

"But if you opened your door, you might have let her in."

"I don't think I would have," he said stubbornly. "She's wanted to get her claws into me ever since I came back to the Cove. Both you and I have made it clear to her that's not going to happen."

"Nevertheless, I think she did slip you the drug, Dylan. I think she's the one who texted me so I would find the two of you together."

A shadow crossed his face. "And with your track record, you would've thought I was cheating on you," he said dully. "Willow, I don't know what to say."

"I know you would never do that to me, Dylan. We love each other. We will get through this."

He glanced to his deputy. "You said Missy is in custody?"

Oswald nodded. "Picked her up at Serenity Salon an hour ago. She hasn't lawyered up yet. I haven't told her why she's in custody. You know we can hold her twenty-four hours without charging her, but you'll need to question her, Sheriff."

"When can I get out of here?" Dylan asked Dr. Peterson.

"I would prefer to keep you overnight for observation, but I can release you at seven tomorrow morning."

Determination filled Dylan's face. "Then I will head straight from here to the interrogation room. Willow, I'll need you to bring me a uniform. I don't want to stop at home and waste any time. I want to confront Missy Newton as soon as possible."

DYLAN SHOWERED with Willow's help. He was still a bit unsteady on his feet and asked her to remain close by. She had brought his razor and volunteered to shave him, for which he was grateful. His hands still shook some. He insisted on dressing himself, though, taking his time as he sat on the bed and slowly pulled his clothes on.

Rage filled him at having Missy take advantage of him. Not only had she wiped a part of his memory, she had also tried to sabotage his relationship with Willow. He couldn't imagine what Willow had seen when she had walked in on the two of them. It surprised him she had remained in town long enough to have Carter bring her to the hospital and explain the situation to her.

They waited for the doctor now. At seven on the dot, Dr. Peterson entered the room, along with a nurse who took Dylan's vitals. The physician listened to Dylan's heart and checked his eyes.

"How's the headache?" Peterson asked jovially.

"A dull ache now. No more violent pounding."

"Good to hear. Physically, you are almost back to normal. Pulse and heart rate good. BP still slightly elevated, but that should resolve itself in a day or so."

"I'm supposed to get married on Friday, Doc," he said. "Can I still do that?"

"No," Willow protested. "We can put that off."

He took her hand. "That is the last thing we'll do. I love you, Willow. I want the world to know you're mine. I want us married and this ugly incident put behind us. Please?"

When she hesitated, Dr. Peterson said, "He should be fine, Miss Martin. Today is Tuesday. If the wedding isn't until Friday, I don't see any problems arising."

"Can he fly to L.A., Doctor?" Willow asked. "That's where we're getting married."

"Flying would be preferable to driving. A long

road trip might tire him out. No, a short flight would be fine."

"That settles it," Dylan said. "I hope you didn't have Jackson cancel our plans."

"I haven't even talked to Jackson," she admitted.

"Then we're good. I can be discharged now?"

"Yes, Sheriff," Peterson said. "But I'd like to see you in a week. Just a quick follow-up." He handed Dylan a card. "You can make an appointment with my office."

The doctor left and the nurse handed him a clipboard with some paperwork to sign so he could be officially discharged.

"I'll bring the car around," Willow said, taking the stairs as the nurse wheeled him to the elevator.

By the time they exited the hospital, Willow's SUV awaited him. He got in, thanking the nurse, and they set out for Maple Cove.

"I already talked to Oswald this morning. Missy still hasn't requested a lawyer. I'm hoping to draw a confession from her."

"Do you actually think she will admit to drugging you?" Willow asked, doubt in her voice. "I don't see that happening. Missy knew we were committed to one another, yet look at the lengths she went to in order to tear us apart. She won't roll over, Dylan. If anything, she'll clam up."

"We'll see."

They arrived at the station shortly after eight. He saw the anxious faces as he entered, everyone watching him carefully.

"I'm fine," he growled, glaring at the gathered group. "Jones, you're with me."

He reached for Willow's hand, pulling her along as they went down the corridor to the interrogation room.

"Camera ready to go?" he asked.

"Yup," Oswald said. "Missy's had her breakfast already and has been complaining nonstop. Still hasn't asked for a lawyer, though. It surprises me a little. But then again, I've heard she's having money troubles. Maybe she thinks she can't afford one."

"Bring her here," Dylan ordered. After his deputy left, he told Willow, "We don't have any fancy two-way mirror here, but in the next room, you can watch the live feed from the camera."

He led her to the room and closed the door. Taking her into his arms, he kissed her, enjoying the feel of her body flush against his and his mouth on hers. Breaking the kiss, he gazed into her eyes.

"I am going to marry you on Friday, Bear. And we are going to have a wonderful life together. I promise. Do you believe me?"

"I do. Dylan, I need to tell you something."

He felt the tension in her body. "Go ahead."

"After... after I saw you... with Missy, I lost faith in you. In us. I was so hurt, I was ready to leave the Cove and never come back."

"I can't blame you," he said softly, stroking her cheek.

"If I would've taken the time to think things through, I would have realized this wasn't you. I apologize for jumping to some pretty damning conclusions."

He kissed her softly. "It's all right. It might have taken some time, but you know in your heart I'll never leave you. I'll never hurt you." He paused. "I may occasionally leave the cap off the toothpaste or drink milk straight from the carton. Things that might irritate the hell out of you. But I love you, Willow Martin. So very much. I will protect you always."

"I know," she whispered and touched her lips to his. "I promise I will always trust you. If I'm ever mad —and you know that will definitely happen—that I will talk it out with you." She kissed him again. "Now, go get Missy's confession."

"Yes, ma'am."

Dylan glanced up at the TV and saw Oswald had already brought Missy into the interrogation room and now stood, arms crossed, leaning against the wall. Dylan returned to the room and watched as Missy's face grew hot, her eyes downcast.

He indicted for Oswald to turn on the camera and then stated the date and time, along with his and Missy's names. Then he seated himself across from her, turning his sternest look on her, watching her face crumble after a good minute of stony silence from him.

"I'm sorry, Dylan," she said, tears running down her face.

"Sorry for what?" he asked, his voice low.

"I just wanted you to love me. I know I can love you more than Willow ever could. She's all wrong for you."

"But Willow *is* the woman I love, Missy. Not you. Drugging me. Climbing into bed with me. Texting Willow to come over so she could see us together. It's wrong on absolutely every single level. You understand that, don't you?"

Missy sniffed. "I thought if she saw us together, she'd leave town. And then you'd finally *see* me. I've been here for years, Dylan. Waiting for you to really notice me. To realize how much I love you."

"You don't love me, Missy. You're in love with the idea of loving someone who doesn't even exist anymore. You want the popular quarterback who gets all the attention and cheers on Friday nights. I stopped being that guy a dozen years ago. I've moved on. It's time you do, too."

He pushed a yellow legal tablet and pen sitting on the desk toward her. "Write it down. Everything you did. Where you got the Rohypnol. How you gave it to me. What you texted to Willow."

Her mouth quivered. "He said you wouldn't remember anything. You remember a lot."

"I do. Now, write it all down—and then we'll talk."

Dylan nudged the pad an inch closer to her. He picked up the pen and handed it to her. Missy took it, sniffing again, and began to quickly scribble on the page.

He didn't try to read upside down as she wrote. He also didn't leave. He wanted Missy to feel his presence across from her. Leaving would be like taking his foot off the gas pedal. Dylan was here to get her confession.

Forty-five minutes later, she rested the pen on the table and pushed the tablet back toward him. He took it and read through her confession, learning that Rick Mercer had given her the name of a guy in Portland who would sell her the Rohypnol. It was too bad he couldn't charge his nemesis with anything. Surprise filled him as he read how she had had rough sex with Mercer, who liked to choke his partners. It had given her an idea, and Missy had used the bruises Mercer had put on her throat and then used a baseball bat to strike her torso and limbs several times, causing multiple bruises.

Those added bruises had been what convinced him to let her stay the night. Missy had told him she wanted to press charges against who hurt her but told Dylan she was afraid of retaliation from her lover. He had offered her his bed for the night, while he slept on the couch. She had convinced him to drink a cup of tea with her, and while he was getting her towels, she poured the Rohypnol into his drink.

The rest was staged. She stripped Dylan of his clothes. She tried to give him a blow job to arouse him, wanting to attempt to have sex with him while he was unconscious. Fortunately, that had been an epic failure. Missy had texted Willow early the next morning and left the door unlocked so she would come in and catch the two of them in bed together. Then Missy had left, worried that if Dylan awakened and saw her there, he would remember her story and want her to press charges against Mercer. She hoped what she had done would force Willow from the Cove —and Missy would be there to pick up the pieces of Dylan's broken heart.

He set the confession aside, anger mixed with pity for this woman. Still, under federal law, Missy could face a prison term of three years if she were convicted of being in possession of Rohypnol. He would have to get a search warrant for her residence and vehicle to see if she had any of the drug left, as well as checking his apartment. Dylan thought she would have been smart enough to thoroughly wash the cup which had the Rohypnol in it. She might have used up what she'd bought, so making the possession charge stick would be iffy.

As for giving him the drug without his consent, her confession made it clear she was liable for inflicting bodily harm. Oregon law would allow them to charge Missy with possession with intent to distribute, with distribute being broadly defined to include giving the drug to just one other person. The distribution charge would carry a far greater penalty, from ten years up to life in prison, along with a fine.

What he worried about was the lack of physical evidence, though. His blood test showed no trace of the Rohypnol in his system. His doctor could attest to his symptoms. Carter could too, his word taken more seriously because of his EMT certification. But in truth, all they had at this point was Missy's written confession of what she had done.

He stood, picking up the legal pad. "Stay with her," he ordered Oswald, who nodded.

Dylan left the room. Willow rushed into the hall.

"Did she admit she drugged you?"

"Yes. It's all here." Quickly, he explained to her about the need to execute a search warrant.

"You take care of that," she said. "I'll get out of your hair."

He reached for her hand. "I'll call you. Keep you in the loop."

"Thank you."

Dylan walked her to the front and the moment Willow left the station, he turned to Pam.

"Get me Judge Baker. I need a search warrant."

Grim satisfaction filled him. Missy would be going to prison, thanks to her confession.

And Dylan could make Willow his.

EPILOGUE

THREE DAYS LATER—LOS
ANGELES, CALIFORNIA

Willow awoke, nestled in Dylan's arms. She stroked his forearm lightly, and soon her husband-to-be was making slow, sweet love to her. Although they had only experienced this deep, physical intimacy for a short while, already their bodies were in tune with one another. Dylan knew every touch, every stroke which would make her body come alive. She had never known the joys of such a liberating, physical relationship and once again, gave thanks that circumstances had led them back to one another. Dylan had been right. They were soulmates, bound together in every way possible.

In the afterglow, she rested in his strong arms. Today, they would be married. They would start their new lives together, becoming one.

"Want to be lazy and order breakfast from room service?" he asked, stroking her hair softly.

"Sounds wonderful."

They had flown into LAX the night before, not wanting to leave anything to chance. Dylan had pointed out they still needed to buy wedding bands, and he mentioned wanting to purchase a new suit for the occasion since he had none. He'd gone straight from wearing his military uniforms to those of the sheriff's department, with only casual clothes for off-duty hours. Willow, who had led a fairly bohemian lifestyle for the last decade, only had two cocktail dresses, which she wore to gallery openings. Both were black, which she didn't feel appropriate for her wedding. She had agreed she would shop for a wedding dress at the same time he looked for a suit.

They enjoyed a leisurely breakfast and then made love again before dressing for the day. She had texted Jackson to let him know they were already in town and asked about where to shop for both clothes and rings. He gave her a few suggestions, and they set out for the jeweler's first.

When they arrived, Dylan said, "We're engaged—but I never even gave you an engagement ring, Bear."

"I don't really want one," she told him. "I prefer a simple, gold band. I don't often wear jewelry, and a band would be easy to slip off when I'm painting."

He grinned at her. "So, you're not the flashy-diamond kind of girl?"

She snagged his shirt and pulled him down for a kiss. "No, I'm the invest-in-kisses-instead-of-diamonds kind of girl." She gave him a scorching kiss to prove her point.

They entered the jewelry store, and a clerk directed them to the wedding ring section once they told him they needed bands for today's ceremony. They found a matching set, and she thought it a good sign that neither would have to be sized since both fit perfectly.

Willow asked, "Would it be possible to have these engraved now? I'd like to have our wedding date inscribed inside both bands."

The clerk said, "Of course." He pulled out a pad and pen from underneath the counter and handed it to her. "If you can put exactly what you want here, we can have it done in fifteen minutes."

She gazed up at Dylan. "Do you want anything besides the date?"

"How about our names?"

She wrote *Dylan & Willow* and the day's date.

"Ah. I see you've gone European-style on me," he noted. "You've placed the date and then the month and year following it."

She chuckled. "It's what I'm used to. Is that okay?'

"More than okay," he assured her.

Handing the pad and pen to the clerk, he lifted both rings from the black velvet they rested upon.

"Browse the store and see if you find anything else you'd like," he said, disappearing into the back.

They strolled through the store, looking in the various glass cases at rings, watches, and necklaces, until he returned.

Giving them the rings, he said, "I think you'll be pleased."

Willow looked inside her ring at the inscription, and then she traded with Dylan and viewed his, as well.

"This is exactly what I wanted. Thank you so much."

Dylan paid for both rings, despite her protests, saying, "My money is now yours. It doesn't matter whose pocket it came from."

They headed directly to a men's store, where she and Dylan narrowed their choices down to three suits for him to try on. One was black, another a deep gray, and the final one a midnight blue. Willow insisted he try on all three and thought he looked more handsome each time he came out wearing a different one.

They had trouble making up their minds, and she finally said, "Get both the black and the blue. Every man should have a choice when it comes to dressing up."

Dylan allowed her to choose a shirt and tie, since she had a good eye and better taste than he did. She went with a crisp, white dress shirt and selected two different ties that matched each suit. The salesman helping them noted no tailoring would be necessary, and they paid for their purchases.

"Next stop? Your dress," he said.

They went to a bridal boutique shop, having received a text message from Jackson, who had told his paralegal that Willow was in town shopping for her wedding dress. While she would not be purchasing the traditional long, white wedding gown, the store also carried mother-of-the-bride dresses and stylish cocktail dresses. She found two that would be appropriate for a courthouse wedding, which she could also wear to professional events. One was a sleeveless teal dress which struck her just above the knee. The other was a beautiful magenta with short sleeves. It was a bit shorter than the teal, showing off her legs to spectacular advantage.

"Do you have a preference?" she asked her groom.

He gave her a wicked smile. "I prefer you in nothing if you want me to be honest, but I supposed that would get you arrested at the courthouse. I like both—but I think the purplish one flatters your hair and skin. It really makes your eyes pop."

"Then that's the one," she confirmed.

They purchased the dress and then decided they better stop for a late lunch. A little mom-and-pop place was a few doors down from the boutique, so they ate there. Excitement filled Willow, and she opted for a Cobb salad, not wanting anything heavy on her stomach.

They returned to the hotel and showered. She took her time applying makeup and blow-drying her hair so that it fell in soft waves around her shoulders. Although Willow told Dylan she liked the stubbled look on him, he insisted on being clean-shaven for their wedding.

When they reached the lobby, he stopped at the concierge desk, and she wondered if he might make dinner reservations for this evening. Instead, the concierge nodded at him in recognition and picked up the phone, dialing an extension, and saying, "Bring it now, please."

A couple of minutes later, a bellman appeared with a beautiful bridal bouquet of roses and tulips. Tears welled in Willow's eyes, and she said, "Thank you, Dylan."

"Every bride needs a bouquet," he told her. He grinned at the concierge. "Thanks for your help."

"Happy to accommodate you, Mr. Taylor," the woman said. "Best wishes on your marriage."

They had decided to Uber to the courthouse, not knowing where to park and thinking downtown might be crowded on a Friday afternoon. Once inside the car, Willow called Jackson's office and spoke to his paralegal, thanking her for providing the name of the dress shop and asking what court her brother's case was being tried in. Armed with that information, they went through the metal detectors and made their way upstairs to the courtroom. They slipped inside and took a seat on the back row. The room was about three-quarters full, and Willow supposed it included journalists and members of both parties' families.

Jackson was cross-examining a witness, and she sat enthralled, watching her brother in action for the very first time. He was impressive in a charcoal gray suit, his demeanor professional, brimming with confidence. He never raised his voice to the witness on the stand, and yet he eviscerated the man's previous testimony. By the time Jackson finished, Willow knew this witness had been discredited in the jury's eyes.

The district attorney called the next witness and spent twenty minutes questioning her. She was a blood spatter expert with the L.A. Police Department, and the questioning was a bit technical at times.

Once more, Jackson approached the witness, his questions clear and concise. Though she was unshakeable, her brother did cast doubt on one point she had made. Willow knew he was pleased by the job he had done.

The judge excused the witness and then said, "Since it is Friday afternoon, we will adjourn for the day. I will remind jurors that they are not to speak to anyone about this case. Not each other. Not family members or friends. Especially not anyone from the press," he finished sternly.

"All rise!" the bailiff said in a loud voice, and the courtroom did as asked, the judge exiting to his chambers.

Willow and Dylan sat, watching the spectators leave the courtroom. Gerald McGreer, Dylan's client, was handcuffed and led away by deputies of the court.

Only then did she and Dylan go to greet Jackson, who was placing file folders inside his briefcase. He snapped it shut and looked up, a broad smile appearing on his handsome face. He drew Willow in for a long hug and then shook hands with Dylan.

"You have landed yourself a spitfire," he jokingly warned Dylan. "I always thought Willow got a bit of Boo's temper. I suppose it's because they both have that artistic bent."

"I am the lucky one, Jackson," Dylan replied. "I still can't believe that I'm about to marry the woman I love."

Jackson glanced at his watch. "Right at four," he commented. "Just on time. Let's walk over to the county clerk's office."

They arrived and Jackson introduced them to the head clerk, who assured them their paperwork was in order. She asked to see a photo ID from each of them. Willow produced her passport, once again thinking she needed to get her Oregon driver's license soon. She and Dylan would not be taking a honeymoon right away since he had only been in office a short while. She had told him it didn't bother her in the least, because every day would be a honeymoon for them.

The clerk returned their IDs, and a man who had stood off to the side stepped up to join them.

"Willow, Dylan, I'd like you to meet my partner, Bill Watterscheim. We went to law school together. Bill is going to serve as your second witness."

Bill shook hands with both of them. "Jackson has been a good friend to me and an ideal partner. I can't think of anyone else I'd rather be in business with," Bill praised.

Willow glanced to Jackson and realized her brother had not mentioned anything to his partner about leaving their joint practice once this trial ended.

"Thank you for coming today," she said. "Jackson

thinks so much of you. We are happy to have you serve as one of our witnesses."

The clerk told them that Judge Sanders would return the marriage certificate to her and that she would file it with the county before mailing them a certified copy.

"Unless I could simply let Jackson pick it up for you if that would be easier."

"I can do that," her brother said. "I'm hoping to sneak up to the Cove the weekend before Christmas. The courthouse will be closed Monday due to the holiday. If I can book a flight for Friday night, I could stay the weekend and then fly back Christmas Eve or Christmas Day." He smiled. "That is, if the newlyweds have room for me."

Dylan slapped Jackson on the back. "You bet we do."

The four of them walked to Judge Sanders' chambers, and the judge's secretary showed them into his office. The judge rose to greet them, and Willow saw he must be at least six-five or six-six in height.

Jackson introduced them, and she said, "No wonder my brother likes having you on his team. I'm sure he feeds you the ball all the time."

"Not often enough," Sanders joked as he came from behind his desk. "But I won't hold that against you, Willow. I know you and Dylan are eager to get this show on the road."

Judge Sanders instructed the witnesses where to stand and then had Willow and Dylan join hands. He said a few brief words about the sanctity of marriage and then said, "Do you have anything you wish to say to one another before I get to your vows?"

Dylan spoke up. "Yes."

He gazed into her eyes, and Willow knew this man saw into her soul.

"I don't know how you do it—but you bring out all the best things in me, Willow. You make me want to be a better man. For you and for myself. Thank you for being the woman you are. The woman I loved all those years ago. The one I love here and now. The one I will love throughout eternity."

She trembled hearing his heartfelt words and said, "I choose you, Dylan. Forever."

He started to lean in to kiss her, and the judge said, "Wait a minute. Let's make this good and legal."

Everyone laughed and Judge Sanders took them through their vows. She and Dylan made their promises to one another, exchanging rings, and then she heard the sweetest words ever spoken.

"I now pronounce you man and wife."

Before the judge could tell Dylan to kiss her, his mouth was already on hers, his arms banded about her, holding her close. The kiss was incredible tender. Willow tasted Dylan's love for her in it and his faith in them as a couple.

When he finally broke it, Judge Sanders proclaimed, "You may be my favorite couple I've married. That is, until I get the chance to hitch Jackson to a good woman."

They all laughed and Dylan led her from the judge's chambers. At the elevator, they paused as he pushed the button.

Dylan wrapped her in an embrace again. "I never would have guessed that we would have a second chance. Now, we have a lifetime to live in love. You were worth the wait, Bear."

As he kissed her, Willow believed the same.

READ A NEW BEGINNING, BOOK 2 IN THE MAPLE COVE SERIES!

Did you enjoy Dylan and Willow's second chance romance? Then look for them in *A New Beginning, Book 2 in the Maple Cove series*!

Willow's college roommate Tenley will visit Maple Cove after her life turns upside down. Dylan's best friend Carter will strike up a friendship with Tenley—and love will bloom.

Widowed firefighter Carter Clark meets aspiring writer Tenley Thompson, who is coming off an annulment after she's learned her husband is a bigamist.

Though reluctant to become involved so quickly after her annulment, Tenley throws caution to the wind. Their whirlwind romance is celebrated by their friends, but it doesn't sit well with one citizen in the Cove.

Will Tenley run to protect the only man she's ever loved—or will she stay and fight for Carter and the happiness they both deserve?

ALSO BY ALEXA ASTON

A Bit of Heaven on Earth

A Knight for Kallen

SECOND SONS OF LONDON:

Educated by the Earl

Debating with the Duke

DUKES DONE WRONG:

Discouraging the Duke

Deflecting the Duke

Disrupting the Duke

Delighting the Duke

Destiny with a Duke

DUKES OF DISTINCTION:

Duke of Renown

Duke of Charm

Duke of Disrepute

Duke of Arrogance

Duke of Honor

MEDIEVAL RUNAWAY WIVES:

Song of the Heart

A Promise of Tomorrow

Destined for Love

SOLDIERS AND SOULMATES:

To Heal an Earl

To Tame a Rogue

To Trust a Duke

To Save a Love

To Win a Widow

ABOUT THE AUTHOR

A native Texan and former history teacher, award-winning and internationally bestselling author Alexa Aston lives with her husband in a Dallas suburb, where she eats her fair share of dark chocolate and plots out stories while she walks every morning. She enjoys travel, sports, and binge-watching—and never misses an episode of *Survivor*.

Alexa brings her characters to life in steamy historicals, contemporary romances, and romantic suspense novels that resonate with passion, intensity, and heart.

KEEP UP WITH ALEXA
Visit her website
Newsletter Sign-Up

MORE WAYS TO CONNECT WITH ALEXA